G.K.CHESTERTON
THIRTEEN DETECTIVES

SELECTED AND ARRANGED BY

Marie Smith

Dodd, Mead & Company · New York

First published in the United States in 1987

This selection copyright © Marie Smith and Xanadu
Publications Limited 1987; Introduction copyright
© Marie Smith 1987

Published by Dodd, Mead & Company, Inc.
71 Fifth Avenue, New York, N.Y. 10003

Manufactured in Great Britain

First edition

Library of Congress Cataloging-in-Publication Data

Chesterton, G.K. (Gilbert Keith), 1874–1936
  Thirteen detectives
  1. Detective and mystery stories, English.
  I. Title.
  PR4453.C4A6   1987d   823'.912   87-15469

ISBN 0-396-09211-X

1 2 3 4 5 6 7 8 9 10

Contents

Introduction

"Do you promise that your detectives shall well and truly detect the crimes presented to them using those wits which it may please you to bestow upon them and not placing reliance on nor making use of Divine Revelation, Feminine Intuition, Mumbo Jumbo, Jiggery-Pokery, Coincidence or Act of God?"

CANDIDATE: "I do."

And quite right too. By 1930, when the Detection Club was founded, writers and readers alike had had enough of omniscient detectives and fudged solutions, and the admission procedure, of which this is an extract, required the candidate solemnly to forswear such nonsense, together with Mysterious Chinamen, Ghosts, Hypnotism and Death-Rays, in the stern presence of the skull Eric. G.K. Chesterton, the Club's first President, must have officiated at many such ceremonies, but by then his own reputation as a creator of detectives was secure; with seven collections of stories under his ample belt, including several about his detective-priest Father Brown, plus that remarkable book *The Man Who Was Thursday*, he was already among the immortals.

A few years after Chesterton's death in 1936, Frederic Dannay and Manfred B. Lee (the two halves of Ellery Queen) wrote in *Queen's Quorum*, their definitive history of the detective story, "The miracle-book of 1911 introduced Father Brown to an eternally grateful public. The position of Father Brown has been expressed pertinently by Barnaby Ross [another Dannay-Lee *persona*!], who wrote: 'If there is one character in detective fiction who possesses the innocence and wisdom to sit beside the immortal Holmes, it is that apotheosis of incredulity, Father Brown.' You will find in G.K. Chesterton's *The Innocence of Father Brown* ... all the wondrous qualities of Chesterton's genius: his extraordinary cleverness of plot, his unique style, and his brilliant use of paradox both in language and in the counterplay of the supernatural and the natural. In a letter to a famous *aficionado* we once wrote that Father Brown is 'one of the three greatest detective characters ever invented.' The correspondent replied with some puzzlement: he assumed (correctly) that another of the 'Three

7

Greatest' was Sherlock Holmes, but he wasn't sure whom we meant for the third. This is a perfect example in literature of not seeing the forest for the trees: the third is, of course, the *first*—Poe's Dupin."

By the 1970s tastes had changed drastically, but Chesterton's reputation survived where many others had not. In *Bloody Murder*, his history of the *genre*, Julian Symons is scathing about many of the humdrum authors of the earlier period, but "the short detective stories written by Gilbert Keith Chesterton were as pungent, paradoxical and romantic as the novels, poems, literary criticism and journalism that streamed from his occasionally too-ready pen ... stories in which reality is made to seem like fantasy. The best of these tales are among the finest short crime stories ever written ... A reading of Chesterton reinforces the truth that the best detective stories have been written by artists and not by artisans." And in the most recent critical work on the subject, *Crime and Mystery: the 100 Best Books* (1987), H.R.F. Keating writes:

> Chesterton's gift of paradox came, perhaps, most into its own in his detective stories. The ability to see paradoxes is something any detective-story writer might well ask as a gift from his fairy god-mother. Essentially, detective stories depend on a sudden seeing of something the right way up, which often means turning it upside down. Poe showed us that the best place to hide a letter is in a letter-rack. Conan Doyle told us that the really significant thing was that the dog did *not* bark in the night-time. The gift was all the better in Chesterton's case for being powered not just by a puzzler's delight in producing conundrums but by the whole man and his beliefs. He saw everything, as often as not, upside-down. And nowhere is this more so than in his running portrait of Father Brown ... the little Catholic priest who is somehow also one of the band of Great Detectives.

We may take it, then, that Chesterton's position at the top of detectival tree is as safe as ever, but the very celebrity of the Father Brown stories—of all Chesterton's books they are the ones that are constantly reprinted—has led to a neglect of his *other* detectives that is in my view quite unwarranted, and this present collection is an attempt to set that matter right, by bringing together the best of them. Which, given this author's very high standard, means that here we have some of the most ingeniously-plotted, dashingly-written and cleverly-argued detective stories in the whole history of crime writing.

II

> The first essential value of the detective story lies in this, that it is the earliest and only form of popular literature in which is expressed some sense of the poetry of modern life. Men lived among mighty mountains and eternal forests for ages before they realised that they were poetical; it may reasonably be

inferred that some of our descendants may see the chimney-pots as rich a purple as the mountain-peaks, and find the lamp-posts as old and natural as the trees. Of this realisation of a great city itself as something wild and obvious the detective story is certainly the *Iliad*. No one can have failed to notice that in these stories the hero or the investigator crosses London with something of the loneliness and liberty of a prince in a tale of elfand, that in the course of that incalculable journey the casual omnibus assumes the primal colours of a fairy ship. The lights of the city begin to glow like innumerable goblin eyes, since they are the guardians of some secret, however crude, which the writer knows and the reader does not. Every twist of the road is like a finger pointing to it; every fantastic skyline of chimney-pots seems wildly and derisively signalling the meaning of the mystery."

So wrote Chesterton in 1901, just a few days before his marriage. He was 27, he had been working for some years as a publisher's assistant, and was now just beginning to make a name for himself in the literary world. Two books of verse had appeared, a series of articles in *The Speaker* would soon be collected as *The Defendant*, and the next few years would see a flood of criticisism, essay, novels and philosophy. But first there would be an attempt to put into practice his theories about the detective story in the shape of 'The Tremendous Adventure of Major Brown', introducing Rupert and Basil Grant. Rupert is ostensibly the detective, racing about London following false clues in a less-than-successful attempt to emulate the great Sherlock Holmes, while his brother Basil, a judge who (as we shall see) retired from the Bench in alarming circumstances, actually solves the case. Other stories followed, and they were eventually collected as *The Club of Queer Trades*, a wonderfully amusing book.

Rupert and Basil are, perhaps, not unlike Chesterton and his own brother Cecil, with G.K. very much the man of ideas in contrast with Cecil's man of action. He had once remarked to Cecil, "It would be a fine thing to write a philosophic detective story," and here he began to do exactly that—and it is significant that the knight-errant who succeeds in solving the mysteries and righting the wrongs is the dreamer rather than the practical man. All of the stories in *The Club of Queer Trades* are good, but space permits only two; 'Major Brown', in which the characters are introduced, has to be one of them, and for the other I have chosen 'The Singular Speculation of the House Agent' as a nicely self-contained episode as well as a hugely entertaining tale.

III

'The Garden of Smoke' dates from 1919, by which time Father Brown had been well and truly established in the detectival hierarchy. It was appended to the stories in the original edition of *The Man Who Knew Too Much*, but inexplicably omitted from the American edition and from later reprints, to the dismay of critics such as Kingsley Amis. A weird, haunting story with a strangely modern theme, it belongs to no series and features a one-off detective in the person of Mr. Traill. He is not exactly the hero of the story, however: one reason that I have chosen it for this collection is that, most unusually in Chesterton's work, it features a female protagonist.

It was Horne Fisher who actually was The Man Who Knew Too Much (Hitchcock borrowed the title, but that was all), and here we enter a very different world to any that Chesterton had explored hitherto, a world jaded by Chesterton's experiences in the Marconi Scandal of 1912, and influenced by his own developing political theories. Fisher, anticipating T.S. Eliot by a year or so, occupies his own particular Waste Land: he is connected by blood or by marriage to (seemingly) every member of the ruling class and, world-weary and ineffective, cannot betray that class even when he despises it. He has been described as a sort of political counterpart to Father Brown, and we see him through the eyes of Harold March, who becomes very rapidly disillusioned as Chesterton himself had been when his ideals came up against the harsh realities of practical politics. The suggestion that he was modelled upon Marice Baring can, from what I know of Baring, be true in only the most superficial sense.

Both C. Day Lewis (as 'Nicholas Blake') and W.H. Auden have posited the detective story as a form of contemporary fairy-tale; it is scarcely a fashionable view nowadays, when truth is equated with realism, but I think that we should consider Chesterton's stories as fairy-tales—he would certainly have taken this as high praise—which can express a greater truth, and nowhere is this more evident than in the two Horne Fisher stories included here. Yet for all their cynicism, they are highly ingenious puzzles which can be enjoyed purely as entertainments.

IV

In Mr. Pond and Gabriel Gale we have two more of Chesterton's serial detectives, both of whose adventures appeared in magazines before they were collected into books. Mr. Pond is another of Chesterton's 'political' detectives, a mild-mannered Civil Servant not unlike Edgar Wallace's Mr. J.G. Reeder, given to dropping into his conversation some seemingly outrageous remark ("Naturally, having no legs, he won the walking race easily"). It is a characteristic of Chesterton's detectives that they are often considered mad until the rightness of their remarks is ultimately revealed, and both Mr. Pond and Gabriel Gale suffer this annoyance repeatedly. Some of these 'paradoxes' have passed into legend, for example Mr. Pond's "They say travel broadens the mind, but you must have the mind."

Jorge Luis Borges, that acute critic and admirer of Chesterton wrote: "One must anticipate an era in which Poe's invention, the detective story, will vanish. It is the most artificial of all literary *genres*, the one most like a game. Chesterton himself wrote that if the novel is a game of faces, then the detective story is a game of masks. But in spite of this I am sure that Chesterton's stories will always be read, since a mystery that so imaginatively suggests an impossible, fantastic occurrence is interesting for more than the logical explanation contained in the last few lines." Borges considered 'The Three Horsemen of the Apocalypse', one of the Mr. Pond stories included here, to be the best of all Chesterton's tales, with its "long white road, white hussars and white horses, and a fascinating struggle of wills".

Gabriel Gale, the poet in *The Poet and the Lunatics*, has been described as an older version of Gabriel Syme, the poet in *The Man Who Was Thursday*, and he anticipates R.D. Laing's proposition that the apparent madman may be the only truly sane person. Gale represents the common people against the ruling elite, solving crimes through his poetic sensibility and his sensitivity to atmospheres and personalities. In these stories the anarchic high spirits of the early stories is replaced by a sort of nostalgia for better times, now that England is ruled by crooks. That said, it must be added that the stories are wonderful set-pieces, which highly ingenious crimes—although 'The Finger of Stone' contains one of the most outrageous explanations in the entire history of detective fiction; within its own framework it is 'fair', but it requires a cheerful abandonment of disbelief on the part of the reader. Incidentally, an interesting article could be written (though not by me) about the victim, Boyg, an odd figure who crops up a number of times in Chesterton's writings.

V

Finally, a wonderful bonus in the form of a newly-discovered Father Brown story! Lost for decades in the pages of an obscure magazine called *The Premier*, this came to light a few years ago and was reprinted in *The Chesterton Review* (to which many thanks), and this marks its first appearance in any book. It also renders all editions of *The Complete Father Brown* incomplete!

A distinct curiosity, 'The Donnington Affair' was devised by Sir Max Pemberton, who invited the leading mystery writers of the day to solve crimes that he set for them. In 1914 Chesterton and Father Brown were, as we have seen, enormously famous, so, in the October issue of the magazine appeared Pemberton's first part of the story to be followed in the November issue by Chesterton and Father Brown's solution of it. The story would have been a great deal better if Chesterton had written the first part too, of course, and had devised the puzzle himself, but it is delightful to meet Father Brown again after all these years, and it is good to report that his conversation is as stimulating as ever.

We begin, however, with another rarity: an uncollected story called 'The White Pillars Murder' that appeared in another obscure magazine, *English Life*, in 1925. It was discovered by Ellery Queen and published in the 1949 collection, *To the Queen's Taste*—now itself a rare book. This marks its first appearance in any collection of Chesterton's own works.

Queen described it as "the paradoxical detective story to end all paradoxical detective stories", with "a clue so daring in conception as to take one's breath away". It is indeed a virtuoso performance: one of those stories where the reader needs to be suspicious about *everything* if he is to make sense of it, yet which stands up to the most rigorous analysis. I will detain you no longer.

—MARIE SMITH

DR. ADRIAN HYDE, JOHN BRANDON
& WALTER WEIR

IN

The White Pillars Murder

The White Pillars Murder

Those who have discussed the secret of the success of the great detective, Dr. Adrian Hyde, could find no finer example of his remarkable methods than the affair which came to be called "The White Pillars Mystery." But that extraordinary man left no personal notes and we owe our record of it to his two young assistants, John Brandon and Walter Weir. Indeed, as will be seen, it was they who could best describe the first investigations in detail, from the outside; and that for a rather remarkable reason.

They were both men of exceptional ability; they had fought bravely and even brilliantly in the Great War; they were cultivated, they were capable, they were trustworthy, and they were starving. For such was the reward which England in the hour of victory accorded to the deliverers of the world. It was a long time before they consented in desperation to consider anything so remote from their instincts as employment in a private detective agency. Jack Brandon, who was a dark, compact, resolute, restless youth, with a boyish appetite for detective tales and talk, regarded the notion with a half-fascinated apprehension, but his friend Weir, who was long and fair and languid, a lover of music and metaphysics, with a candid disgust.

"I believe it might be frightfully interesting," said Brandon. "Haven't you ever had the detective fever when you couldn't help overhearing somebody say something—'If only he knew what she did to the Archdeacon,' or 'And then the whole business about Susan and the dog will come out.'?"

"Yes," replied Weir, "but you only heard snatches because you didn't mean to listen and almost immediately left off listening. If you were a detective, you'd have to crawl under the bed or hide in the dust-bin to hear the whole secret, till your dignity was as dirty as your clothes."

"Isn't it better than stealing," asked Brandon, gloomily, "which seems to be the next step?"

"Why, no; I'm not sure that it is!" answered his friend.

Then, after a pause, he added, reflectively, "Besides, it isn't as if we'd get the sort of work that's relatively decent. We can't claim to know the wretched trade. Clumsy eavesdropping must be worse than the blind spying on the blind. You've not only got to know what is said, but what is meant. There's a lot of difference between listening and hearing. I don't say I'm exactly in a position to fling away a handsome salary offered me by a great criminologist like Dr. Adrian Hyde, but, unfortunately, he isn't likely to offer it."

But Dr. Adrian Hyde was an unusual person in more ways than one, and a better judge of applicants than most modern employers. He was a very tall man with a chin so sunk on his chest as to give him, in spite of his height, almost a look of being hunchbacked; but though the face seemed thus fixed as in a frame, the eyes were as active as a bird's, shifting and darting everywhere and observing everything; his long limbs ended in large hands and feet, the former being almost always thrust into his trouser-pockets, and the latter being loaded with more than appropriately large boots. With all his awkward figure he was not without gaiety and a taste for good things, especially good wine and tobacco; his manner was grimly genial and his insight and personal judgment marvellously rapid. Which was how it came about that John Brandon and Walter Weir were established at comfortable desks in the detective's private office, when Mr. Alfred Morse was shown in, bringing with him the problem of White Pillars.

Mr. Alfred Morse was a very stolid and serious person with stiffly-brushed brown hair, a heavy brown face and a heavy black suit of mourning of a cut somewhat provincial, or perhaps colonial. His first words were accompanied with an inoffensive but dubious cough and a glance at the two assistants.

"This is rather confidential business," he said.

"Mr. Morse," said Dr. Hyde, with quiet good humour, "if you were knocked down by a cab and carried to a hospital, your life might be saved by the first surgeon in the land: but you couldn't complain if he let students learn from the operation. These are my two cleverest pupils, and if you want good detectives, you must let them be trained."

"Oh, very well," said the visitor, "perhaps it is not quite so easy to talk of the personal tragedy as if we were alone; but I think I can lay the main facts before you.

"I am the brother of Melchior Morse, whose dreadful death is so generally deplored. I need not tell you about him; he was a public man of more than average public spirit; and I suppose his benefactions and social work are known throughout the world. I had not seen so much of him as I could wish till the last few years; for I have been much abroad; I suppose some would call me the rolling stone of the family, compared with my brother, but I was deeply attached to him, and all the resources of the family estate will be open to anyone ready to avenge his death. You will understand I shall not lightly abandon that duty.

"The crime occurred, as you probably know, at his country place called 'White Pillars,' after its rather unique classical architecture; a colonnade in the shape of a crescent, like that at St. Peter's, runs half-way round an artificial lake, to which the descent is by a flight of curved stone steps. It is in the lake that my brother's body was found floating in the moonlight; but as his neck was broken, apparently with a blow, he had clearly been killed elsewhere. When the butler found the body, the moon was on the other side of the house and threw the inner crescent of the colonnade and steps into profound shadow. But the butler swears he saw the figure of the fleeing man in dark outline against the moonlight as it turned the corner of the house. He says it was a striking outline, and he would know it again."

"Those outlines are very vivid sometimes," said the detective, thoughtfully, "but of course very difficult to prove. Were there any other traces? Any footprints or fingerprints?"

"There were no fingerprints," said Morse, gravely, "and the murderer must have meant to take equal care to leave no footprints. That is why the crime was probably committed on the great flight of stone steps. But they say the cleverest murderer forgets something; and when he threw the body in the lake there must have been a splash, which was not quite dry when it was discovered; and it showed the edge of a pretty clear footprint. I have a copy of the thing here, the original is at home.' He passed a brown slip across to Hyde, who looked at it and nodded. "The only other thing on the stone steps that might be a clue was a cigar-stump. My brother did not smoke."

"Well, we will look into those clues more closely in due course," said Dr. Hyde. "Now tell me something about the house and the people in it."

Mr. Morse shrugged his shoulders, as if the family in question did not impress him.

"There were not many people in it," he replied, "putting aside a fairly large staff of servants, headed by the butler, Barton, who has been devoted to my brother for years. The servants all bear a good character; but of course you will consider all that. The other occupants of the house at the time were my brother's wife, a rather silent elderly woman, devoted almost entirely to religion and good works; a niece, of whose prolonged visits the old lady did not perhaps altogether approve, for Miss Barbara Butler is half Irish and rather flighty and excitable; my brother's secretary, Mr. Graves, a very silent young man (I confess I could never make out whether he was shy or sly), and my brother's solicitor, Mr. Caxton, who is an ordinary snuffy lawyer, and happened to be down there on legal business. They might all be guilty in theory, I suppose, but I'm a practical man, and I don't imagine such things in practice."

"Yes, I realized you were a practical man when you first came in," said Dr. Hyde, rather dryly. 'I realized a few other details as well. Is that all you have to tell me?"

"Yes," replied Morse, "I hope I have made myself clear."

"It is well not to forget anything," went on Adrian Hyde, gazing at him calmly. "It is still better not to suppress anything, when confiding in a professional man. You may have heard, perhaps, of a knack I have of noticing things about people. I knew some of the things you told me before you opened your mouth; as that you long lived abroad and had just come up from the country. And it was easy to infer from your own words that you are the heir of your brother's considerable fortune."

"Well, yes, I am," replied Alfred Morse, stolidly.

"When you said you were a rolling stone," went on Adrian Hyde, with the same placid politeness, "I fear some might say you were a stone which the builders were justified in rejecting. Your adventures abroad have not all been happy. I perceive that you deserted from some foreign navy, and that you were once in prison for robbing a bank. If it comes to an inquiry into your brother's death and your present inheritance——"

"Are you trying to suggest," cried the other fiercely, "that appearances are against me?"

"My dear sir," said Dr. Adrian Hyde blandly, "appearances are most damnably against you. But I don't always go by appearances. It all depends. Good day."

When the visitor had withdrawn, looking rather black, the impetuous Brandon broke out into admiration of the Master's methods and besieged him with questions.

"Look here," said the great man, good-humouredly, "you've no business to be asking how I guessed right. You ought to be guessing at the guesses yourselves. Think it out."

"The desertion from a foreign navy," said Weir, slowly, 'might be something to do with those bluish marks on his wrist. Perhaps they were some special tattooing and he'd tried to rub them out."

"That's better," said Dr. Hyde, "you're getting on."

"I know!" cried Brandon, more excitedly, "I know about the prison! They always say, if you once shave your moustache it never grows the same; perhaps there's something like that about hair that's been cropped in gaol. Yes, I thought so. The only thing I can't imagine, is why you should guess he had robbed a bank."

"Well, you think that out too," said Adrian Hyde. "I think you'll find it's the key to the whole of this riddle. And now I'm going to leave this case to you. I'm going to have a half-holiday." As a signal that his own working hours were over, he lit a large and sumptuous cigar, and began pishing and poohing over the newspapers.

"Lord, what rubbish!" he cried. "My God, what headlines! Look at this about White Pillars: 'Whose Was the Hand?' They've murdered even murder with clichés like clubs of wood. Look here, you two fellows had better go down to White Pillars and try to put some sense into them. I'll come down later and clear up the mess."

The two young detectives had originally intended to hire a car, but by the end of their journey they were very glad they had decided to travel by train with the common herd. Even as they were in the act of leaving the train, they had a stroke of luck in the matter of that collecting of stray words and whispers which Weir found the least congenial, but Brandon desperately clung to as the most practicable, of all forms of detective inquiry. The steady scream of a steam-whistle, which was covering all the shouted conversation, stopped suddenly in the fashion that makes a shout shrivel into a whisper. But there was one whisper caught in the silence and sounding clear as a bell; a voice that said, "There were excellent reasons for killing him. I know them, if nobody else does."

Brandon managed to trace the voice to its origin; a sallow face with a long shaven chin and a rather scornful lower lip. He saw the same face more than once on the remainder of his journey, passing the ticket collector, appearing in a car behind them on the road, haunting him so significantly, that he was not surprised to meet the man eventually in the garden of White Pillars, and to have him presented as Mr. Claxton, the solicitor.

"That man evidently knows more than he's told the authorities," said Brandon to his friend, "but I can't get anything more out of him."

"My dear fellow," cried Weir, "that's just what they're all like. Don't you feel by this time that it's the atmosphere of the whole place? It's not a bit like those delightful detective stories. In a detective story all the people in the house are gaping imbeciles, who can't understand anything, and in the midst stands the brilliant sleuth who understands everything. Here am I standing in the midst, a brilliant sleuth, and I believe, on my soul, I'm the only person in the house who doesn't know all about the crime."

"There's one other anyhow," said Brandon, with gloom, "two brilliant sleuths."

"Everybody else knows except the detective," went on Weir; "everybody knows something, anyhow, if it isn't everything. There's something odd even about old Mrs. Morse; she's devoted to charity, yet she doesn't seem to have agreed with her husband's philanthropy. It's as if they'd quarrelled about it. Then there's the secretary, the quiet, good-looking young man, with a square face like Napoleon. He looks as if he would get what he wants, and I've very little doubt that what he wants is that red-haired Irish girl they call Barbara. I think she wants the same thing; but if so there's really no reason for them to hide it. And they are hiding it, or hiding something. Even the butler is secretive. They can't all have been in a conspiracy to kill the old man."

"Anyhow, it all comes back to what I said first," observed Brandon. "If they're in a conspiracy, we can only hope to overhear their talk. It's the only way."

"It's an excessively beastly way," said Weir, calmly, "and we will proceed to follow it."

They were walking slowly round the great semicircle of colonnade that looked inwards upon the lake, that shone like a silver mirror to the moon. It was of the same stretch of clear moonlit

nights as that recent one, on which old Morse had died mysteriously
in the same spot. They could imagine him as he was in many
portraits, a little figure in a skull cap with a white beard thrust
forward, standing on those steps, till a dreadful figure that had no
face in their dreams descended the stairway and struck him down.
They were standing at one end of the colonnade, full of these
visions, when Brandon said suddenly:

"Did you speak?"

"I? No," replied his friend staring.

"Somebody spoke," said Brandon, in a low voice, "yet we seem
to be quite alone."

Then their blood ran cold for an instant. For the wall behind
them spoke; and it seemed to say quite plainly, in a rather harsh
voice:

"Do you remember exactly what you said?"

Weir stared at the wall for an instant; then he slapped it with his
hand with a shaky laugh.

"My God," he cried, "what a miracle! And what a satire! We've
sold ourselves to the devil as a couple of damned eavesdroppers; and
he's put us in the very chamber of eavesdropping—into the ear of
Dionysius, the Tyrant. Don't you see this is a whispering gallery,
and people at the other end of it are whispering?"

"No, they're talking too loud to hear us, I think," whispered
Brandon, "but we'd better lower our voices. It's Caxton the lawyer,
and the young secretary."

The secretary's unmistakable and vigorous voice sounded along
the wall saying:

"I told him I was sick of the whole business; and if I'd known he
was such a tyrant, I'd never have had to do with him. I think I told
him he ought to be shot. I was sorry enough for it afterwards."

Then they heard the lawyer's more croaking tones saying, "Oh,
you said that, did you? Well, there seems no more to be said now.
We had better go in," which was followed by echoing feet and then
silence.

The next day Weir attached himself to the lawyer with a peculiar
pertinacity and made a new effort to get something more out of that
oyster. He was pondering deeply on the very little that he had got,
when Brandon rushed up to him with hardly-restrained excitement.

"I've been at that place again," he cried. "I suppose you'll say I've
sunk lower in the pit of slime, and perhaps I have, but it's got to be

done. I've been listening to the young people this time, and I believe I begin to see something; though heaven knows, it's not what I want to see. The secretary and the girl are in love all right, or have been; and when love is loose pretty dreadful things can happen. They were talking about getting married, of course, at least she was, and what do you think she said? 'He made an excuse of my being under age.' So it's pretty clear the old man opposed the match. No doubt that was what the secretary meant by talking about his tyranny."

"And what did the secretary say when the girl said that?"

"That's the queer thing," answered Brandon, "rather an ugly thing, I begin to fancy. The young man only answered, rather sulkily, I thought: 'Well, he was within his rights there; and perhaps it was for the best.' She broke out in protest: 'How can you say such a thing'; and certainly it was a strange thing for a lover to say."

"What are you driving at?" asked his friend.

"Do you know anything about women?" asked Brandon. "Suppose the old man was not only trying to break off the engagement but *succeeding* in breaking it off. Suppose the young man was weakening and beginning to wonder whether she was worth losing his job for. The woman might have waited any time or eloped any time. But if she thought she was in danger of losing him altogether, don't you think she might have turned on the tempter with the fury of despair? I fear we have got a glimpse of a very heart-rending tragedy. Don't you believe it, too?"

Walter Weir unfolded his long limbs and got slowly to his feet, filling a pipe and looking at his friend with a sort of quizzical melancholy.

"No, I don't believe it," he said, "but that's because I'm such an unbeliever. You see, I don't believe in all this eavesdropping business; I don't think we shine at it. Or, rather, I think you shine too much at it and dazzle yourself blind. I don't believe in all this detective romance about deducing everything from a trifle. I don't believe in your little glimpse of a great tragedy. It would be a great tragedy no doubt, and does you credit as literature or a symbol of life; you can build imaginative things of that sort on a trifle. You can build everything on the trifle except the truth. But in the present practical issue, I don't believe there's a word of truth in it. I don't believe the old man was opposed to the engagement; I don't believe the young man was backing out of it; I believe the young people are perfectly happy and ready to be married tomorrow. I don't believe anybody in this house had any motive to kill Morse or has any notion of how he was killed. In spite of what I said, the poor shabby old sleuth enjoys his own again. I believe I am the only person who knows the truth; and it only came to me in a flash a few minutes ago."

"Why, how do you mean?" asked the other.

"It came to me in a final flash," said Weir, "when you repeated those words of the girl: 'He made the excuse that I was under age'."

After a few puffs of his pipe, he resumed reflectively: "One queer thing is, that the error of the eavesdropper often comes from a thing being too clear. We're so sure that people mean what we mean, that we can't believe they mean what they say. Didn't I once tell you that it's one thing to listen and another to hear? And sometimes the voice talks too plain. For instance, when young Graves, the secretary, said that he was sick of the business, he meant it literally, and not metaphorically. He meant he was sick of Morse's trade, because it was tyrannical."

"Morse's trade? What trade?" asked Brandon, staring.

"Our saintly old philanthropist was a money-lender," replied Weir, "and as great a rascal as his rascally brother. That is the great central fact that explains everything. That is what the girl meant by talking about being under age. She wasn't talking about her love-affair at all, but about some small loan she'd tried to get from the old man and which he refused because she was a minor. Her fiancé made the very sensible comment that perhaps it was all for the best; meaning that she had escaped the net of a usurer. And her momentary protest was only a spirited young lady's lawful privilege of insisting on her lover agreeing with all the silly things she says. That is an example of the error of the eavesdropper, or the fallacy of detection by trifles. But, as I say, it's the moneylending business that's the clue to everything in this house. That's what all of them, even the secretary and solicitor, out of a sort of family pride, are trying to hush up and hide from detectives and newspapers. But the old man's murder was much more likely to get it into the newspapers. They had no motive to murder him, and they didn't murder him."

"Then who did?" demanded Brandon.

"Ah," replied his friend, but with less than his usual languor in the ejaculation and something a little like a hissing intake of the breath. He had seated himself once more, with his elbows on his knees, but the other was surprised to realize something rigid about his new attitude; almost like a creature crouching for a spring. He still spoke quite dryly, however, and merely said:

"In order to answer that, I fancy we must go back to the first talk that we overheard, before we came to the house; the very first of all."

"Oh, I see," said Brandon, a light dawning on his face. "You mean what we heard the solicitor say in the train."

"No," replied Weir, in the same motionless manner, "that was only another illustration touching the secret trade. Of course his solicitor knew he was a money-lender; and knew that any such money-lender has a crowd of victims, who might kill him. It's quite true he was killed by one of those victims. But it wasn't the lawyer's remark in the train that I was talking about, for a very simple reason."

"And why not?" inquired his companion.

"Because that was not the first conversation we overheard."

Walter Weir clutched his knees with his long bony hands, and seemed to stiffen still more as if in a trance, but he went on talking steadily.

"I have told you the moral and the burden of all these things; that it is one thing to hear what men say and another to hear what they mean. And it was at the very first talk that we heard all the words and missed all the meaning. We did not overhear that first talk slinking about in moonlit gardens and whispering galleries. We overheard that first talk sitting openly at our regular desks in broad daylight, in a bright and businesslike office. But we no more made sense of that talk than if it had been half a whisper, heard in a black forest or a cave."

He sprang to his feet as if a stiff spring were released and began striding up and down, with what was for him an unnatural animation.

"That was the talk we really misunderstood," he cried. "That was the conversation that we heard word for word, and yet missed entirely! Fools that we were! Deaf and dumb and imbecile, sitting there like dummies and being stuffed with a stage play! We were actually allowed to be eavesdroppers, tolerated, ticketed, given special permits to be eavesdroppers; and still we could not eavesdrop! I never even guessed till ten minutes ago the meaning of that conversation in the office. That terrible conversation! That terrible meaning! Hate and hateful fear and shameless wickedness and mortal peril—death and hell wrestled naked before our eyes in that office, and we never saw them. A man accused another man of murder across a table, and we never heard it."

"Oh," gasped Brandon at last, "you mean that the Master accused the brother of murder?"

"No!" retorted Weir, in a voice like a volley, "I mean that the brother accused the Master of murder."

"The Master!"

"Yes," answered Weir, and his high voice fell suddenly, "and the accusation was true. The man who murdered old Morse was our employer, Dr. Adrian Hyde."

"What can it all mean?" asked Brandon, and thrust his hand through his thick brown hair.

"That was our mistake at the beginning," went on the other calmly, "that we did not think what it could all mean. Why was the brother so careful to say the reproduction of the footprint was a proof and not the original? Why did Dr. Hyde say the outline of the fugitive would be difficult to prove? Why did he tell us, with that sardonic grin, that the brother having robbed a bank was the key of the riddle? Because the whole of that consultation of the client and the specialist was a fiction for our benefit. The whole course of events was determined by that first thing that happened; that the young and innocent detectives were allowed to remain in the room. Didn't you think yourself the interview was a little too like that at the beginning of every damned detective story? Go over it speech by speech, and you will see that every speech was a thrust or parry under a cloak. That blackmailing blackguard Alfred hunted out Doctor Hyde simply to accuse and squeeze him. Seeing us there, he said, 'This is confidential,' meaning, 'You don't want to be accused before them.' Dr. Hyde answered, 'They're my favourite pupils,' meaning, 'I'm less likely to be blackmailed before them; they shall stay.' Alfred answered, 'Well, I can state my business, if not quite so personally,' meaning, 'I can accuse you so that you understand, if they don't.' And he did. He presented his proofs like pistols across the table; things that sounded rather thin, but, in Hyde's case, happened to be pretty thick. His boots, for instance, happened to be very thick. His huge footprint would be unique enough to be a clue. So would the cigar-end; for very few people can afford to smoke his cigars. Of course, that's what got him tangled up with the money-lender—extravagance. You see how much money you get through if you smoke those cigars all day and never drink anything but the best vintage champagne. And though a black silhouette against the moon sounds as vague as moonshine, Hyde's huge figure and hunched shoulders would be rather marked. Well, you know how the blackmailed man hit back: 'I perceive by your left eyebrow that you are a deserter; I deduce from the pimple on your nose that you were once in gaol,' meaning, 'I know you, and you're as much a crook as I am; expose me and I'll expose you.' Then he said he had deduced in the Sherlock Holmes manner that Alfred had robbed a bank, and that was where he went too far. He presumed on the incredible credulity, which is the mark of the modern mind when anyone has uttered the magic word 'science.' He presumed on the priestcraft of our time; but he presumed the least little bit too much, so far as I was concerned. It was then I first began to doubt. A man might possibly deduce by scientific detection that another man had been in a certain navy or prison, but by no possibility could he deduce from a man's appearance that what he had once robbed was a bank. It was simply impossible. Dr. Hyde knew it was his biggest bluff; that was why he told you in mockery, that it was the key to the riddle. It was; and I managed to get hold of the key."

He chuckled in a hollow fashion as he laid down his pipe. "That jibe at his own bluff was like him; he really is a remarkable man or a remarkable devil. He has a sort of horrible sense of humour. Do you know, I've got a notion that sounds rather a nightmare, about what happened on that great slope of steps that night. I believe Hyde jeered at the journalistic catchword, 'Whose Was the Hand?' partly because he, himself, had managed it without hands. I believe he managed to commit a murder entirely with his feet. I believe he tripped up the poor old usurer and stamped on him on the stone steps with those monstrous boots. An idyllic moonlight scene, isn't it? But there's something that seems to make it worse. I think he had the habit anyhow, partly to avoid leaving his fingerprints, which may be known to the police. Anyhow, I believe he did the whole murder with his hands in his trouser-pockets."

Brandon shuddered suddenly; then collected himself and said, rather weakly:

"Then you don't think the science of observation——"

"Science of observation be damned!" cried Weir. "Do you still think private detectives get to know about criminals by smelling their hair-oil, or counting their buttons? They do it, a whole gang of them do it just as Hyde did. They get to know about criminals by being half criminals themselves, by being of the same rotten world, by belonging to it and by betraying it, by setting a thief to catch a thief, and proving there is no honour among thieves. I don't say there are no honest private detectives, but if there are, you don't get into their service as easily as you and I got into the office of the distinguished Dr. Adrian Hyde. You ask what all this means, and I tell you one thing it means. It means that you and I are going to sweep crossings or scrub out drains. I feel as if I should like a clean job."

RUPERT GRANT & BASIL GRANT
IN

The Tremendous Adventure of Major Brown

The Tremendous
Adventure
of Major Brown

Rabelais, or his wild illustrator Gustave Doré, must have had something to do with the designing of the things called flats in England and America. There is something entirely Gargantuan in the idea of economising space by piling houses on top of each other, front doors and all. And in the chaos and complexity of those perpendicular streets anything may dwell or happen, and it is in one of them, I believe, that the inquirer may find the offices of the Club of Queer Trades. It may be thought at the first glance that the name would attract and startle the passer-by, but nothing attracts or startles in these dim immense hives. The passer-by is only looking for his own melancholy destination, the Montenegro Shipping Agency or the London office of the *Rutland Sentinel*, and passes through the twilight passages as one passes through the twilight corridors of a dream. If the Thugs set up a Strangers' Assassination Company in one of the great buildings in Norfolk Street, and sent in a mild man in spectacles to answer inquiries, no inquiries would be made. And the Club of Queer Trades reigns in a great edifice hidden like a fossil in a mighty cliff of fossils.

The nature of this society, such as we afterwards discovered it to be, is soon and simply told. It is an eccentric and Bohemian Club, of which the absolute condition of membership lies in this, that the candidate must have invented the method by which he earns his living. It must be an entirely new trade. The exact definition of this requirement is given in the two principal rules. First, it must not be a mere application or variation of an existing trade. Thus, for instance, the Club would not admit an insurance agent simply because instead of insuring men's furniture against being burnt in a fire, he insured, let us say, their trousers against being torn by a mad dog. The principle (as Sir Bradcock Burnaby-Bradcock, in the extraordinarily eloquent and soaring speech to the Club on the occasion of the question being raised in the Stormby Smith affair, said wittily and keenly) is the same. Secondly, the trade must be a genuine commercial source of income, the support of its inventor. Thus the Club would not receive a man simply because he chose to pass his days collecting broken sardine tins, unless he could drive a roaring trade in them. Professor Chick made that quite clear. And when one remembers what Professor Chick's own new trade was, one doesn't know whether to laugh or cry.

The discovery of this strange society was a curiously refreshing thing; to realise that there were ten new trades in the world was like looking at the first ship or the first plough. It made a man feel what he should feel, that he was still in the childhood of the world. That I should have come at last upon so singular a body was, I may say without vanity, not altogether singular, for I have a mania for belonging to as many societies as possible: I may be said to collect clubs, and I have accumulated a vast and fantastic variety of specimens ever since, in my audacious youth, I collected the Athenaeum. At some future day, perhaps, I may tell tales, of some of the other bodies to which I have belonged. I will recount the doings of the Dead Man's Shoes Society (that superficially immoral, but darkly justifiable communion); I will explain the curious origin of the Cat and Christian, the name of which has been so shamefully misinterpreted; and the world shall know at least why the Institute of Typewriters coalesced with the Red Tulip League. Of the Ten Teacups, of course I dare not say a word. The first of my revelations, at any rate, shall be concerned with the Club of Queer Trades, which, as I have said, was one of this class, one which I was almost bound to come across sooner or later, because of my singular hobby. The wild youth of the metropolis call me facetiously "The King of Clubs." They also call me "The Cherub," in allusion to the roseate and youthful appearance I have presented in my declining years. I only hope the spirits in the better world have as good dinners as I have. But the finding of the Club of Queer Trades has one very curious thing about it. The most curious thing about it is that it was not discovered by me: it was discovered by my friend Basil Grant, a star-gazer, a mystic, and a man who scarcely stirred out of his attic.

Very few people knew anything of Basil; not because he was in the least unsociable, for if a man out of the street had walked into his rooms he would have kept him talking till morning. Few people knew him, because, like all poets, he could do without them; he welcomed a human face as he might welcome a sudden blend of colour in a sunset; but he no more felt the need of going out to parties than he felt the need of altering the sunset clouds. He lived in a queer and comfortable garret in the roofs of Lambeth. He was surrounded by a chaos of things that were in odd contrast to the slums around him: old fantastic books, swords, armour—the whole dust-hole of romanticism. But his face, amid all these quixotic relics, appeared curiously keen and modern—a powerful, legal face. And no one but I knew who he was.

Long ago as it is, every one remembers the terrible and grotesque scene that occurred in ——, when one of the most acute and forcible of the English judges suddenly went mad on the bench. I had my own view of that occurrence; but about the facts themselves there is no question at all. For some months, indeed for some years, people had detected something curious in the judge's conduct. He seemed to have lost interest in the law, in which he had been beyond expression brilliant and terrible as a K.C., and to be occupied in giving personal and moral advice to the people concerned. He talked more like a priest or a doctor, and a very outspoken one at that. The first thrill was probably given when he said to a man who had attempted a crime of passion: "I sentence you to three years' imprisonment, under the firm, and solemn, and God-given conviction, that what you require is three months at the seaside." He accused criminals from the bench, not so much of their obvious legal crimes, but of things that had never been heard of in a court of justice, monstrous egoism, lack of humour, and morbidity deliberately encouraged. Things came to a head in that celebrated diamond case in which the Prime Minister himself, that brilliant patrician, had to come forward, gracefully and reluctantly, to give evidence against his valet. After the detailed life of the household had been thoroughly exhibited, the judge requested the Premier again to step forward, which he did with quiet dignity. The judge then said, in a sudden, grating voice: "Get a new soul. That thing's not fit for a dog. Get a new soul." All this, of course, in the eyes of the sagacious, was premonitory of that melancholy and farcical day when his wits actually deserted him in open court. It was a libel case between two very eminent and powerful financiers, against both of whom charges of considerable defalcation were brought. The case was long and complex; the advocates were long and eloquent; but at

last, after weeks of work and rhetoric, the time came for the great
judge to give a summing-up; and one of his celebrated masterpieces
of lucidity and pulverising logic was eagerly looked for. He had
spoken very little during the prolonged affair, and he looked sad
and lowering at the end of it. He was silent for a few moments, and
then burst into a stentorian song. His remarks (as reported) were as
follows:—

> "O Rowty-owty tiddly-owty
> Tiddly-owty tiddly-owty
> Highty-ighty tiddly-ighty
> Tiddly-ighty ow."

He then retired from public life and took the garret in Lambeth.

I was sitting there one evening, about six o'clock, over a glass of
that gorgeous Burgundy which he kept behind a pile of black-letter
folios; he was striding about the room, fingering, after a habit of his,
one of the great swords in his collection; the red glare of the strong
fire struck his square features and his fierce grey hair; his blue eyes
were even unusually full of dreams, and he had opened his mouth to
speak dreamily, when the door was flung open, and a pale, fiery
man, with red hair and a huge furred overcoat, swung himself
panting into the room.

"Sorry to bother you, Basil," he gasped. "I took a liberty—made
an appointment here with a man—a client—in five minutes—I beg
your pardon, sir," and he gave me a bow of apology.

Basil smiled at me. "You didn't know," he said, "that I had a
practical brother. This is Rupert Grant, Esquire, who can and does
all there is to be done. Just as I was a failure at one thing, he is a
success at everything. I remember him as a journalist, a house-agent,
a naturalist, an inventor, a publisher, a schoolmaster, a—what are
you now, Rupert?"

"I am and have been for some time," said Rupert, with some
dignity, "a private detective, and there's my client."

A loud rap at the door had cut him short, and, on permission
being given, the door was thrown sharply open and a stout, dapper
man walked swiftly into the room, set his silk hat with a clap on the
table, and said, "Good evening, gentlemen," with a stress on the last
syllable that somehow marked him out as a martinet, military,
literary and social. He had a large head streaked with black and
grey, and an abrupt black moustache, which gave him a look of

fierceness which was contradicted by his sad sea-blue eyes.

Basil immediately said to me, "Let us come into the next room, Gully," and was moving towards the door, but the stranger said:—

"Not at all. Friends remain. Assistance possibly."

The moment I heard him speak I remembered who he was, a certain Major Brown I had met years before in Basil's society. I had forgotten altogether the black dandified figure and the large solemn head, but I remembered the peculiar speech, which consisted of only saying about a quarter of each sentence, and that sharply, like the crack of a gun. I do not know, it may have come from giving orders to troops.

Major Brown was a V.C., and an able and distinguished soldier, but he was anything but a warlike person. Like many among the iron men who recovered British India, he was a man with the natural belief and tastes of an old maid. In his dress he was dapper and yet demure; in his habits he was precise to the point of the exact adjustment of a tea-cup. One enthusiasm he had, which was of the nature of a religion—the cultivation of pansies. And when he talked about his collection, his blue eyes glittered like a child's at a new toy, the eyes that had remained untroubled when the troops were roaring victory round Roberts at Candahar.

"Well, Major," said Rupert Grant, with a lordly heartiness, flinging himself into a chair, "what is the matter with you?"

"Yellow pansies. Coal cellar. P. G. Northover," said the Major, with righteous indignation.

We glanced at each other with inquisitiveness. Basil, who had his eyes shut in his abstracted way, said simply:—

"I beg your pardon."

"Fact is. Street, you know, man, pansies. On wall. Death to me. Something. Preposterous."

We shook our heads gently. Bit by bit, and mainly by the seemingly sleepy assistance of Basil Grant, we pieced together the Major's fragmentary, but excited narration. It would be infamous to submit the reader to what we endured; therefore I will tell the story of Major Brown in my own words. But the reader must imagine the scene. The eyes of Basil closed as in a trance, after his habit, and the eyes of Rupert and myself getting rounder and rounder as we listened to one of the most astounding stories in the world, from the lips of the little man in black, sitting bolt upright in his chair and talking like a telegram.

Major Brown was, I have said, a successful soldier, but by no means an enthusiastic one. So far from regretting his retirement on half-pay, it was with delight that he took a small neat villa, very like a doll's house, and devoted the rest of his life to pansies and weak tea. The thought that battles were over when he had once hung up his sword in the little front hall (along with two patent stew-pots and a bad water-colour), and betaken himself instead to wielding the rake in his little sunlit garden, was to him like having come into a harbour in heaven. He was Dutch-like and precise in his taste in gardening, and had, perhaps, some tendency to drill his flowers like soldiers. He was one of those men who are capable of putting four umbrellas in the stand rather than three, so that two may lean one way and two another; he saw life like a pattern in a freehand drawing-book. And assuredly he would not have believed, or even understood, any one who had told him that within a few yards of his brick paradise he was destined to be caught in a whirlpool of incredible adventures, such as he had never seen or dreamed of in the horrible jungle, or the heart of battle.

One certain bright and windy afternoon, the Major, attired in his usual faultless manner, had set out for his usual constitutional. In crossing from one great residential thoroughfare to another, he happened to pass along one of those aimless looking lanes which lie along the back-garden walls of a row of mansions, and which in their empty and discoloured appearance give one an odd sensation as of being behind the scenes of a theatre. But mean and sulky as the scene might be in the eyes of most of us, it was not altogether so in the Major's, for along the coarse gravel footway was coming a thing which was to him what the passing of a religious procession is to a devout person. A large, heavy man, with fish blue eyes and a ring of irradiating red beard, was pushing before him a barrow, which was ablaze with incomparable flowers. There were splendid specimens of almost every order, but the Major's own favourite pansies predominated. The Major stopped and fell into conversation, and then into bargaining. He treated the man after the manner of collectors and other mad men, that is to say, he carefully and with a sort of anguish selected the best roots from the less excellent, praised some, disparaged others, made a subtle scale ranging from a thrilling worth and rarity to a degraded insignificance, and then bought them all. The man was just pushing off his barrow when he stopped and came close to the Major.

"I'll tell you what, sir," he said. "If you're interested in them things, you just get on to that wall."

"On the wall!" cried the scandalised Major, whose conventional soul quailed within him at the thought of such fantastic trespass.

"Finest show of yellow pansies in England in that there garden, sir," hissed the tempter. "I'll help you up, sir."

How it happened no one will ever know, but that positive enthusiasm of the Major's life triumphed over all its negative traditions, and with an easy leap and swing that showed that he was in no need of physical assistance, he stood on the wall at the end of the strange garden. The second after, the flapping of the frock-coat at his knees made him feel inexpressibly a fool. But the next instant all such trifling sentiments were swallowed up by the most appalling shock of surprise the old soldier had ever felt in all his bold and wandering existence. His eyes fell upon the garden, and there across a large bed in the centre of the lawn was a vast pattern of pansies; they were splendid flowers, but for once it was not their horticultural aspects that Major Brown beheld, for the pansies were arranged in gigantic capital letters so as to form the sentence—

"DEATH TO MAJOR BROWN"

A kindly looking old man, with white whiskers, was watering them.

Brown looked sharply back at the road behind him; the man with the barrow had suddenly vanished. Then he looked again at the lawn with its incredible inscription. Another man might have thought he had gone mad, but Brown did not. When romantic ladies gushed over his V.C. and his military exploits, he sometimes felt himself to be a painfully prosaic person, but by the same token he knew he was incurably sane. Another man, again, might have thought himself a victim of a passing practical joke, but Brown could not easily believe this. He knew from his own quaint learning that the garden arrangement was an elaborate and expensive one; he thought it extravagantly improbable that any one would pour out money like water for a joke against him. Having no explanation whatever to offer, he admitted the fact to himself, like a clear-headed man, and waited as he would have done in the presence of a man with six legs.

At this moment the stout old man with white whiskers looked up, and the watering-can fell from his hand, shooting a swirl of water down the gravel path.

"Who on earth are you?" he gasped, trembling violently.

"I am Major Brown," said that individual, who was always cool in the hour of action.

The old man gaped helplessly like some monstrous fish. At last he stammered wildly, "Come down—come down here!"

"At your service," said the Major, and alighted at a bound on the grass beside him, without disarranging his silk hat.

The old man turned his broad back and set off at a sort of waddling run towards the house, followed with swift steps by the Major. His guide led him through the back passages of a gloomy, but gorgeously appointed house, until they reached the door of the front room. Then the old man turned with a face of apoplectic terror dimly showing in the twilight.

"For heaven's sake," he said, "don't mention jackals."

Then he threw open the door, releasing a burst of red lamplight, and ran downstairs with a clatter.

The Major stepped into a rich, glowing room, full of red copper, and peacock and purple hangings, hat in hand. He had the finest manners in the world, and though mystified, was not in the least embarrassed to see that the only occupant was a lady, sitting by the window, looking out.

"Madam," he said, bowing simply, "I am Major Brown."

"Sit down," said the lady; but she did not turn her head.

She was a graceful, green-clad figure, with fiery red hair and a flavour of Bedford Park. "You have come, I suppose," she said mournfully, "to tax me about the hateful title-deeds."

"I have come, madam," he said, "to know what is the matter. To know why my name is written across your garden. Not amicably either."

He spoke grimly, for the thing had hit him. It is impossible to describe the effect produced on the mind by that quiet and sunny garden scene, the frame for a stunning and brutal personality. The evening air was still, and the grass was golden in the place where the little flowers he studied cried to heaven for his blood.

"You know I must not turn round," said the lady; "every afternoon till the stroke of six I must keep my face turned to the street."

Some queer and unusual inspiration made the prosaic soldier resolute to accept these outrageous riddles without surprise.

"It is almost six," he said; and even as he spoke the barbaric copper clock upon the wall clanged the first stroke of the hour. At the sixth the lady sprung up and turned on the Major one of the queerest and yet most attractive faces he had even seen in his life; open, and yet tantalising, the face of an elf.

"That makes the third year I have waited," she cried. "This is an anniversary. The waiting almost makes one wish the frightful thing would happen once and for all."

And even as she spoke, a sudden rending cry broke the stillness. From low down on the pavement of the dim street (it was already twilight) a voice cried out with a raucous and merciless distinctness:—

"Major Brown, Major Brown, where does the jackal dwell?"

Brown was decisive and silent in action. He strode to the front door and looked out. There was no sign of life in the blue gloaming of the street, where one or two lamps were beginning to light their lemon sparks. On returning, he found the lady in green trembling.

"It is the end," she cried, with shaking lips; "it may be death for both of us. Whenever——"

But even as she spoke her speech was cloven by another hoarse proclamation from the dark street, again horribly articulate.

"Major Brown, Major Brown, how did the jackal die?"

Brown dashed out of the door and down the steps, but again he was frustrated; there was no figure in sight, and the street was far too long and empty for the shouter to have run away. Even the rational Major was a little shaken as he returned at a certain time to the drawing-room. Scarcely had he done so than the terrific voice came:—

"Major Brown, Major Brown, where did——"

Brown was in the street almost at a bound, and he was in time—in time to see something which at first glance froze the blood. The cries appeared to come from a decapitated head resting on the pavement.

The next moment the pale Major understood. It was the head of a man thrust through the coal-hole in the street. The next moment again, it had vanished, and Major Brown turned to the lady. "Where's your coal cellar?" he said, and stepped out into the passage.

She looked at him with wild grey eyes. "You will not go down," she cried, "alone, into the dark hole, with that beast?"

"Is this the way?" replied Brown, and descended the kitchen stairs three at a time. He flung open the door of a black cavity and stepped in, feeling in his pocket for matches. As his right hand was thus occupied, a pair of great slimy hands came out of the darkness, hands clearly belonging to a man of gigantic stature, and seized him by the back of the head. They forced him down, down in the suffocating darkness, a brutal image of destiny. But the Major's head, though upside down, was perfectly clear and intellectual. He gave quietly under the pressure until he had slid down almost to his hands and knees. Then finding the knees of the invisible monster within a foot of him, he simply put out one of his long, bony, and skilful hands, and gripping the leg by a muscle pulled it off the ground, and laid the huge living man, with a crash, along the floor. He strove to rise, but Brown was on top like a cat. They rolled over and over. Big as the man was, he had evidently now no desire but to escape; he made sprawls hither and thither to get past the Major to the door, but that tenacious person had him hard by the coat collar and hung with the other hand to a beam. At length there came a strain in holding back this human bull, a strain under which Brown expected his hand to rend and part from the arm. But something else rent and parted; and the dim fat figure of the giant vanished out of the cellar, leaving the torn coat in the Major's hand; the only fruit of his adventure and the only clue to the mystery. For when he went up and out at the front door, the lady, the rich hangings, and the whole equipment of the house had disappeared. It had only bare boards and whitewashed walls.

"The lady was in the conspiracy, of course," said Rupert, nodding. Major Brown turned brick red. "I beg your pardon," he said, "I think not."

Rupert raised his eyebrows and looked at him for a moment, but said nothing. When next he spoke he asked:—

"Was there anything in the pockets of the coat?"

"There was sevenpence halfpenny in coppers and a threepenny-bit," said the Major, carefully; "there was a cigarette-holder, a piece of string, and this letter," and he laid it on the table. It ran as follows:—

"DEAR MR. PLOVER,

"I am annoyed to hear that some delay has occurred in the arrangements re Major Brown. Please see that he is attacked as per arrangement to-morrow. The coal-cellar, of course.
'Yours faithfully,
"P. G. NORTHOVER."

Rupert Grant was leaning forward listening with hawk-like eyes. He cut in:—

"Is it dated from anywhere?"

"No—oh, yes!" replied Brown, glancing upon the paper; "14 Tanner's Court, North——"

Rupert sprang up and struck his hands together.

"Then why are we hanging here? Let's get along. Basil, lend me your revolver."

Basil was staring into the embers like a man in a trance; and it was some time before he answered:—

"I don't think you'll need it."

"Perhaps not," said Rupert, getting into his fur coat. "One never knows. But going down a dark court to see criminals—"

"Do you think they are criminals?" asked his brother.

Rupert laughed stoutly. "Giving orders to a subordinate to strangle a harmless stranger in a coal-cellar may strike you as a very blameless experiment, but——"

"Do you think they wanted to strangle the Major?" asked Basil, in the same distant and monotonous voice.

"My dear fellow, you've been asleep. Look at the letter."

"I am looking at the letter," said the mad judge calmly; though, as a matter of fact he was looking at the fire. "I don't think it's the sort of letter one criminal would write to another."

"My dear boy, you are glorious," cried Rupert, turning round, with laughter in his bright blue eyes. "Your methods amaze me. Why, there *is* the letter. It *is* written, and it does give orders for a crime. You might as well say that the Nelson Column was not at all the sort of thing that was likely to be set up in Trafalgar Square."

Basil Grant shook all over with a sort of silent laughter, but did not otherwise move.

"That's rather good," he said; "but, of course, logic like that's not what is really wanted. It's a question of spiritual atmosphere. It's not a criminal letter."

"It is. It's a matter of fact," cried the other in an agony of reasonableness.

"Facts," murmured Basil, like one mentioning some strange, far-off animals, "how facts obscure the truth. I may be silly—in fact, I'm off my head—but I never could believe in that man—what's his name, in those capital stories?—Sherlock Holmes. Every detail points to something, certainly; but generally to the wrong thing. Facts point in all directions, it seems to me, like the thousands of twigs on a tree. It's only the life of the tree that has unity and goes up—only the green blood that springs, like a fountain, at the stars."

"But what the deuce else can the letter be but criminal?"

"We have eternity to stretch our legs in," replied the mystic. "It can be an infinity of things. I haven't seen any of them—I've only seen the letter. I look at that, and say it's not criminal."

"Then what's the origin of it?"

"I haven't the vaguest idea."

"Then why don't you accept the ordinary explanation?"

Basil continued for a little to glare at the coals, and seemed collecting his thoughts in a humble and even painful way. Then he said:—

"Suppose you went out into the moonlight. Suppose you passed through silent, silvery streets and squares until you came into an open and deserted space, set with a few monuments, and you beheld one dressed as a ballet girl dancing in the argent glimmer. And suppose you looked, and saw it was a man disguised. And suppose you looked again, and saw it was Lord Kitchener. What would you think?"

He paused a moment, and went on:—

"You could not adopt the ordinary explanation. The ordinary explanation of putting on singular clothes is that you look nice in them; you would not think that Lord Kitchener dressed up like a ballet girl out of ordinary personal vanity. You would think it much more likely that he inherited a dancing madness from a great grandmother; or had been hypnotised at a séance; or threatened by a secret society with death if he refused the ordeal. With Baden-Powell, say, it might be a bet—but not with Kitchener. I should know all that, because in my public days I knew him quite well. So I know that letter quite well, and criminals quite well. It's not a criminal's letter. It's all atmospheres." And he closed his eyes and passed his hand over his forehead.

Rupert and the Major were regarding him with a mixture of respect and pity. The former said:—

"Well, I'm going, anyhow, and shall continue to think—until your spiritual mystery turns up—that a man who sends a note recommending a crime, that is, actually a crime that is actually carried out, at least tentatively, is, in all probability, a little casual in his moral tastes. Can I have that revolver?"

"Certainly," said Basil, getting up. "But I am coming with you." And he flung an old cape or cloak round him, and took a sword-stick from the corner.

"You!" said Rupert, with some surprise, "you scarcely ever leave your hole to look at anything on the face of the earth."

Basil fitted on a formidable old white hat.

"I scarcely ever," he said, with an unconscious and colossal arrogance, "hear of anything on the face of the earth that I do not understand at once, without going to see it."

And he led the way out into the purple night.

We four swung along the flaring Lambeth streets, across Westminster Bridge, and along the Embankment in the direction of that part of Fleet Street which contained Tanner's Court. The erect, black figure of Major Brown, seen from behind, was a quaint contrast to the hound-like stoop and flapping mantle of young Rupert Grant, who adopted, with childlike delight, all the dramatic poses of the detective of fiction. The finest among his many fine qualities was his boyish appetite for the colour and poetry of London. Basil, who walked behind, with his face turned blindly to the stars, had the look of a somnambulist.

Rupert paused at the corner of Tanner's Court, with a quiver of delight at danger, and gripped Basil's revolver in his greatcoat pocket.

"Shall we go in now?" he asked.

"Not get police?" asked Major Brown, glancing sharply up and down the street.

"I am not sure," answered Rupert, knitting his brows. "Of course, it's quite clear, the thing's all crooked. But there are three of us, and——"

"I shouldn't get the police," said Basil in a queer voice. Rupert glanced at him and stared hard.

"Basil," he cried, "you're trembling. What's the matter—are you afraid?"

"Cold, perhaps," said the Major, eyeing him. There was no doubt that he was shaking.

At last, after a few moments' scrutiny, Rupert broke into a curse.

"You're laughing," he cried. "I know that confounded, silent, shaky laugh of yours. What the deuce is the amusement, Basil? Here we are, all three of us, within a yard of a den of ruffians——"

"But I shouldn't call the police," said Basil. "We four heroes are quite equal to a host," and he continued to quake with his mysterious mirth.

Rupert turned with impatience and strode swiftly down the court, the rest of us following. When he reached the door of No. 14 he turned abruptly, the revolver glittering in his hand.

"Stand close," he said in the voice of a commander. "The scoundrel may be attempting an escape at this moment. We must fling open the door and rush in."

The four of us cowered instantly under the archway, rigid, except for the old judge and his convulsion of merriment.

"Now," hissed Rupert Grant, turning his pale face and burning eyes suddenly over his shoulder, "when I say 'Four,' follow me with a rush. If I say 'Hold him,' pin the fellows down, whoever they are. If I say 'Stop,' stop. I shall say that if there is more than three. If they attack us I shall empty my revolver on them. Basil, have your sword-stick ready. Now—one, two, three, four!"

With the sound of the word the door burst open, and we fell into the room like an invasion, only to stop dead.

The room, which was an ordinary and neatly-appointed office, appeared, at the first glance, to be empty. But on a second and more careful glance, we saw seated behind a very large desk with pigeon-holes and drawers of bewildering multiplicity, a small man with a black waxed moustache, and the air of a very average clerk, writing hard. He looked up as we came to a standstill.

"Did you knock?" he asked pleasantly. "I am sorry if I did not hear. What can I do for you?"

There was a doubtful pause, and then, by general consent, the Major himself, the victim of the outrage, stepped forward.

The letter was in his hand, and he looked unusually grim.

"Is your name P. G. Northover?" he asked.

"That is my name," replied the other, smiling.

"I think," said Major Brown, with an increase in the dark glow of his face, "that this letter was written by you." And with a loud clap he struck open the letter on the desk with his clenched fist. The man called Northover looked at it with unaffected interest, and merely nodded.

"Well, sir," said the Major, breathing hard, "what about that?"

"What about it, precisely," said the man with the moustache.

"I am Major Brown," said that gentleman sternly.

Northover bowed. "Pleased to meet you, sir. What have you to say to me?"

"Say!" cried the Major, loosing a sudden tempest: "why, I want this confounded thing settled. I want——"

"Certainly, sir," said Northover, jumping up with a slight elevation of the eyebrows. "Will you take a chair for a moment." And he pressed an electric bell just above him, which thrilled and tinkled in a room beyond. The Major put his hand on the back of the chair offered him, but stood chafing and beating the floor with his polished boot.

The next moment an inner glass door was opened, and a fair, weedy, young man, in a frock-coat, entered from within.

"Mr. Hopson," said Northover, "this is Major Brown. Will you please finish that thing for him I gave you this morning and bring it in?"

"Yes, sir," said Mr. Hopson, and vanished like lightning.

"You will excuse me, gentlemen," said the egregious Northover, with his radiant smile, "if I continue to work until Mr. Hopson is ready. I have some books that must be cleared up before I get away on my holiday to-morrow. And we all like a whiff of the country, don't we? Ha! ha!"

The criminal took up his pen with a childlike laugh, and a silence ensued; a placid and busy silence on the part of Mr. P. G. Northover; a raging silence on the part of everybody else.

At length the scratching of Northover's pen in the stillness was mingled with a knock at the door, almost instantaneous with the turning of the handle, and Mr. Hopson came in again with the same silent rapidity, placed a paper before his principal, and disappeared again.

The man at the desk pulled and twisted his spiky moustache for a few moments as he ran his eye up and down the paper presented to him. He took up his pen, with a slight, instantaneous frown, and altered something, muttering—"Careless." Then he read it again with the same impenetrable reflectiveness, and finally handed it to the frantic Brown, whose hand was beating the devil's tattoo on the back of the chair.

"I think you will find that all right, Major," he said briefly.

The Major looked at it; whether he found it all right or not will appear later, but he found it like this:

Major Brown to P. G. Northover

	£	s.	d.
January 1, to account rendered	5	6	0
May 9, to potting and embedding of 200 pansies	2	0	0
To cost of trolley with flowers	0	15	0
To hiring of man with trolley	0	5	0
To hire of house and garden for one day	1	0	0
To furnishing of room in peacock curtains, copper ornaments, &c.	3	0	0
To salary of Miss Jameson	1	0	0
To salary of Mr. Plover	1	0	0
Total	£14	6	0

A remittance will oblige.

"What," said Brown, after a dead pause, and with eyes that seemed slowly rising out of his head. "What in heaven's name is this?"

"What is it?" repeated Northover, cocking his eyebrow with amusement. "It's your account, of course."

"My account!" The Major's ideas appeared to be in a vague stampede. "My account. And what have I got to do with it?"

"Well," said Northover, laughing outright, "naturally I prefer you to pay it."

The Major's hand was still resting on the back of the chair as the words came. He scarcely stirred otherwise, but he lifted the chair bodily into the air with one hand and hurled it at Northover's head.

The legs crashed against the desk, so that Northover only got a blow on the elbow as he sprang up with clenched fists, only to be seized by the united rush of the rest of us. The chair had fallen clattering on the empty floor.

"Let me go, you scamps," he shouted. "Let me——"

"Stand still," cried Rupert, authoritatively. "Major Brown's action is excusable. The abominable crime you have attempted——"

"A customer has a perfect right," said Northover hotly, "to question an alleged overcharge, but confound it all, not to throw furniture."

"What, in God's name, do you mean by your customers and overcharges?" shrieked Major Brown, whose keen feminine nature, steady in pain or danger, became almost hysterical in the presence of a long and exasperating mystery. "Who are you? I've never seen you or your insolent tomfool bills. I know one of your cursed brutes tried to choke me——"

"Mad," said Northover, gazing blankly round; "all of them mad. I didn't know they travelled in quartettes."

"Enough of this prevarication," said Rupert; "your crimes are discovered. A policeman is stationed at the corner of the court. Though only a private detective myself, I will take the responsibility of telling you that anything you say——"

"Mad," repeated Northover, with a weary air.

And at this moment, for the first time, there struck in among them the strange, sleepy voice of Basil Grant.

"Major Brown," he said, "may I ask you a question?"

The Major turned his head with an increased bewilderment.

"You?" he cried; "certainly, Mr. Grant."

"Can you tell me," said the mystic, with sunken head and lowering brow, as he traced a pattern in the dust with his sword-stick, "can you tell me what was the name of the man who lived in your house before you?"

The unhappy Major was only faintly more disturbed by this last and futile irrelevancy, and he answered vaguely:

"Yes, I think so; a man named Gurney something—a name with a hyphen—Gurney-Brown; that was it."

"And when did the house change hands?" said Basil, looking up sharply. His strange eyes were burning brilliantly.

"I came in last month," said the Major.

And at the mere word the criminal Northover suddenly fell into his great office chair and shouted with a volleying laughter.

"Oh! it's too perfect—it's too exquisite," he gasped, beating the arms with his fists. He was laughing deafeningly; Basil Grant was laughing voicelessly; and the rest of us only felt that our heads were like weathercocks in a whirlwind.

"Confound it, Basil," cried Rupert, stamping. "If you don't want me to go mad and blow your metaphysical brains out, tell me what all this means?"

Northover rose.

"Permit me, sir, to explain," he said. "And, first of all, permit me to apologise to you, Major Brown, for a most abominable and unpardonable blunder, which has caused you menace and incon-venience, in which, if you will allow me to say so, you have behaved with astonishing courage and dignity. Of course you need not trouble about the bill. We will stand the loss." And, tearing the paper across, he flung the halves into the waste-paper basket and bowed.

Poor Brown's face was still a picture of distraction. "But I don't even begin to understand," he cried. "What bill? what blunder? what loss?"

Mr. P. G. Northover advanced in the centre of the room, thoughtfully, and with a great deal of unconscious dignity. On closer consideration, there were apparent about him other things beside a screwed moustache, especially a lean, sallow face, hawk-like, and not without a care-worn intelligence. Then he looked up abruptly.

"Do you know where you are, Major?" he said.

"God knows I don't," said the warrior, with fervour.

"You are standing," replied Northover, "in the office of the Adventure and Romance Agency, Limited."

"And what's that?" blankly inquired Brown.

The man of business leaned over the back of the chair, and fixed his dark eyes on the other's face.

"Major," said he, "did you ever, as you walked along the empty street upon some idle afternoon, feel the utter hunger for something to happen—something, in the splendid words of Walt Whitman: 'Something pernicious and dread; something far removed from a puny and pious life; something unproved; something in a trance; something loosed from its anchorage, and driving free.' Did you ever feel that?"

"Certainly not," said the Major shortly.

"Then I must explain with more elaboration," said Mr. North-over, with a sigh. "The Adventure and Romance Agency has been started to meet a great modern desire. On every side, in conversation and in literature, we hear of the desire for a larger theatre of events—for something to waylay us and lead us splendidly astray. Now the man who feels this desire for a varied life pays a yearly or a quarterly sum to the Adventure and Romance Agency; in return, the Adventure and Romance Agency undertakes to surround him with startling and weird events. As a man is leaving his front door, an excited sweep approaches him and assures him of a plot against his life; he gets into a cab, and is driven to an opium den; he receives a mysterious telegram or a dramatic visit, and is immediately in a

THE TREMENDOUS ADVENTURE OF MAJOR BROWN 49

vortex of incidents. A very picturesque and moving story is first
written by one of the staff of distinguished novelists who are at
present hard at work in the adjoining room. Yours, Major Brown
(designed by our Mr. Grigsby), I consider peculiarly forcible and
pointed; it is almost a pity you did not see the end of it. I need
scarcely explain further the monstrous mistake. Your predecessor in
your present house, Mr. Gurney-Brown, was a subscriber to our
agency, and our foolish clerks, ignoring alike the dignity of the
hyphen and the glory of military rank, positively imagined that
Major Brown and Mr. Gurney-Brown were the same person. Thus
you were suddenly hurled into the middle of another man's story."

"How on earth does the thing work?" asked Rupert Grant, with
bright and fascinated eyes.

"We believe that we are doing a noble work," said Northover
warmly. "It has continually struck us that there is no element in
modern life that is more lamentable than the fact that the modern
man has to seek all artistic existence in a sedentary state. If he wishes
to float into fairyland, he reads a book; if he wishes to dash into the
thick of battle, he reads a book; if he wishes to soar into heaven, he
reads a book; if he wishes to slide down the banisters, he reads a
book. We give him these visions, but we give him exercise at the
same time, the necessity of leaping from wall to wall, of fighting
strange gentlemen, of running down long streets from pursuers—all
healthy and pleasant exercises. We give him a glimpse of that great
morning world of Robin Hood or the Knights Errant, when one
great game was played under the splendid sky. We give him back his
childhood, that godlike time when we can act stories, be our own
heroes, and at the same instant dance and dream."

Basil gazed at him curiously. The most singular psychological
discovery had been reserved to the end, for as the little business man
ceased speaking he had the blazing eyes of a fanatic.

Major Brown received the explanation with complete simplicity
and good humour.

"Of course; awfully dense sir," he said. "No doubt at all, the
scheme excellent. But I don't think—" He paused a moment, and
looked dreamily out of the window. "I don't think you will find me
in it. Somehow, when one's seen—seen the thing itself, you
know—blood and men screaming, one feels about having a little
house and a little hobby; in the Bible, you know, 'There remaineth a
rest.'"

Northover bowed. Then after a pause, he said:

"Gentlemen, may I offer you my card. If any of the rest of you desire, at any time, to communicate with me, despite Major Brown's view of the matter——"

"I should be obliged for your card, sir," said the Major, in his abrupt but courteous voice. "Pay for chair."

The agent of Romance and Adventure handed his card, laughing. It ran, "P. G. Northover, B.A., C.Q.T., Adventure and Romance Agency, 14 Tanner's Court, Fleet Street."

"What on earth is 'C.Q.T.?'" asked Rupert Grant, looking over the Major's shoulder.

"Don't you know?" returned Northover. "Haven't you ever heard of the Club of Queer Trades?"

"There seems to be a confounded lot of funny things we haven't heard of," said the little Major, reflectively. "What's this one?"

"The Club of Queer Trades is a society consisting exclusively of people who have invented some new and curious way of making money. I was one of the earliest members."

"You deserve to be," said Basil, taking up his great white hat, with a smile, and speaking for the last time that evening.

When they had passed out the Adventure and Romance agent wore a queer smile, as he trod down the fire and locked his desk up. "A fine chap, that Major; when one hasn't a touch of the poet one stands some chance of being a poem. But to think of such a clockwork little creature of all people getting into the nets of one of Grigsby's tales," and he laughed out aloud in the silence.

Just as the laugh echoed away, there came a sharp knock at the door. An owlish head, with dark moustaches, was thrust in, with deprecating and somewhat absurd inquiry.

"What! back again, Major?" cried Northover in surprise. "What can I do for you?"

The Major shuffled feverishly into the room.

"It's horribly absurd," he said. "Something must have got started in me that I never knew before. But upon my soul I feel the most desperate desire to know the end of it all."

"The end of it all?"

"Yes," said the Major, "'Jackals,' and the title-deeds, and 'death to Major Brown.'"

The agent's face grew grave, but his eyes were amused.

"I am terribly sorry, Major," said he, "but what you ask is

impossible. I don't know anyone I would sooner oblige than you; but the rules of the agency are strict. The Adventures are confidential; you are an outsider; I am not allowed to let you know an inch more than I can help. I do hope you understand——"

"There is no one," said Brown, "who understands discipline better than I do. Thank you very much. Good-night."

And the little man withdrew for the last time.

He married Miss Jameson, the lady with the red hair and the green garments. She was an actress, employed (with many others) by the Romance Agency; and her marriage with the prim old veteran caused some stir in her languid and intellectualised set. She always replied very quietly that she had met scores of men who acted splendidly in the charades provided for them by Northover, but that she had only met one man who went down into a coal-cellar when he really thought it contained a murderer.

The Major and she are living as happily as birds, in an absurd villa, and the former has taken to smoking. Otherwise he is unchanged—except, perhaps, there are moments when, alert and full of feminine unselfishness as the Major is by nature, he falls into a trance of abstraction. Then his wife recognises with a concealed smile, by the blind look in his blue eyes, that he is wondering what were the title-deeds, and why he was not allowed to mention jackals. But, like so many old soldiers, Brown is religious, and believes that he will realise the rest of those purple adventures in a better world.

RUPERT GRANT & BASIL GRANT
IN

The Singular
Speculation of
the House Agent

The Singular Speculation of the House Agent

Lieutenant Drummond Keith was a man about whom conversation always burst like a thunderstorm the moment he left the room. This arose from many separate touches about him. He was a light, loose person, who wore light, loose clothes, generally white, as if he were in the tropics; he was lean and graceful, like a panther, and he had restless black eyes.

He was very impecunious. He had one of the habits of the poor in a degree so exaggerated as immeasurably to eclipse the most miserable of the unemployed: I mean the habit of continual change of lodgings. There are inland tracts of London where, in the very heart of artificial civilisation, humanity has almost become nomadic once more. But in that restless interior there was no ragged tramp so restless as the elegant officer in the loose white clothes. He had shot a great many things in his time, to judge from his conversation, from partridges to elephants, but his slangier acquaintances were of opinion that "the moon" had been not unfrequently amid the victims of his victorious rifle. The phrase is a fine one, and suggests a mystic, elvish, nocturnal hunting.

He carried from house to house and from parish to parish a kit which consisted practically of five articles. Two odd-looking, large-bladed spears, tied together, the weapons, I suppose, of some savage tribe, a green umbrella, a huge and tattered copy of the "Pickwick Papers," a big game rifle, and a large sealed jar of some unholy Oriental wine. These always went into every new lodging, even for one night; and they went in quite undisguised, tied up in wisps of string or straw, to the delight of the poetic gutter boys in the little grey streets.

I had forgotten to mention that he always carried also his old regimental sword. But this raised another odd question about him. Slim and active as he was, he was no longer very young. His hair, indeed, was quite grey, though his rather wild almost Italian moustache retained its blackness, and his face was careworn under its almost Italian gaiety. To find a middle-aged man who has left the army at the primitive rank of lieutenant is unusual and not necessarily encouraging. With the more cautious and solid this fact, like his endless flitting, did the mysterious gentleman no good.

Lastly, he was a man who told the kind of adventures which win a man admiration, but not respect. They came out of queer places, where a good man would scarcely find himself, out of opium dens and gambling hells; they had the heat of the thieves' kitchens or smelled of a strange smoke from cannibal incantations. These are the kind of stories which discredit a person almost equally whether they are believed or no. If Keith's tales were false he was a liar; if they were true he had had, at any rate, every opportunity of being a scamp.

He had just left the room in which I sat with Basil Grant and his brother Rupert, the voluble amateur detective. And as I say was invariably the case, we were all talking about him. Rupert Grant was a clever young fellow, but he had that tendency which youth and cleverness, when sharply combined, so often produce, a somewhat extravagant scepticism. He saw doubt and guilt everywhere, and it was meat and drink to him. I had often got irritated with this boyish incredulity of his, but on this particular occasion I am bound to say that I thought him so obviously right that I was astounded at Basil's opposing him, however banteringly.

I could swallow a good deal, being naturally of a simple turn, but I could not swallow Lieutenant Keith's autobiography.

"You don't seriously mean, Basil," I said, "that you think that that fellow really did go as a stowaway with Nansen and pretend to be the Mad Mullah and——"

"He has one fault," said Basil, thoughtfully, "or virtue, as you may happen to regard it. He tells the truth in too exact and bald a style; he is too veracious."

"Oh! if you are going to be paradoxical," said Rupert contemptuously, "be a bit funnier than that. Say, for instance, that he has lived all his life in one ancestral manor."

"No, he's extremely fond of change of scene," replied Basil dispassionately, "and of living in odd places. That doesn't prevent his chief trait being verbal exactitude. What you people don't understand is that telling a thing crudely and coarsely as it happened makes it sound frightfully strange. The sort of things Keith recounts are not the sort of things that a man would make up to cover himself with honour; they are too absurd. But they are the sort of things that a man would do if he were sufficiently filled with the soul of skylarking."

"So far from paradox," said his brother, with something rather like a sneer, "you seem to be going in for journalese proberbs. Do you believe that truth is stranger than fiction?"

"Truth must of necessity be stranger than fiction," said Basil placidly. "For fiction is the creation of the human mind, and therefore is congenial to it."

"Well, you lieutenant's truth is stranger, if it is truth, than anything I ever heard of," said Rupert, relapsing into flippancy. "Do you, on your soul, believe in all that about the shark and the camera?"

"I believe Keith's words," answered the other. "He is an honest man."

"I should like to question a regiment of his landladies," said Rupert cynically.

"I must say, I think you can hardly regard him as unimpeachable merely in himself," I said mildly; "his mode of life——"

Before I could complete the sentence the door was flung open and Drummond Keith appeared again on the threshold, his white Panama on his head.

"I say, Grant," he said, knocking off his cigarette ash against the door, "I've got no money in the world till next April. Could you lend me a hundred pounds? There's a good chap."

Rupert and I looked at each other in an ironical silence. Basil, who was sitting by his desk, swung the chair round idly on its screw and picked up a quill-pen.

"Shall I cross it?" he asked, opening a cheque-book.

"Really," began Rupert, with a rather nervous loudness, "since Lieutenant Keith has seen fit to make this suggestion to Basil before his family, I——"

"Here you are, Ugly," said Basil, fluttering a cheque in the direction of the quite nonchalant officer. "Are you in a hurry?"

"Yes," replied Keith, in a rather abrupt way. "As a matter of fact I want it now. I want to see my—er—business man."

Rupert was eyeing him sarcastically, and I could see that it was on the tip of his tongue to say, inquiringly, "Receiver of stolen goods, perhaps." What he did say was:

"A business man? That's rather a general description, Lieutenant Keith."

Keith looked at him sharply, and then said, with something rather like ill-temper:

"He's a thingum-my-bob, a house-agent, say. I'm going to see him."

"Oh, you're going to see a house-agent, are you?" said Rupert Grant grimly. "Do you know, Mr. Keith, I think I should very much like to go with you?"

Basil shook with his soundless laughter. Lieutenant Keith started a little; his brow blackened sharply.

"I beg your pardon," he said. "What did you say?"

Rupert's face had been growing from stage to stage of ferocious irony, and he answered:

"I was saying that I wondered whether you would mind our strolling along with you to this house-agent's."

The visitor swung his stick with a sudden whirling violence.

"Oh, in God's name, come to my house-agent's! Come to my bedroom. Look under my bed. Examine my dust-bin. Come along!" And with a furious energy which took away our breath he banged his way out of the room.

Rupert Grant, his restless blue eyes dancing with his detective excitement, soon shouldered alongside him, talking to him with that transparent camaraderie which he imagined to be appropriate from the disguised policeman to the disguised criminal. His interpretation was certainly corroborated by one particular detail, the unmistakable unrest, annoyance, and nervousness of the man with whom he walked. Basil and I tramped behind, and it was not necessary for us to tell each other that we had both noticed this.

Lieutenant Drummond Keith led us through very extraordinary and unpromising neighbourhoods in the search for his remarkable house-agent. Neither of the brothers Grant failed to notice this fact. As the streets grew closer and more crooked and the roofs lower and the gutters grosser with mud, a darker curiosity deepened on the brows of Basil, and the figure of Rupert seen from behind seemed to fill the street with a gigantic swagger of success. At length, at the end of the fourth or fifth lean grey street in that sterile district we came suddenly to a halt, the mysterious lieutenant looking once more about him with a sort of sulky desperation. Above a row of shutters and a door, all indescribably dingy in appearance and in size scarce sufficient even for a penny toyshop, ran the inscription: "P. Montmorency, House-Agent."

"This is the office of which I spoke," said Keith, in a cutting voice. "Will you wait here a moment, or does your astonishing tenderness about my welfare lead you to wish to overhear everything I have to say to my business adviser?"

Rupert's face was white and shaking with excitement; nothing on earth would have induced him now to have abandoned his prey.

"If you will excuse me," he said, clenching his hands behind his back, "I think I should feel myself justified in——"

"Oh! Come along in," exploded the lieutenant. He made the same gesture of savage surrender. And he slammed into the office, the rest of us at his heels.

P. Montmorency, house-agent, was a solitary old gentleman sitting behind a bare brown counter. He had an egglike head, froglike jaws, and a grey hairy fringe of aureole round the lower part of his face; the whole combined with a reddish, aquiline nose. He wore a shabby black frock coat, a sort of semi-clerical tie worn at a very unclerical angle, and looked, generally speaking, about as unlike a house-agent as anything could look, short of something like a sandwich-man or a Scotch Highlander.

We stood inside the room for fully forty seconds, and the odd old gentleman did not look at us. Neither, to tell the truth, odd as he was, did we look at him. Our eyes were fixed, where his were fixed, upon something that was crawling about on the counter in front of him. It was a ferret.

The silence was broken by Rupert Grant. He spoke in that sweet and steely voice which he reserved for great occasions and practised for hours together in his bedroom. He said:

"Mr. Montmorency, I think?"

The old gentleman started, lifted his eyes with a bland bewilderment, picked up the ferret by the neck, stuffed it alive into his trousers pocket, smiled apologetically, and said:

"Sir."

"You are a house-agent, are you not?" asked Rupert.

To the delight of that criminal investigator, Mr. Montmorency's eyes wandered unquietly towards Lieutenant Keith, the only man present that he knew.

"A house-agent," cried Rupert again, bringing out the word as if it were "burglar."

"Yes ... oh, yes," said the man, with a quavering and almost coquettish smile. "I am a house-agent ... oh, yes."

"Well, I think," said Rupert, with a sardonic sleekness, "that Lieutenant Keith wants to speak to you. We have come in by his request."

Lieutenant Keith was lowering gloomily, and now he spoke.

"I have come, Mr. Montmorency, about that house of mine."

"Yes, sir," said Montmorency, spreading his fingers on the flat counter. "It's all ready, sir. I've attended to all your suggestions—er—about the br——"

"Right," cried Keith, cutting the word short with the startling neatness of a gunshot. "We needn't bother about all that. If you've done what I told you, all right."

And he turned sharply towards the door.

Mr. Montmorency, house-agent, presented a picture of pathos. After stammering a moment he said: "Excuse me ... Mr. Keith ... there was another matter ... about which I wasn't quite sure. I tried to get all the heating apparatus possible under the circumstances ... but in winter ... at that elevation ..."

"Can't expect much, eh?" said the lieutenant, cutting in with the same sudden skill. "No, of course not. That's all right, Montmorency. There can't be any more difficulties," and he put his hand on the handle of the door.

"I think," said Rupert Grant, with a satanic suavity, "that Mr. Montmorency has something further to say to you, lieutenant."

"Only," said the house-agent, in desperation, "what about the birds?"

"I beg your pardon," said Rupert, in a general blank.

"What about the birds?" said the house-agent, doggedly.

Basil, who had remained throughout the proceedings in a state of Napoleonic calm, which might be more accurately described as a state of Napoleonic stupidity, suddenly lifted his leonine head.

"Before you go, Lieutenant Keith," he said. "Come now. Really, what about the birds?"

"I'll take care of them," said Lieutenant Keith, still with his long back turned to us; "they sha'n't suffer."

"Thank you, sir, thank you," cried the incomprehensible house-agent, with an air of ecstasy. "You'll excuse my concern, sir. You know I'm wild on wild animals. I'm as wild as any of them on that.

Thank you, sir. But there's another thing . . ."

The lieutenant, with his back turned to us, exploded with an indescribable laugh and swung round to face us. It was a laugh, the purport of which was direct and essential, and yet which one cannot exactly express. As near as it said anything, verbally speaking, it said: "Well, if you must spoil it, you must. But you don't know what you're spoiling."

"There is another thing," continued Mr. Montmorency weakly. "Of course if you don't want to be visited you'll paint the house green, but——"

"Green!" shouted Keith. "Green! Let it be green or nothing. I won't have a house of another colour. Green!" and before we could realise anything the door had banged between us and the street.

Rupert Grant seemed to take a little time to collect himself; but he spoke before the echoes of the door died away.

"Your client, Lieutenant Keith, appears somewhat excited," he said. "What is the matter with him? Is he unwell."

"Oh, I should think not," said Mr. Montmorency, in some confusion. "The negotiations have been somewhat difficult—the house is rather——"

"Green," said Rupert calmly. "That appears to be a very important point. It must be rather green. May I ask you, Mr. Montmorency, before I rejoin my companion outside, whether, in your business, it is usual to ask for houses by their colour? Do clients write to a house-agent asking for a pink house or a blue house? Or, to take another instance, for a green house?"

"Only," said Montmorency, trembling, "only to be inconspicuous."

Rupert had his ruthless smile. "Can you tell me any place on earth in which a green house would be inconspicuous?"

The house-agent was fidgeting nervously in his pocket. Slowly drawing out a couple of lizards and leaving them to run on the counter, he said:

"No; I can't."

"You can't suggest an explanation?"

"No," said Mr. Montmorency, rising slowly and yet in such a way as to suggest a sudden situation. "I can't. And may I, as a busy man, be excused if I ask you, gentlemen, if you have any demand to make of me in connection with my business. What kind of house would you desire me to get for you, sir?"

He opened his blank blue eyes on Rupert, who seemed for the second staggered. Then he recovered himself with perfect common sense and answered:

"I am sorry, Mr. Montmorency. The fascination of your remarks has unduly delayed us from joining our friend outside. Pray excuse my apparent impertinence."

"Not at all, sir," said the house-agent, taking a South American spider idly from his waistcoat pocket and letting it climb up the slope of his desk. "Not at all, sir. I hope you will favour me again."

Rupert Grant dashed out of the office in a gust of anger, anxious to face Lieutenant Keith. He was gone. The dull, starlit street was deserted.

"What do you say now?" cried Rupert to his brother. His brother said nothing now.

We all three strode down the street in silence, Rupert feverish, myself dazed, Basil, to all appearance, merely dull. We walked through grey street after grey street, turning corners, traversing squares, scarcely meeting any one, except occasional drunken knots of two or three.

In one small street, however, the knots of two or three began abruptly to thicken into knots of five or six and then into great groups and then into a crowd. The crowd was stirring very slightly. But any one with a knowledge of the eternal populace knows that if the outside rim of a crowd stirs ever so slightly it means that there is madness in the heart and core of the mob. It soon became evident that something really important had happened in the centre of this excitement. We wormed our way to the front, with the cunning which is known only to cockneys, and once there we soon learned the nature of the difficulty. There had been a brawl concerned with some six men, and one of them lay almost dead on the stones of the street. Of the other four, all interesting matters were, as far as we were concerned, swallowed up in one stupendous fact. One of the four survivors of the brutal and perhaps fatal scuffle was the immaculate Lieutenant Keith, his clothes torn to ribbons, his eyes blazing, blood on his knuckles. One other thing, however, pointed at him in a worse manner. A short sword, or very long knife, had been drawn out of his elegant walking-stick, and lay in front of him upon the stones. It did not, however, appear to be bloody.

The police had already pushed into the centre with their ponderous omnipotence, and even as they did so, Rupert Grant sprang forward with his incontrollable and intolerable secret.

"That is the man, constable," he shouted, pointing at the battered lieutenant. "He is a suspicious character. He did the murder."

"There's been no murder done, sir," said the policeman, with his automatic civility. "The poor man's only hurt. I shall only be able to take the names and addresses of the men in the scuffle and have a good eye kept on them."

"Have a good eye kept on that one," said Rupert, pale to the lips, and pointing to the ragged Keith.

"All right, sir," said the policeman, unemotionally, and went the round of the people present, collecting the addresses. When he had completed his task the dusk had fallen and most of the people not immediately connected with the examination had gone away. He still found, however, one eager-faced stranger lingering on the outskirts of the affair. It was Rupert Grant.

"Constable," he said, "I have a very particular reason for asking you a question. Would you mind telling me whether that military fellow who dropped his swordstick in the row gave you an address or not?"

"Yes, sir," said the policeman, after a reflective pause; "yes, he gave me his address."

"My name is Rupert Grant," said that individual, with some pomp. "I have assisted the police on more than one occasion. I wonder whether you would tell me, as a special favour, what address?"

The constable looked at him.

"Yes," he said slowly, "if you like. His address is: 'The Elms, Buxton Common, near Purley, Surrey.'"

"Thank you," said Rupert, and ran home through the gathering night as fast as his legs could carry him, repeating the address to himself.

Rupert Grant generally came down late in a rather lordly way to breakfast; he contrived, I don't know how, to achieve always the attitude of the indulged younger brother. Next morning, however, when Basil and I came down we found him ready and restless.

"Well," he said, sharply to his brother almost before we sat down to the meal. "What do you think of your Drummond Keith now?"

"What do I think of him?" inquired Basil slowly. "I don't think anything of him."

"I'm glad to hear it," said Rupert, buttering his toast with an energy that was somewhat exultant. "I thought you'd come round to my view, but I own I was startled at your not seeing it from the beginning. The man is a translucent liar and knave."

"I think," said Basil, in the same heavy monotone as before, "that I did not make myself clear. When I said that I thought nothing of him I meant grammatically what I said. I meant that I did not think about him; that he did not occupy my mind. You, however, seem to me to think a lot of him, since you think him a knave. I should say he was glaringly good myself."

"I sometimes think you talk paradox for its own sake," said Rupert, breaking an egg with unnecessary sharpness. "What the deuce is the sense of it? Here's a man whose original position was, by our common agreement, dubious. He's a wanderer, a teller of tall tales, a man who doesn't conceal his acquaintance with all the blackest and bloodiest scenes on earth. We take the trouble to follow him to one of his appointments, and if ever two human beings were plotting together and lying to every one else, he and that impossible house-agent were doing it. We followed him home, and the very same night he is in the thick of a fatal, or nearly fatal, brawl, in which he is the only man armed. Really, if this is being glaringly good, I must confess that the glare does not dazzle me."

Basil was quite unmoved. "I admit his moral goodness is of a certain kind, a quaint, perhaps a casual kind. He is very fond of change and experiment. But all the points you so ingeniously make against him are mere coincidence or special pleading. It's true he didn't want to talk about his house business in front of us. No man would. It's true that he carries a swordstick. Any man might. It's true he drew it in the shock of a street fight. Any man would. But there's nothing really dubious in all this. There's nothing to confirm——"

As he spoke a knock came at the door.

"If you please, sir," said the landlady, with an alarmed air, "there's a policeman wants to see you."

"Show him in," said Basil, amid the blank silence.

The heavy, handsome constable who appeared at the door spoke almost as soon as he appeared there.

"I think one of you gentlemen," he said, curtly but respectfully, "was present at the affair in Copper Street last night, and drew my attention very strongly to a particular man."

Rupert half rose from his chair, with eyes like diamonds, but the constable went on calmly, referring to a paper.

"A young man with grey hair. Had light grey clothes, very good, but torn in the struggle. Gave his name as Drummond Keith."

"This is amusing," said Basil, laughing. "I was in the very act of clearing that poor officer's character of rather fanciful aspersions. What about him?"

"Well, sir," said the constable, "I took all the men's addresses and had them watched. It wasn't serious enough to do more than that. All the other addresses are all right. But this man Keith gave a false address. The place doesn't exist."

The breakfast table was nearly flung over as Rupert sprang up, slapping both his thighs.

"Well, by all that's good," he cried. "This is a sign from heaven."

"It's certainly very extraordinary," said Basil quietly, with knitted brows. "It's odd the fellow should have given a false address, considering he was perfectly innocent in the——"

"Oh, you jolly old early Christian duffer," cried Rupert, in a sort of rapture, "I don't wonder you couldn't be a judge. You think every one as good as yourself. Isn't the thing plain enough now? A doubtful acquaintance; rowdy stories, a most suspicious conversation, mean streets, a concealed knife, a man nearly killed, and, finally, a false address. That's what we call glaring goodness."

"It's certainly very extraordinary," repeated Basil. And he strolled moodily about the room. Then he said: "You are quite sure, constable, that there's no mistake? You got the address right, and the police have really gone to it and found it was a fraud?"

"It was very simple, sir," said the policeman, chuckling. "The place he named was a well-known common quite near London, and our people were down there this morning before any of you were awake. And there's no such house. In fact, there are hardly any houses at all. Though it is so near London, it's a blank moor with hardly five trees on it, to say nothing of Christians. Oh, no, sir, the address was a fraud right enough. He was a clever rascal, and chose one of those scraps of lost England that people know nothing about. Nobody could say off-hand that there was not a particular house dropped somewhere about the heath. But as a fact, there isn't."

Basil's face during this sensible speech had been growing darker and darker with a sort of desperate sagacity. He was cornered almost for the first time since I had known him; and to tell the truth I rather wondered at the almost childish obstinacy which kept him so close to his original prejudice in favour of the wildly questionable lieutenant. At length he said:

"You really searched the common? And the address was really not known in the district—by the way, what was the address?"

The constable selected one of his slips of paper and consulted it, but before he could speak Rupert Grant, who was leaning in the window in a perfect posture of the quiet and triumphant detective, struck in with the sharp and suave voice he loved so much to use.

"Why, I can tell you that, Basil," he said graciously, as he idly plucked leaves from a plant in the window. "I took the precaution to get this man's address from the constable last night."

"And what was it?" asked his brother gruffly.

"The constable will correct me if I am wrong," said Rupert, looking sweetly at the ceiling. "It was 'The Elms, Buxton Common, near Purley, Surrey.'"

"Right, sir," said the policeman, laughing and folding up his papers.

There was a silence, and the blue eyes of Basil looked blindly for a few seconds into the void. Then his head fell back in his chair so suddenly that I started up, thinking him ill. But before I could move further his lips had flown apart (I can use no other phrase) and a peal of gigantic laughter struck and shook the ceiling—laughter that shook the laughter, laughter redoubled, laughter incurable, laughter that could not stop.

Two whole minutes afterwards it was still unended; Basil was ill with laughter; but still he laughed. The rest of us were by this time ill almost with terror.

"Excuse me," said the insane creature, getting at last to his feet. "I am awfully sorry. It is horribly rude. And stupid, too. And also unpractical, because we have not much time to lose if we're to get down to that place. The train service is confoundedly bad, as I happen to know. It's quite out of proportion to the comparatively small distance."

"Get down to that place?" I repeated blankly. "Get down to what place?"

"I have forgotten its name," said Basil vaguely, putting his hands in his pockets as he rose. "Something Common near Purley. Has any one got a time-table?"

"You don't seriously mean," cried Rupert, who had been staring in a sort of confusion of emotions. "You don't mean that you want to go to Buxton Common, do you? You can't mean that!"

"Why shouldn't I go to Buxton Common?" asked Basil, smiling.

"Why should you?" said his brother, catching hold again restlessly of the plant in the window and staring at the speaker.

"To find our friend, the lieutenant, of course," said Basil Grant. "I thought you wanted to find him?"

Rupert broke a branch brutally from the plant and flung it impatiently on the floor. "And in order to find him," he said, "you suggest the admirable expedient of going to the only place on the habitable earth where we know he can't be."

The constable and I could not avoid breaking into a kind of assenting laugh, and Rupert, who had family eloquence, was encouraged to go on with a reiterated gesture:

"He may be in Buckingham Palace; he may be sitting astride the cross of St. Paul's; he may be in jail (which I think most likely); he may be in the Great Wheel; he may be in my pantry; he may be in your store cupboard; but out of all the innumerable points of space, there is only one where he has just been systematically looked for and where we know that he is not to be found—and that, if I understand you rightly, is where you want us to go."

"Exactly," said Basil calmly, getting into his great coat; "I thought you might care to accompany me. If not, of course, make yourselves jolly here till I come back."

It is our nature always to follow vanishing things and value them if they really show a resolution to depart. We all followed Basil, and I cannot say why, except that he was a vanishing thing, that he vanished decisively with his great coat and his stick. Rupert ran after him with a considerable flurry of rationality.

"My dear chap," he cried, "do you really mean that you see any good in going down to this ridiculous scrub, where there is nothing but beaten tracks and a few twisted trees, simply because it was the first place that came into a rowdy lieutenant's head when he wanted to give a lying reference in a scrape?"

"Yes," said Basil, taking out his watch, "and, what's worse, we've lost the train."

He paused a moment and then added: "As a matter of fact, I think we may just as well go down later in the day. I have some writing to do, and I think you told me, Rupert, that you thought of going to the Dulwich Gallery. I was rather too impetuous. Very likely he wouldn't be in. But if we get down by the 5.15, which gets to Purley about 6, I expect we shall just catch him."

"Catch him!" cried his brother, in a kind of final anger. "I wish we could. Where the deuce shall we catch him now?"

"I keep forgetting the name of the common," said Basil, as he buttoned up his coat. "The Elms—what is it? Buxton Common, near Purley. That's where we shall find him."

"But there is no such place," groaned Rupert; but he followed his brother downstairs.

We all followed him. We snatched our hats from the hat-stand and our sticks from the umbrella-stand; and why we followed him we did not and do not know. But we always followed him, whatever was the meaning of the fact, whatever was the nature of his mastery. And the strange thing was that we followed him the more completely the more nonsensical appeared the thing which he said. At bottom, I believe, if he had risen from our breakfast table and said, "I am going to find the Holy Pig with Ten Tails," we should have followed him to the end of the world.

I don't know whether this mystical feeling of mine about Basil on this occasion has gone any of the dark and cloudy colour, so to speak, of the strange journey that we made the same evening. It was already very dense twilight when we struck southward from Purley. Suburbs and things on the London border may be, in most cases, commonplace and comfortable. But if ever by any chance they really are empty solitudes they are to the human spirit more desolate and dehumanised than any Yorkshire moors or Highland hills, because the suddenness with which the traveller drops into that silence has something about it as of evil elf-land. It seems to be one of the ragged suburbs of the cosmos half-forgotten by God— such a place was Buxton Common, near Purley.

There was certainly a sort of grey futility in the landscape itself. But it was enormously increased by the sense of grey futility in our expedition. The tracts of drab turf looked useless, the occasional wind-stricken trees looked useless, but we, the human beings, more useless than the hopeless turf or the idle trees. We were maniacs akin to the foolish landscape, for we were come to chase the wild goose which has led men and left men in bogs from the beginning. We were three dazed men under the captaincy of a madman going to look for a man whom we knew was not there in a house that had no existence. A livid sunset seemed to look at us with a sort of sickly smile before it died.

Basil went on in front with his coat collar turned up, looking in the gloom rather like a grotesque Napoleon. We crossed swell after swell of the windy common in increasing darkness and entire silence. Suddenly Basil stopped and turned to us, his hands in his pockets. Through the dusk I could just detect that he wore a broad grin as of comfortable success.

"Well," he cried, taking his heavily gloved hands out of his pockets and slapping them together, "here we are at last."

The wind swirled sadly over the homeless heath; two desolate elms rocked above us in the sky like shapeless clouds of grey. There was not a sign of man or beast to the sullen circle of the horizon, and in the midst of that wilderness Basil Grant stood rubbing his hands with the air of an innkeeper standing at an open door.

"How jolly it is," he cried, "to get back to civilisation. That notion that civilisation isn't poetical is a civilised delusion. Wait till you've really lost yourself in nature, among the devilish woodlands and the cruel flowers. Then you'll know that there's no star like the red star of man that he lights on his hearth-stone; no river like the red river of man, the good red wine, which you, Mr. Rupert Grant, if I have any knowledge of you, will be drinking in two or three minutes in enormous quantities."

Rupert and I exchanged glances of fear. Basil went on heartily, as the wind died in the dreary trees.

"You'll find our host a much more simple kind of fellow in his own house. I did when I visited him when he lived in the cabin at Yarmouth, and again in the loft at the city warehouse. He's really a very good fellow. But his greatest virtue remains what I said originally."

"What do you mean?" I asked, finding his speech straying towards a sort of sanity. "What is his greatest virtue?"

"His greatest virtue," replied Basil, "is that he always tells the literal truth."

"Well, really," cried Rupert, stamping about between cold and anger, and slapping himself like a cabman, "he doesn't seem to have been very literal or truthful in this case, nor you either. Why the deuce, may I ask, have you brought us out to this infernal place?"

"He was too truthful, I confess," said Basil, leaning against the tree; "too hardly veracious, too severely accurate. He should have indulged in a little more suggestiveness and legitimate romance. But come, it's time we went in. We shall be late for dinner."

Rupert whispered to me with a white face:

"Is it a hallucination, do you think? Does he really fancy he sees a house?"

"I suppose so," I said. then I added aloud, in what was meant to be a cheery and sensible voice, but which sounded in my ears almost as strange as the wind:

"Come, come, Basil, my dear fellow. Where do you want us to go?"

"Why, up here," cried Basil, and with a bound and a swing he was above our heads, swarming up the grey column of the colossal tree.

"Come up, all of you," he shouted out of the darkness, with the voice of a schoolboy. "Come up. You'll be late for dinner."

The two great elms stood so close together that there was hardly a yard anywhere, and in some places not more than a foot, between them. Thus occasional branches and even bosses and boles formed a series of footholds that almost amounted to a rude natural ladder. They must, I supposed, have been some sort of Growth, Siamese twins of vegetation.

Why we did it I cannot think; perhaps, as I have said, the mystery of the waste and dark had brought out and made primary something wholly mystical in Basil's supremacy. But we only felt that there was a giant's staircase going somewhere, perhaps to the stars; and the victorious voice above called to us out of heaven. We hoisted ourselves up after him.

Half-way up some cold tongue of the night air struck and sobered me suddenly. The hypnotism of the madman above fell from me, and I saw the whole map of our silly actions as clearly as if it were printed. I saw three modern men in black coats who had begun with a perfectly sensible suspicion of a doubtful adventurer and who had ended, God knows how, half-way up a naked tree on a naked moorland, far from that adventurer and all his works, that adventurer who was at that moment, in all probability, laughing at us in some dirty Soho restaurant. He had plenty to laugh at us about, and no doubt he was laughing his loudest; but when I thought what his laughter would be if he knew we were at that moment, I nearly let go of the tree and fell.

"Swinburne," said Rupert, suddenly, from above, "what are we doing? Let's get down again," and by the mere sound of his voice I knew that he too felt the shock of wakening to reality.

"We can't leave poor Basil," I said. "Can't you call to him or get hold of him by the leg?"

"He's too far ahead," answered Rupert; "he's nearly at the top of the beastly thing. Looking for Lieutenant Keith in the rooks' nests, I suppose."

We were ourselves by this time far on our frantic vertical journey. The mighty trunks were beginning to sway and shake slightly in the wind. Then I looked down and saw something which made me feel that we were far from the world in a sense and to a degree that I cannot easily describe. I saw that the almost straight lines of the tall elm trees diminished a little in perspective as they fell. I was used to seeing parallel lines taper towards the sky. But to see them taper towards the earth made me feel lost in space, like a falling star.

"Can nothing be done to stop Basil?" I called out.

"No," answered my fellow climber. "He's too far up. He must get to the top, and when he finds nothing but wind and leaves he may go sane again. Hark at him above there; you can just hear him talking to himself."

"Perhaps he's talking to us," I said.

"No," said Rupert, "he'd shout if he was. I've never known him to talk to himself before; I'm afraid he really is bad to-night; it's a known sign of the brain going."

"Yes," I said sadly, and listened. Basil's voice certainly was sounding above us, and not by any means in the rich and riotous tones in which he had hailed us before. He was speaking quietly, and laughing every now and then, up there among the leaves and stars.

After a silence mingled with this murmur, Rupert Grant suddenly said, "My God!" with a violent voice.

"What's the matter—are you hurt?" I cried alarmed.

"No. Listen to Basil," said the other in a very strange voice. "He's not talking to himself."

"Then he is talking to us," I cried.

"No," said Rupert simply, "he's talking to somebody else."

Great branches of the elm loaded with leaves swung about us in a sudden burst of wind, but when it died down I could still hear the conversational voice above. I could hear two voices.

Suddenly from aloft came Basil's boisterous hailing voice as before: "Come up, you fellows. Here's Lieutenant Keith."

And a second afterwards came the half-American voice we had heard in our chambers more than once. It called out:

"Happy to see you, gentlemen; pray come in."

Out of a hole in an enormous dark egg-shaped thing pendant in the branches like a wasp's nest, was protruding the pale face and fierce moustache of the lieutenant, his teeth shining with that slightly Southern air that belonged to him.

Somehow or other, stunned and speechless, we lifted ourselves heavily into the opening. We fell into the full glow of a lamp-lit, cushioned, tiny room, with a circular wall lined with books, a circular table, and a circular seat around it. At this table sat three people. One was Basil, who, in the instant after alighting there, had fallen into an attitude of marmoreal ease as if he had been there from boyhood; he was smoking a cigar with a slow pleasure. The second was Lieutenant Drummond Keith, who looked happy also, but feverish and doubtful compared with his granite guest. The third was the little bald-headed house-agent with the wild whiskers, who called himself Montmorency. The spears, the green umbrella, and the cavalry sword hung in parallels on the wall. The sealed jar of strange wine was on the mantelpiece, the enormous rifle in the corner. In the middle of the table was a magnum of champagne. Glasses were already set for us.

The wind of the night roared far below us, like an ocean at the foot of a light-house. The room stirred slightly, as a cabin might in a mild sea.

Our glasses were filled, and we still sat there dazed and dumb. Then Basil spoke.

"You seem still a little doubtful, Rupert. Surely there is no further question about the cold veracity of our injured host."

"I don't quite grasp it all," said Rupert, blinking still in the sudden glare. "Lieutenant Keith said his address was——"

"It's really quite right, sir," said Keith, with an open smile. "The bobby asked me where I lived. And I said, quite truthfully, that I lived in the elms on Buxton Common, near Purley. So I do. This gentleman, Mr. Montmorency, whom I think you have met before, is an agent for houses of this kind. He has a special line in arboreal villas. It's being kept rather quiet at present, because the people who want these houses don't want them to get too common. But it's just the sort of thing that a fellow like myself, racketing about in all sorts of queer corners of London, naturally knocks up against."

"Are you really an agent for arboreal villas?" asked Rupert eagerly, recovering his ease with the romance of the reality.

Mr. Montmorency, in his embarrassment, fingered one of his pockets and nervously pulled out a snake, which crawled about the table.

"W-well, yes, sir," he said. "The fact was—er—my people wanted me very much to go into the house-agency business. But I never cared myself for anything but natural history and botany and things like that. My poor parents have been dead some years now, but—naturally I like to respect their wishes. And I thought somehow that an arboreal villa agency was a sort of—of compromise between being a botanist and being a house-agent."

Rupert could not help laughing. "Do you have much custom?" he asked.

"N-not much," replied Mr. Montmorency, and then he glanced at Keith, who was (I am convinced) his only client. "But what there is—very select."

"My dear friends," said Basil, puffing his cigar, "always remember two facts. The first is that though, when you are guessing about any one who is sane, the sanest thing is the most likely; when you are guessing about any one who is, like our host, insane, the maddest thing is the most likely. The second is to remember that very plain literal fact always seems fantastic. If Keith had taken a little brick box of a house in Clapham with nothing but railings in front of it and had written 'The Elms' over it, you wouldn't have thought there was anything fantastic about that. Simply because it was a great blaring, swaggering lie you would have believed it."

"Drink your wine, gentlemen," said Keith, laughing, "for this confounded wind will upset it."

We drank, and as we did so, although the hanging house, by a cunning mechanism, swung only slightly, we knew that the great head of the elm-tree swayed in the sky like a stricken thistle.

MR. TRAILL
IN

The Garden of Smoke

The Garden of Smoke

The end of London looked very like the end of the world; and the last lamp-post of the suburbs like a lonely star in the fields of space. It also resembled the end of the world in another respect; that it was a long time coming. The girl Catharine Crawford was a good walker; she had the fine figure of the mountaineer, and there almost went with her a wind from the hills through all the grey labyrinths of London. For she came from the high villages of Westmorland, and seemed to carry the quiet colours of them in her light brown hair, her open features, irregular yet the reverse of plain, the framework of two grave and very beautiful grey eyes. But the mountaineer began to feel the labyrinth of London suburbs interminable and intolerable, swiftly as she walked. She knew little of the details of her destination, save the address of the house, and the fact that she was going there as a companion to a Mrs. Mowbray, or rather to *the* Mrs. Mowbray—a famous lady novelist and fashionable poet, married, it was said, to some matter-of-fact medical man, reduced to the permanent status of Mrs. Mowbray's husband. And when she found the house eventually, it was at the end of the very last line of houses, where the suburban gardens faded into the open fields.

The whole heavens were full of the hues of evening, though still as luminous as noon; as if in a land of endless sunset. It settled down in a shower of gold amid the twinkling leaves of the thin trees of the gardens, most of which had low fences and hedges, and lay almost as open to the yellow sky as the fields beyond. The air was so still that occasional voices, talking or laughing on distant lawns, could be heard like clear bells. One voice, more recurrent than the rest, seemed to be whistling and singing the old sailors' song of "Spanish Ladies"; it drew nearer and nearer; and when she turned into the last garden gate at the corner, the singer was the first figure she encountered. He stood in a garden red with very gorgeous ranks of standard roses, and against a background of the golden sky and a white cottage with touches of rather fanciful colour; the sort of cottage that is not built for cottagers.

He was a lean not ungraceful man in grey with a limp straw hat pulled forward above his dark face and black beard, out of which projected an almost blacker cigar; which he removed when he saw the lady.

"Good evening," he said politely. "I think you must be Miss Crawford. Mrs. Mowbray asked me to tell you that she would be out here in a minute or two, if you cared to look round the garden first. I hope you don't mind my smoking. I do it to kill the insects, you know, on the roses. Need I say that this is the one and only origin of all smoking? Too little credit, perhaps, is given to the self-sacrifice of my sex, from the clubmen in smoking-rooms to the navvies on scaffoldings, all steadily and firmly smoking, on the mere chance that a rose may be growing somewhere in the neighbour-hood. Handicapped, like most of my comrades, with a strong natural dislike of tobacco, I contrive to conquer it and——"

He broke off, because the grey eyes regarding him were a little blank and even bleak. He spoke with gravity and even gloom; and she was conscious of humour, but was not sure that it was good-humour. Indeed she felt, at first sight, something faintly sinister about him; his face was aquiline and his figure feline, almost as in the fabulous griffin; a creature moulded of the eagle and the lion, or perhaps the leopard. She was not sure that she approved of fabulous animals.

"Are you Dr. Mowbray?" she asked, rather stiffly.

"No such luck," he replied. "I haven't got such beautiful roses, or such a beautiful—household, shall we say. But Mowbray is about the garden somewhere, spraying the roses with some low scientific instrument called a syringe. He's a great gardener; but you won't find him spraying with the same perpetual, uncomplaining patience as you'll find me smoking."

With these words he turned on his heel and hallooed his friend's name across the garden in a style which, along with the echo of his song, somehow suggested a ship's captain; which was indeed his trade. A stooping figure disengaged itself from a distant rose bush and came forward apologetically.

Dr. Mowbray also had a loose straw hat and a beard, but there the resemblance ended; his beard was fair and he was burly and big of shoulder; his face was good-humoured and would have been good-looking but that his blue and smiling eyes were a little wide apart, which rather increased the pleasant candour of his expression. By comparison, the more deep sunken eyes on either side of the dark captain's beak seemed to be too close together.

"I was explaining to Miss Crawford," said the latter gentleman, "the superiority of my way of curing your roses of any of their little maladies. In scientific circles the cigar has wholly superseded the syringe."

"Your cigars look as if they'd kill the roses," replied the doctor. "Why are you always smoking your very strongest cigars here?"

"On the contrary, I am smoking my mildest," answered the captain, grimly. "I've got another sort here if anybody wants them."

He turned back the lapel of his square jacket, and showed some dangerous-looking sticks of twisted leaf in his upper waistcoat pocket. As he did so they noticed also that he had a broad leather belt round his waist, to which was buckled a big crooked knife in a leather sheath.

"Well, I prefer health to tobacco," said Mowbray, laughing. "I may be a doctor, but I take my own medicine; which is fresh air. People cultivate these tastes till they can't taste the air, or the smell of the earth, or any of the elementary things. I agree with Thoreau—that the sunrise is a better beginning of the day than tea or coffee."

"So it is; but not better than beer or rum," replied the sailor. "But it is a matter of taste, as you say. Hallo, who's this?"

As they spoke the french windows of the house opened abruptly, and a man in black came out and passed them going out at the garden gate. He was walking rapidly, as if irritably, and putting his hat and gloves on as he went. Before he put on his hat he showed a head half bald and bumpy, with a semicircle of red hair; and before he put on his gloves he tore a small piece of paper into yet smaller pieces, and tossed it away among the roses by the road.

"Oh, one of Marion's friends from the Theosophical or Ethical Society, I think," said the doctor. "His name's Miall, a tradesman in the town, a chemist or something."

"He doesn't seem in the best or most ethical of tempers," observed the captain. "I thought you nature-worshippers were always serene. Well, he's released our hostess at any rate; and here she comes."

Marion Mowbray really looked like an artist, which an artist is not supposed to do. This did not come from her clinging green drapery and halo of Pre-Raphaelite brown hair, which need only have made her look like an aesthete. But in her face there was a true intensity; her keen eyes were full of distances, that is, of desires, but of desires too large to be sensuous. If such a soul was wasted by a flame, it seemed one of purely spiritual ambition. A moment after she had given her hand to the guest, with very graceful apologies, she stretched it out towards the flowers with a gesture that was quite natural, yet so decisive as to be almost dramatic.

"I simply must have some more of those roses in the house," she said, "and I've lost my scissors. I know it sounds silly, but when the fit comes over me I feel I must tear them off with my hands. Don't you love roses, Miss Crawford? I simply can't do without them sometimes."

The captain's hand had gone to his hip, and the queer crooked knife was naked in the sun; a shining but ugly shape. In a few flashes he had hacked and lopped away a long spray or two of blossom, and handed them to her with a bow, like a bouquet on the stage.

"Oh, thank you," she said rather faintly; and one could fancy, somehow, a tragic irony behind the masquerade. The next moment she recovered herself and laughed a little. "It's absurd, I know; but I do so hate ugly things, and living in the London suburbs, though only on the edge of them. Do you know, Miss Crawford, the next door neighbour walks about his garden in a top-hat. Positively in a top-hat. I see it passing just above that laurel hedge about sunset; when he's come back from the city, I suppose. Think of the laurel, that we poor poets are supposed to worship," and she laughed more naturally, "and then think of my feelings, looking up and seeing it wreathed round a top-hat."

And indeed, before the party entered the house to prepare for an evening meal, Catharine had actually seen the offending head-dress appear above the hedge, a shadow of respectability in the sunshine of that romantic plot of roses.

At dinner they were served by a man in black, like a butler, and Catharine felt an unmeaning embarrassment in the mere fact. A man-servant seemed out of place in that artistic toy cottage; and there was nothing notable about the man addressed as Parker except that he seemed especially so; a tall man with a wooden face and dark flat hair like a Dutch doll's. He would have been proper enough if the doctor had lived in Harley Street; but he was too big for the suburbs. Nor was he the only incongruous element, nor the principal one. The captain, whose name seemed to be Fonblanque, still puzzled her and did not altogether please her. Her northern Puritanism found something obscurely rowdy about his attitude. It would be hardly adequate to say he acted as if he were at home; it would be truer to say he acted as if he were abroad, in a café or tavern in some foreign port. Mrs. Mowbray was a vegetarian; and though her husband lived the simple life in a rather simpler fashion, he was sufficiently sophisticated to drink water. But Captain Fonblanque had a great flagon of rum all to himself, and did not disguise his relish; and the meal ended in smoke of the most rich and reeking description. And throughout the captain continued to fence with his hostess and with the stranger with the same flippancies that had fallen from him in the garden.

"It's my childlike innocence that makes me drink and smoke," he explained. "I can enjoy a cigar as I could a sugar-stick; but you jaded dissipated vegetarians look down on such sugar-sticks. And rum, too, if it comes to that, is itself a sort of liquid sugar-stick. They say it makes sailors drunk; but after all, what is being drunk but another form of infantile faith and confidence? How saintly must be the innocence of a sailor who can trust himself entirely to a policeman? I do so hate this cynical suspicious habit of being sober at all sorts of odd times to catch other people napping."

"When you have done talking nonsense," said Mrs. Mowbray, rising, "we will go into the other room." The nonsense made no particular impression on her or on her feminine companion; but the latter still regarded the speaker with a subdued antagonism, chiefly because he really seemed in an equally subdued degree to be an antagonist. His irony was partly provocative, whether of her hosts or herself; and she was conscious of something slightly Mephistophelian about his blue-black beard and ivory yellow face amid the fumes.

In passing out, the ladies paused accidentally at the open french windows, and Catharine looked out upon the darkening lawn. She was surprised to see that clouds had already come up out of the coloured west and the twilight was troubled with rain. There was a silence, and then Catharine said, rather suddenly:

"That neighbour of yours must be very fond of his garden. Almost as fond of the roses as you are, Mrs. Mowbray."

"Why, what do you mean?" asked that lady, turning back.

"He's still standing among his flowers in the pouring rain," said Catharine, staring, "and will soon be standing in the pitch dark too. . . . I can still see his black hat in the dusk."

"Who knows," said the lady poet, softly; "perhaps a sense of beauty has really stirred in him in a strange, sudden way. If seeds under black earth can grow into those glorious roses, what will souls even under black hats grow into at last? Everything moves upwards; even our sins are steps upwards; there is nowhere any downward turning in the great spiral road, the winding staircase of the stars. Perhaps the black hat may turn into the laurel wreath after all."

She glanced behind her, and saw that the two men had already strolled out of the room; and her voice fell into a tone more casual and yet confidential.

"Besides," she added, "I'm not sure he isn't right; and perhaps rain is as beautiful as sun or anything else in the wonderful wheel of things. Don't you like the smell of the damp earth, and that deep noise of all the roses drinking?"

"All the roses are teetotallers, anyhow," remarked Catharine, with a smile.

Her hostess smiled also. "I'm afraid Captain Fonblanque shocked you a little; he's rather eccentric, wearing that crooked eastern dagger just because he's travelled in the East, and drinking rum, of all ridiculous things, just to show he's a sailor. But he's an old friend, you know; I knew him well many years ago; and he's done his duty on the sea at least, and even gained distinction there. I'm afraid he's still rather on the animal plane, but at least he's a fighting animal."

"Yes, he reminds me of a pirate in a play," said Catharine, laughing. "He might be stalking round this house looking for hidden treasure of gold and silver."

Mrs. Mowbray seemed to start a little, and then stared out into the dark in silence. At last she said, in a changed voice:

"It is strange that you should say that."

"And why?" inquired her companion, in some wonder.

"Because there is a hidden treasure in this house," said Mrs. Mowbray, "and such a thief might well steal it. It's not exactly gold or silver, but it's almost as valuable, I believe, even in money. I don't know why I tell you this; but at least you can see I don't distrust you. Let's go into the other room." And she rather abruptly led the way in that direction.

Catharine Crawford was a woman whose conscious mind was full of practicality; but her unconscious mind had its own poetry, which was all on the note of purity. She loved white light and clear waters, boulders washed smooth in rivers, and the sweeping curves of wind. It was perhaps the poetry that Wordsworth, at his finest, found in the lakes of her own land; and in principle it could repose in the artistic austerity of Marion Mowbray's home. But whether the stage was filled too much by the almost fantastic figure of the piratical Fonblanque, or whether the summer heat, with its hint of storm, obscured such clarity, she felt an oppression. Even the rose-garden seemed more like a chamber curtained with red and green than an open place. Her own chamber was curtained in sufficiently cool and soothing colours; but she fell asleep later than usual, and then heavily.

She woke with a start from some tangled dream of which she recalled no trace; and with senses sharpened by darkness, she was vividly conscious of a strange smell. It was vaporous and heavy, not unpleasant to the nostrils, yet somehow all the more unpleasant to the nerves. It was not the smell of any tobacco she knew; and yet she connected it with those sinister black cigars to which the captain's brown finger had pointed. She thought half-consciously that he might be still smoking in the garden; and that those dark and dreadful weeds might well be smoked in the dark. But it was only half consciously that she thought or moved at all; she remembered half rising from her bed; and then remembered nothing but more dreams, which left a little more recollection in their track. They were but a medley of the smoking and the strange smell and the scents of the rose garden, but they seemed to make up a mystery as well as a medley. Sometimes the roses were themselves a sort of purple smoke. Sometimes they glowed from purple to fiery crimson, like the butts of a giant's cigars. And that garden of smoke was haunted by the pale yellow face and blue-black beard; and she awoke with the word "Bluebeard" on her mind and almost on her mouth.

Morning was so much of a relief as to be almost a surprise; the rooms were full of the white light that she loved, and which might well be the light of a primeval wonder. As she passed the half-opened door of the doctor's scientific study or consulting-room, she paused by a window, and saw the silver daybreak brightening over the garden. She was idly counting the birds that began to dart by the house; and as she counted the fourth she heard the shock of a falling chair, followed by a voice crying out and cursing again and again.

The voice was strained and unnatural; but after the first few syllables she recognized it as that of the doctor.

"It's gone," he was saying. "The stuff's gone, I tell you!"

The reply was inaudible; but she already suspected that it came from the servant Parker, whose voice proved to be as baffling as was his face.

The doctor answered again in unabated agitation.

"The drug, you devil or dunce or whatever you are! The drug I told you to keep an eye on!"

This time she heard the dull tones of the other, who seemed to be saying: "There's very little of it gone, sir."

"Why has any of it gone?" cried Doctor Mowbray. "Where's my wife?"

Probably hearing the rustle of a skirt outside, he flung the door open and came face to face with Catharine, falling back before her in consternation. The room into which she now looked in bewilderment was neat and even severe, except for the fallen chair still lying on the carpet. It was fitted with bookcases, and contained a rank of bottles and phials, like those in a chemist's shop, the colours of which looked like jewels in the brilliant early daylight. One glittering green bottle bore a large label of "Poison"; but the present problem seemed to revolve round a glass vessel, rather like a decanter, which stood on the table more than half full of a dust or powder of a rich reddish brown.

Against this strict scientific background the tall servant looked more important and appropriate; in fact, she was soon conscious that he was something more intimate than a servant who waited at table. He had at least the air of a doctor's assistant; and indeed, in comparison with his distracted employer, might almost at that moment have been the attendant in a private asylum.

He was saying, as she doubtfully entered: "I am very sorry this has happened, sir. But at least I kept very careful note of the quantity; and I assure you there is very little gone. Not enough to do anyone much harm."

"It's the damned plague breaking out again," said the doctor hastily. "Go and see if my wife is in the dining-room."

He pulled himself together as Parker left the room, and picked up the chair that had fallen on the carpet, offering it to the girl with a gesture. Then he went and leaned on the window-sill, looking out upon the garden. She could see his large shoulders shift and shake; but there was no sound but the growing noise of the birds in the bushes. At last he said in his natural voice:

"Well, I suppose you ought to have been told. Anyhow, you'll have to be told now."

There was another silence, and then he said: "My wife is a poet, you know; a creative artist, and all that. And all enlightened people know that a genius can't be judged quite by common rules of conduct. A genius lives by a recurrent need for a sort of inspiration."

"What do you mean?" asked Catharine almost impatiently; for the preamble of excuses was a strain on her nerves.

"There's a kind of opium in that bottle," he said abruptly, "a very rare kind. She smokes it occasionally, that's all. I wish Parker would hurry up and find her."

"I can find her, I think," said Catharine, relieved by the chance of doing something; and not a little relieved also to get out of the scientific room. "I think I saw her going down the garden path."

When she went out into the rose garden it was full of the freshness of the sunrise; and all her smoky nightmares were rolled away from it. The roof of her green and crimson room seemed to have been lifted off like a lid. She went down many winding paths without seeing any living thing but the birds hopping here and there; then she came to the corner of one turning and stood still.

In the middle of the sunny path, a few yards from one of the birds, lay something crumpled like a great green rag. But it was really the rich green dress of Marion Mowbray; and beyond it was her fallen face, colourless against its halo of hair and one arm thrust out, in a piteous stiffness towards the roses, as she had stretched it when Catharine saw her for the first time. Catharine gave a little cry, and the bird flashed away into a tree. Then she bent over the fallen figure, and knew, in a blast of all the trumpets of terror, why the face was colourless and why the arm was stiff.

An hour afterwards, still in that world of rigid unreality that remains long after a shock, she was but automatically, though efficiently, helping in the hundred minute and aching utilities of a house of mourning. How she had told them she hardly knew; but there was no need to tell much. Mowbray the doctor soon had bad news for Mowbray the husband, when he had been but a few moments silent and busy over the body of his wife. Then he turned away; and Catharine almost feared he would fall.

A problem confronted him still, however, even as a doctor, when he had so grimly solved his problem as a husband. His medical assistant, whom he had always had reason to trust, still emphatically asserted that the amount of the drug missing was insufficient to kill a kitten. He came down and stood with the little group on the lawn, where the dead woman had been laid on a sofa, to be examined in the best light. He repeated his assertion in the face of the examination, and his wooden face was knotted with obstinacy.

"If he is right," said Captain Fonblanque, "she must have got it from somewhere else as well, that's all. Did any strange people come here lately?"

He had taken a turn or two of pacing up and down the lawn, when he stopped with an arrested gesture.

"Didn't you say that theosophist was also a chemist?" he asked. "He may be as theosophical or ethical as he likes; but he didn't come here on a theosophical errand. No, by God, nor an ethical one."

It was agreed that this question should be followed up first; Parker was dispatched to the High Street of the neighbouring suburb; and about half an hour afterwards the black-clad figure of Mr. Miall came back into the garden, much less swiftly than he had gone out of it. He removed his hat out of respect for the presence of death; and his face under the ring of red hair was whiter than the dead.

But though pale, he also was firm; and that upon a point that brought the inquiry once more to a standstill. He admitted that he had once supplied that peculiar brand of opium; and did not attempt to dissipate the cloud of responsibility that rested on him so far. But he vehemently denied that he had supplied it yesterday, or even lately, or indeed for long past. And he was especially emphatic upon one point, which seemed almost to be a personal grievance: that he could not supply it, because he could not get it.

"She must have got some more somehow," cried the doctor, in

dogmatic and even despotic tones, "and where could she have got it but from you?"

"And where could I have got it from anybody?" demanded the tradesman equally hotly. "You seem to think it's sold like shag. I tell you there's no more of it in England—a chemist can't get it even for desperate cases. I gave her the last I had months ago, more shame to me; and when she wanted more yesterday, I told her I not only wouldn't but couldn't. There's the scraps of the note she sent me, still lying where I tore it up in a temper."

And he pointed a dark-gloved finger at a few white specks lying her and there under the hedge. The captain strode across and silently stamped them into the black soil. He turned again, pale but composed, and said to the doctor quietly: "We must be careful, Mowbray. Poor Marion's death is more of a mystery than we thought."

"There is no mystery," said Mowbray angrily. "Out of his own mouth this fellow owns he had the stuff."

"I've no more got the stuff now than the Crown Jewels," repeated the chemist. "It's about as rare now, and more valuable than a heap of gold and silver."

Catharine's mind had a movement of recollection; and she thought, with a cold thrill, of how the same strange words about a treasure had been on the lips of the unfortunate Marion the night before. Was it possible that the hidden treasure, that had dazzled the dead woman like diamonds, was only this red dust of death?

The doctor seemed to regard the hitch in the inquiry with a sort of harassed fury. He browbeat the pale chemist even more than he had browbeaten his servant about his first and smaller discovery. Indeed, Catharine began to feel about Dr. Mowbray something that can be felt at times in men of such solid amiability. She suspected that his serenity had been a strong stream or tide of steady satisfaction; and that he could bear being baffled less than more bitter men. Perhaps he was of a sort sometimes called the strong man; who is strong in fulfilling his desires, but not in controlling them. Anyhow, his desire at the moment, so concrete as to be comic in such a scene, seemed to be the desire to hang a chemist.

"Look here, Mowbray, you know how we all feel for you, but you really mustn't be so violent," remonstrated the captain. "You'll put us all in the wrong. Mr. Miall has a right to justice, not to mention law; which will probably have a hand in this business."

"If you interfere with me, Fonblanque," said the doctor, "I will say something I have never said before."

"What the devil do you mean?"

The figures in the little group on the lawn had fallen into such angry attitudes that one could almost fancy they would strike each other even in the presence of the dead when an interruption came as soft as the note of the bird but as unexpected as a thunderbolt.

A voice from several yards away said mildly but more or less loudly: 'Permit me to offer you my assistance."

They all looked round and saw the next-door neighbour's top-hat, above a large, loose, heavy-lidded face, leaning over the low fringe of laurels.

"I'm sure I can be of some little help," he said; and the next moment he had calmly taken a high stride over the low hedge, and was walking across the lawn towards them. He was a large, heavily-walking man in a loose frock coat; his clean-shaven face was at once heavy and cadaverous. He spoke in a soft and even sentimental tone, which contrasted with his impudence and, as it soon appeared, with his trade.

"What do you want here?" asked Dr. Mowbray sharply, when he had recovered from a sheer astonishment.

"It is you who want something. Sympathy," said the strange gentleman. "Sympathy ... sympathy, and also light. I think I can offer both. Poor lady, I have watched her sympathetically for many months; and I think I can offer both."

"If you've been watching over the wall," said the captain frowning, "we should like to know why. There are suspicious facts here, and you seem to have behaved in a suspicious manner."

"Suspicion rather than sympathy," said the stranger, with a sigh, "is perhaps the defect in my duties. But my sorrow for this poor lady is perfectly sincere. Do you suspect me of being mixed up in her trouble?"

"Who are you?" asked the angry doctor.

"My name is Traill," said the man in the top-hat. "I have some official title; but it was never used except at the Yard. Scotland Yard, I mean. We needn't use it among neighbours."

"You are a detective, in fact?" observed the captain; but he received no reply, for the new investigator was already examining the corpse, quite respectfully, but with a professional absence of apology. After a few moments he rose again, and looked at them under the large drooping eyelids which were his most prominent features; and said simply: "It is satisfactory to let people go, Dr. Mowbray; and your druggist and your assistant can certainly go. It was not the fault of either of them that the unhappy lady died."

"Do you mean it was a suicide?" asked the other.

"I mean it was a murder," said Mr. Traill. "But I have a very sufficient reason for saying she was not killed by the druggist."

"And why not?"

"Because she was not killed by the drug," said the man from next door.

"What?" exclaimed the captain, with a slight start. "Why, how else could she have been killed?"

"She was killed with a short and sharp instrument, the point of which was prepared in a particular manner for the purpose," said Traill in the level tones of a lecturer. "There was apparently a struggle, but probably a short, or even a slight one. Poor lady, just look at this"; and he lifted one of the dead hands quite gently, and pointed to what appeared to be a prick or puncture on the wrist.

"A hypodermic needle, perhaps," said the doctor in a low voice; "she generally took a drug by smoking it; but she might have used a hypodermic syringe and needle, after all."

The detective shook his head, so that one could almost imagine his hanging eyelids flapping with the loose movement. "If she injected it herself," he said sadly, "she would make a clean perforation. This is more a scratch than a prick, and you can see it has torn the lace on her sleeve a little."

"But how can it have killed her," Catharine was impelled to ask, "if it was only a scratching on the wrist?"

"Ah," said Mr. Traill; and then after a short silence, "I'm sure you'll support me, Dr. Mowbray, when I say it's improbable, after all, that any mere opiate should produce that extreme rigidity in the body. The effect resembles rather that of some direct vegetable poison, especially some of those rapid oriental poisons. Poor lady, poor lady, it is really a very horrible story."

"But what is the story, do you think, in plain words?" asked the captain.

"I think," said Traill, "that when we find the dagger we shall find it a poisoned dagger. Is that plain enough, Captain Fonblanque?"

The next moment he seemed to droop again with his rather morbid and almost maudlin tone of compassion.

"Poor lady," he repeated. "She was so fond of roses, wasn't she? Strew on her roses, roses, as the poet says. I really feel somehow that it might give a sort of rest to her, even now."

He looked round the garden with his heavy half-closed eye, and addressed Fonblanque more sympathetically.

"It was on a happier occasion, Captain, that you last cut flowers for her; I can't help wishing it could be done again now."

Half unconsciously, the captain's hand went to where the hilt of his knife had hung; then his hand dropped, as if in abrupt recollection. But as the flap of his jacket shifted for an instant, they saw that the leather sheath was empty; and the knife was gone.

"Such a very sad story, such a terrible story," murmured the man in the top-hat distantly, as if he were talking of a novel. "Of course, it is a silly fancy about the flowers. It is not such things as that that are our duties to the dead."

The others seemed still a little bewildered; but Catharine was looking at the captain as if she had been turned to stone by a basilisk. Indeed, that moment had been for her the beginning of a monstrous interregnum of imagination, which might well be said to be full of monsters. Something of mythology had hung about the garden since her first fancy about a man like a griffin. It lasted for many days and nights, during which the detective seemed to hover over the house like a vampire; but the vampire was not the most awful of the monsters. She hardly defined to herself what she thought, or rather refused to think. But she was conscious of other unknown emotions coming to the surface and co-existing, somehow, with that sunken thought that was their contrary. For some time past the first unfriendly feelings about the captain had rather faded from her mind; even in that short space he had improved on acquaintance, and his sensible conduct in the crisis was a relief from the wild grief and anger of the husband, however natural these might be. Moreover, the very explosion of the opium secret, in accounting for the cloud upon the house, had cleared away another suspicion she had half entertained about the wife and the piratical guest. This she was now disposed to dismiss, so far at least as he was concerned; and she had lately had an additional reason for doing so. The eyes of Fonblanque had been following her about in a manner about which so humorous and therefore modest a lady was not likely to be mistaken; and she was surprised to find in herself a corresponding recoil from the idea of this comedy of sentiment turning suddenly to a tragedy of suspicion. For the next few nights she again slept uneasily; and as is often the case with a crushed or suppressed thought, the doubt raged and ruled in her dreams. What might be called the Bluebeard motif ran through even wilder scenes of strange lands, full of fantastic cities and giant vegetation, through all of which passed a solitary figure with a blue beard and a red knife. It was as if this sailor not only had a wife, but a murdered wife, in every port. And there recurred again and again, like a distant but distinct voice speaking, the accents of the detective: "If only we could find the dagger, we should find it a poisoned dagger." And yet nothing could have seemed more cool and casual at the moment, on the following morning, when she did find it. She had come down from the upper rooms and gone through the french windows into the garden once more; she was about to pass down the paths among the rose bushes, when she looked round and saw the captain leaning on the garden gate. There was nothing unusual in his idle and somewhat languid attitude, but her eye was fixed, and as it were frozen, on the one bright spot where the sun again shone and shifted on the crooked blade. He was somewhat sullenly hacking with it at the wooden fence, but stopped when their eyes met.

"So you've found it again," was all that she could say.

"Yes, I've found it," he replied, rather gloomily; and then, after a pause: "I've also found several other things, including how I lost it."

"Do you mean," asked Catharine unsteadily, "that you've found out about—about Mrs. Mowbray?"

"It wouldn't be correct to say I've found it out," he answered. "Our depressing neighbour with the top-hat and the eyelids has found it out, and he's upstairs now, finding more of it out. But if you mean do I know how Marion was murdered, yes, I do; and I rather wish I didn't."

After a minute or two of objectless chipping on the fence he struck the point of his knife into the wood and faced her abruptly in a franker fashion.

"Look here," he said. "I should like to explain myself a little. When we first knew each other, I suppose I was very flippant. I admired your gravity and great goodness so much that I had to attack it; can you understand that? But I was not entirely flippant— no, nor entirely wrong. Think again of all the silly things that annoyed you, and of whether they have turned out so very silly? Are not rum and tobacco really more childlike and innocent than some things, my friend? Has any low sailors' tavern seen a worse tragedy than you have seen here? Mine are vulgar tastes, or, if you like, vulgar vices. But there is one thing to be said for our appetites: that they are appetites. Pleasure may be only satisfaction; but it can be satisfied. We drink it because we are thirsty; but not because we want to be thirsty. I tell you that these artists thirst for thirst. They want infinity, and they get it, poor souls. It may be bad to be drunk, but you can't be infinitely drunk; you fall down. A more horrible thing happens to them; they rise and rise, for ever. Isn't it better to fall under the table and snore than to rise through the seven heavens on the smoke of opium?"

She answered at last, with an appearance of thought and hesitation.

"There may be something in what you say, but it doesn't account for all the nonsensical things you said." She smiled a little, and added: "You said you only smoked for the good of the roses, you know. You'll hardly pretend there was any solemn truth behind that."

He started, and then stepped forward, leaving the knife standing and quivering in the fence.

"Yes, by God, there was," he cried. "It may seem the maddest thing of all, but it's true. Death and hell would not be in this house to-day, if they had only trusted to my trick of smoking the roses."

Catharine continued to look at him wildly, but his own gaze did not falter or show a shade of doubt; and he went slowly back to the fence and plucked his knife out of it. There was a long silence in the garden before either of them spoke again. He seemed to be revolving the best way of opening a difficult explanation. At last he spoke; his words were not the least of the riddles of the rose-garden.

"Do you think," he asked in a low voice, "that Marion is really dead?"

"Dead!" repeated Catharine; "why, of course she's dead."

He seemed to nod in brooding acquiescence, staring at his knife; then he added:

"Do you think her ghost walks?"

"What do you mean? Do you think so?" demanded his companion.

"No," he said. "But that drug is still disappearing."

She could only repeat, with a rather pale face: "Still disappearing?"

"In fact, it's nearly disappeared," remarked the captain; "you can come upstairs and see, if you like." He stopped and gazed at her a moment very seriously. "I know you are brave," he said. "Would you really like to see the end of this nightmare?"

"It would be a much worse nightmare if I didn't," she answered. And the captain, with a gesture at once negligent and resolved, tossed his knife among the rose bushes and turned towards the house.

She looked at him with a last flicker of suspicion.

"Why are you leaving your dagger in the garden?" she asked abruptly.

"The garden is full of daggers," said the captain, as he went upstairs.

Mounting the staircase with a catlike swiftness, he was some way ahead of the girl, in spite of her own mountaineering ease of movement. She had time to reflect that the greys and greens of the dados and decorative curtains had never seemed to her so dreary and even inhuman. And when she reached the landing and the door of the doctor's study, she met the captain again face to face. For he stood now with a face as pale as her own, and not any longer as leading her, but rather as barring her way.

"What is the matter?" she cried; and then, by a wild intuition: "Is somebody else dead?"

"Yes," replied Fonblanque; "somebody else is dead."

In the silence they heard within the heavy and yet soft movements of the strange investigator; and Fonblanque spoke again with a new impulsiveness.

"Catharine, my friend, I think you know how I feel about you; but what I am trying to say now is not about myself. It may seem a queer thing for a man like me to say, but somehow I think you will understand. Before you go inside, remember the things outside. I don't mean my things, but yours. I mean the empty sky and all the good grey virtues and the things that are clean and strong, like the wind. Believe me, they are real, after all; more real than the cloud on this accursed house. Hold fast to them still; tell yourself that God's winds and washing rivers are really there; at least as much there as the thing in that room."

"Yes, I think I understand you," she said. "And now let me

pass." Apart from the detective's presence there were but two differences in the doctor's study, as compared with the time when she stood in it last; and though they bulked very unequally to the eye, they seemed almost equal in a deadly significance. On a sofa under the window, covered with a sheet, lay something that could only be a corpse; but the very bulk of it and the way in which the folds of the sheet fell, showed her that it was not the corpse she had already seen. For herself, she had hardly need to glance at it; she knew, almost before she looked, that it was not the wife but the husband. And on the table in the centre stood the glass vessel of the opium and the other green bottle labelled "Poison"; but the opium vessel was quite empty.

The detective came forward with a mildness amounting to embarrassment, and spoke in a tone that seemed more sincerely sympathetic than his old half ironic phrases of sympathy. Without his top hat he looked much older; for his head was bald, with a fringe of grey hair behind standing out in rather neglected wisps. Irrationally enough the absence of the hat, as well as the greyness of the hair, made her feel that this man also improved on acquaintance. And indeed when he spoke to her it was in a paternal and even pathetic tone which she did not resent.

"You are naturally prejudiced against me, my dear," he said, "and you are not far out. You feel I am a morbid person; I think you sometimes felt I was probably a murderer. Well, I think you were right; not about the murder, but about the morbidity. I do live in the wrong atmosphere, as poor Mrs. Mowbray did, and for something of the same reason—because I have something of the artist who has taken the wrong turning. . . . I can't help being interested in the tragedies that are my trade; and you're quite wrong if you think my sentiment's all hypocritical. I've lost a good deal for my living; I can't hope to behave like a gentleman, but I do often feel like a man; only not like a healthy-minded man. The captain here has knocked about in all sorts of wild places; it is often an excellent way of remaining sane. I hope he'll take it as a compliment if I call it an excellent way of remaining commonplace. But we quiet people might really go mad, by digging away at one intellectual pleasure, as the poor lady did. My intellectual pleasure is criminology, which, I sometimes think, is itself a crime. Especially as I specialize in this department of it that concerns drugs. But I often think that in looking for dope I get almost as diseased as the dopers."

Catharine was conscious that he was talking with easy egotism to make her more at home in that unnatural room; and she did not doubt or depreciate his good nature. But the unanswered riddle still rode her imagination; and his last phrase about dope brought them all back to it.

"But I thought you said," she protested, "that Mrs. Mowbray was not killed by the drug."

"True," said Mr. Traill, "but this is a tragedy of dope for all that. She did not die of it, and yet it was the cause of her death."

He was silent again, looking at her wan and wondering face, and then added:

"She was not killed by the drug. She was killed for the drug. Did you notice anything odd about Dr. Mowbray when you were last in this room?"

"He was naturally agitated," said the girl doubtfully.

"No, unnaturally agitated," replied Traill; "more agitated than a man so sturdy would have been even by the revelation of another's weakness. It was his own weakness that rattled him like a storm that morning. He was indeed angry that the drug was stolen by his wife, for the simple reason that he wanted all that was left for himself. I have rather an ear for distant conversation, Miss Crawford, and I once heard you talking at the window about a pirate and a treasure. Can't you picture two pirates stealing the same treasure bit by bit, till one of them killed the other in rage at seeing it vanish? That is what happened in this house; and perhaps we had better call it madness, and then pity it. The drug had become the unhappy man's life, and that a horribly happy life. All his health and high spirits and humanitarianism flowered from that foul root. Can you fancy what it was to him when the last supply was shrinking, like the wild ass's skin in the story? It was like death to him; indeed, it was literally death. He had long resolved that when he had really emptied this bottle," and Traill touched the receptacle of opium, "he would at once turn to this"; and he laid his large lean hand on the green bottle of poison. "And now the end has come at last. All the opium is gone. Very little of the stuff in the green bottle is gone. But it is a more effective opiate."

Catharine did not doubt that a desolate dawn of truth was gradually invading the dark house; but her pale face was still puzzled. "You mean her husband killed her, and then killed himself," she said, in her simple way. "But how did he kill her, if not with the drug? Indeed how did he kill her at all? I left him in this room evidently amazed that the stuff was gone, and then I found her as if just struck down by a thunderbolt at the other end of the garden. How did he manage to kill her?"

"He stabbed her," replied Traill. "He stabbed her in a rather strange fashion, when she was far away at the other end of the garden."

"But he was not there!" cried Catharine. "He was up in this room."

"He was not there when he stabbed her," answered the detective.

"I told Miss Crawford," said the captain, in a low voice, "that the garden was full of daggers."

"Yes, of green daggers that grow on trees," continued Traill. "You may say if you like that she was killed by a wild creature, tied to the earth but armed."

His somewhat morbid fancy in putting things moved in her again her vague feeling of a garden of green mythological monsters; but the daylight was penetrating that thicket, and the daylight was white and terrible.

"He was committing the crime at the moment when you first came into that garden," said Traill. "The crime that he committed with his own hands. You stood in the sunshine and watched him commit it. But few crimes done in darkness have been so secret or so strange."

After a pause he began again, like a man trying different approaches to the same explanation.

"I have told you the deed was done for the drug, but not by the drug. I tell you now it was done with a syringe, but not a hypodermic syringe. It was being done with that ordinary garden implement he was holding in his hand when you saw him first. But the stuff with which he drenched the green rose-trees came out of this green bottle."

"He poisoned the roses," repeated Catharine almost mechanically.

"Yes," said the captain. "He poisoned the roses. And the thorns."

He had not spoken for some time, but the girl was gazing at him rather distractedly, and her next question had the same direction. She only said in a broken phrase: "And the knife. . . ."

"That is soon said," answered Traill. "The presence of the knife had nothing to do with it. The absence of the knife had a great deal. The murderer stole it and hid it, partly, perhaps, with some idea that its loss would look black against the captain; whom I did in fact suspect, as you did, I think. But there was a much more practical reason: the same that had made him steal and hide his wife's scissors. You heard his wife say she always wanted to tear off the roses with her fingers. If there was no instrument to hand, he knew that one fine morning she would do it. And one fine morning she did."

Catharine left the room without looking again at what lay in the light of the window under the sheet. She had no desire but to leave the room, and leave the house, and above all leave the garden behind her. And when she went out into the road she automatically turned her back on the fringe of fanciful cottages, and set her face towards the open fields and the distant woods of England. And she was already snapping bracken and startling birds with her step, before she became conscious of anything incongruous in the fact that Fonblanque was still strolling in her company. But they had fallen into a final companionship, and crossed a borderline together. It was the borderline she had faintly seen on that first evening, and which she had thought was like the end of the world. And, as the tales go, it was like the end of the world in one other respect: that it was the beginning of a better one.

The Hole in the Wall

The Hole
in the Wall

Two men, the one an architect and the other an archaeologist, met
on the steps of the great house at Prior's Park; and their host, Lord
Bulmer, in his breezy way, thought it natural to introduce them. It
must be confessed that he was hazy as well as breezy, and had no
very clear connexion in his mind, beyond the sense that an architect
and an archaeologist begin with the same series of letters. The world
must remain in a reverent doubt as to whether he would, on the
same principles, have presented a diplomatist to a dipsomaniac, or a
ratiocinator to a rat-catcher. He was a big, fair, bull-necked young
man abounding in outward gestures, unconsciously flapping his
gloves and flourishing his stick.

"You two ought to have something to talk about," he said
cheerfully. "Old buildings and all that sort of thing; this is rather an
old building, by the way, though I say it who shouldn't. I must ask
you to excuse me a moment; I've got to go and see about the cards
for this Christmas romp my sister's arranging. We hope to see you
all there, of course. Juliet wants it to be a fancy-dress affair; abbots
and crusaders and all that. My ancestors, I suppose, after all."

"I trust the abbot was not an ancestor," said the archaeological
gentleman with a smile.

"Only a sort of great-uncle, I imagine," answered the other,
laughing. Then his rather rambling eye rolled round the ordered
landscape in front of the house; an artificial sheet of water
ornamented with an antiquated nymph in the centre and surrounded by a park of tall trees now grey and black and frosty, for it
was in the depth of a severe winter.

"It's getting jolly cold," his lordship continued. "My sister hopes
we shall have some skating as well as dancing."

"If the crusaders come in full armour," said the other, "you must
be careful not to drown your ancestors."

101

"Oh, there's no fear of that," answered Bulmer; "this precious lake of ours is not two feet deep anywhere."

And with one of his flourishing gestures he stuck his stick into the water to demonstrate its shallowness. They could see the short end bent in the water; so that he seemed for a moment to lean his large weight on a breaking staff.

"The worst you can expect is to see an abbot sit down rather suddenly," he added, turning away. "Well, au revoir; I'll let you know about it later."

The archaeologist and the architect were left on the great stone steps smiling at each other; but whatever their common interests, they presented a considerable personal contrast; and the fanciful might even have found some contradiction in each considered individually. The former, a Mr. James Haddow, came from a drowsy den in the Inns of Court, full of leather and parchment; for the law was his profession and history only his hobby; he was indeed, among other things, the solicitor and agent of the Prior's Park estate. But he himself was far from drowsy and seemed remarkably wide-awake, with shrewd and prominent blue eyes and red hair brushed as neatly as his very neat costume. The latter, whose name was Leonard Crane, came straight from a crude and almost cockney office of builders and house-agents in the neighbouring suburb, sunning itself at the end of a new row of jerry-built houses with plans in very bright colours and notices in very large letters. But a serious observer, at a second glance, might have seen in his eyes something of that shining sleep that is called vision; and his yellow hair, while not affectedly long, was unaffectedly tidy. It was a manifest if melancholy truth that the architect was an artist. But the artistic temperament was far from explaining him; there was something else about him that was not definable but which some even felt to be dangerous. Despite his dreaminess he would sometimes surprise his friends with arts and even sport apart from his ordinary life, like memories of some previous existence. On this occasion, nevertheless, he hastened to disclaim any authority on the other man's hobby.

"I mustn't appear on false pretences," he said with a smile. "I hardly even know what an archaeologist is; except that a rather rusty remnant of Greek suggests that he is a man who studies old things."

"Yes," replied Haddow grimly. "An archaeologist is a man who studies old things and finds they are new."

Crane looked at him steadily for a moment and then smiled again.

"Dare one suggest," he said, "that some of the things we have been talking about are among the old things that turn out not to be old?"

His companion also was silent for a moment; and the smile on his rugged face was fainter as he replied quietly:

"The wall round the park is really old. The one gate in it is Gothic, and I cannot find any trace of destruction or restoration. But the house and the estate generally—well, the romantic ideas read into these things are often rather recent romances, things almost like fashionable novels. For instance, the very name of this place, Prior's Park, makes everybody think of it as a moonlit medieval abbey; I dare say the spiritualists by this time have discovered the ghost of a monk there. But according to the only authoritative study of the matter I can find the place was simply called Prior's as any rural place is called Podger's. It was the house of a Mr. Prior; a farmhouse probably, that stood here at some time or other and was a local landmark. Oh, there are a great many examples of the same thing, here and everywhere else. This suburb of ours used to be a village, and because some of the people slurred the name and pronounced it Holliwell, many a minor poet indulged in fancies about a Holy Well, with spells and fairies and all the rest of it, filling the suburban drawing-rooms with the Celtic twilight. Whereas anyone acquainted with the facts knows that 'Hollinwall' simply means 'the hole in the wall' and probably referred to some quite trivial accident. That's what I mean when I say that we don't so much find old things as we find new ones."

Crane seemed to have grown somewhat inattentive to the little lecture on antiquities and novelties; and the cause of his restlessness was soon apparent and indeed approaching. Lord Bulmer's sister, Juliet Bray, was coming slowly across the lawn, accompanied by one gentleman and followed by two others. The young architect was in the illogical condition of mind in which he preferred three to one.

The man walking with the lady was no other than the eminent Prince Borodino, who was at least as famous as a distinguished diplomatist ought to be, in the interests of what is called secret diplomacy. He had been paying a round of visits at various English country houses; and exactly what he was doing for diplomacy at

Prior's Park was as much a secret as any diplomatist could desire. The obvious thing to say of his appearance was that he would have been extremely handsome if he had not been entirely bald. But indeed that would itself be a rather bald way of putting it. Fantastic as it sounds, it would fit the case better to say that people would have been surprised to see hair growing on him; as surprised as if they had found hair growing on the bust of a Roman Emperor. His tall figure was buttoned up in a rather tight-waisted fashion that rather accentuated his potential bulk, and he wore a red flower in his button-hole. Of the two men walking behind one also was bald, but in a more partial and also a more premature fashion; for his drooping moustache was still yellow, and if his eyes were somewhat heavy it was with languor and not with age. His name was Horne Fisher; and he talked so easily and idly about everything, that nobody had ever discovered his favourite subject. His companion was a more striking and even more sinister figure; and he had the added importance of being Lord Bulmer's oldest and most intimate friend. He was generally known with a severe simplicity as Mr. Brain; but it was understood that he had been a judge and police official in India; and that he had enemies, who had represented his measures against crime as themselves almost criminal. He was a brown skeleton of a man with dark, deep sunken eyes and a black moustache that hid the meaning of his mouth. Though he had the look of one wasted by some tropical disease, his movements were much more alert than those of his lounging companion.

"It's all settled," announced the lady with great animation when they came within hailing distance. "You've all got to put on masquerade things and very likely skates as well; though the Prince says they don't go with it; but we don't care about that. It's freezing already, and we don't often get such a chance in England."

"Even in India we don't exactly skate all the year round," observed Mr. Brain.

"And even Italy is not primarily associated with ice," said the Italian.

"Italy is primarily associated with ices," remarked Mr. Horne Fisher, "I mean with ice-cream men. Most people in this country imagine that Italy is entirely populated with ice-cream men and organ-grinders. There certainly are a lot of them; perhaps they're an invading army in disguise."

"How do you know they are not the secret emissaries of our

diplomacy?" asked the Prince with a slightly scornful smile. "An army of organ-grinders might pick up hints, and their monkeys might pick up all sorts of things."

"The organs are organized, in fact," said the flippant Mr. Fisher.

"Well, I've known it pretty cold before now in Italy and even in India, up on the Himalayan slopes. The ice on our own little round pond will be quite cosy by comparison."

Juliet Bray was an attractive lady with dark hair and eyebrows and dancing eyes; and there was a geniality and even generosity in her rather imperious ways. In most matters she could command her brother; though that nobleman, like many other men of vague ideas, was not without a touch of the bully when he was at bay. She could certainly command her guests; even to the extent of decking out the most respectable and reluctant of them with her medieval masquerade. And it really seemed as if she could command the elements also, like a witch. For the weather steadily hardened and sharpened; that night the ice of the lake, glimmering in the moonlight, was like a marble floor; and they had begun to dance and skate on it before it was dark.

Prior's Park, or more properly the surrounding district of Hollinwall, was a country-seat that had become a suburb; having once had only a dependent village at its doors, it now found outside all its doors the signals of the expansion of London. Mr. Haddow—who was engaged in historical researches both in the library and the locality could find little assistance in the latter. He had already gathered from the documents that Prior's Park had originally been something like Prior's Farm, named after some local figure; but the new social conditions were all against his tracing the story by its traditions. Had any of the real rustics remained, he would probably have found some lingering legend of Mr. Prior, however remote he might be. But the new nomadic population of clerks and artisans, constantly shifting their homes from one suburb to another, or their children from one school to another, could have no corporate continuity. They had all that forgetfulness of history that goes everywhere with the extension of education.

Nevertheless when he came out of the library next morning, and saw the wintry trees standing round the frozen pond like a black forest, he felt he might well have been far in the depths of the country. The old wall running round the park kept that enclosure itself still entirely rural and romantic; and one could easily imagine that the depth of that dark forest faded away indefinitely into distant vales and hills. The grey and black and silver of the wintry wood were all the more severe or sombre as a contrast to the coloured carnival groups that already stood on and around the frozen pool. For the house-party had already flung themselves impatiently into fancy-dress; and the lawyer, with his neat black suit and red hair, was the only modern figure left among them.

"Aren't you going to dress up?" asked Juliet indignantly, shaking at him a horned and towering blue head-dress of the fourteenth century which framed her face very becomingly, fantastic as it was. "Everybody here has to be in the Middle Ages. Even Mr. Brain has put on a sort of brown dressing-gown and says he's a monk; and Mr. Fisher got hold of some old potato-sacks in the kitchen and sewed them together; he's supposed to be a monk too. As to the Prince, he's perfectly glorious, in great crimson robes, as a cardinal. He looks as if he could poison everybody. You simply must be something."

"I will be something later in the day," he replied; "at present I am nothing but an antiquary and an attorney. I have to see your brother presently, about some legal business and also some local investigations he asked me to make. I must look a little like a steward when I give an account of my stewardship."

"Oh, but my brother has dressed up," cried the girl, "very much so. No end, if I may say so. Why, he's bearing down on you now in all his glory."

The noble lord was indeed marching towards them in a magnificent sixteenth-century costume of purple and gold, with a gold-hilted sword and a plumed cap, and manners to match. Indeed, there was something more than his usual expansiveness of bodily action in his appearance at that moment. It almost seemed, so to speak, that the plumes on his hat had gone to his head. He flapped his great gold-lined cloak like the wings of a fairy king in a pantomime; he even drew his sword with a flourish and waved it about as he did his walking-stick. In the light of after events there seemed to be something monstrous and ominous about that exuberance; something of the spirit that is called *fey*. At the time it merely crossed a few people's minds that he might possibly be drunk.

As he strode towards his sister, the first figure he passed was that of Leonard Crane, clad in Lincoln green with the horn and baldrick and sword appropriate to Robin Hood; for he was standing nearest to the lady, where indeed he might have been found during a disproportionate part of the time. He had displayed one of his buried talents in the matter of skating, and now that the skating was over seemed disposed to prolong the partnership. The boisterous Bulmer playfully made a pass at him with his drawn sword, going forward with the lunge in the proper fencing fashion, and making a somewhat too familiar Shakespearean quotation about a rodent and a Venetian coin.

Probably in Crane also there was a subdued excitement just then; anyhow, in one flash he had drawn his own sword and parried; and then suddenly, to the surprise of everyone, Bulmer's weapon seemed to spring out of his hand into the air and rolled away on the ringing ice.

"Well, I never," said the lady, as if with justifiable indignation, "you never told me you could fence too."

Bulmer put up his sword with an air rather bewildered than annoyed, which increased the impression of something irresponsible in his mood at the moment; then he turned rather abruptly to his lawyer, saying: "We can settle up about the estate after dinner; I've missed nearly all the skating as it is; and I doubt if the ice will hold till to-morrow night. I think I shall get up early and have a spin by myself."

"You won't be disturbed with my company," said Horne Fisher in his weary fashion. "If I have to begin the day with ice, in the American fashion, I prefer it in smaller quantities. But no early hours for me in December. The early bird catches the cold."

"Oh, I shan't die of catching cold," answered Bulmer, and laughed.

A considerable group of the skating party had consisted of the guests staying at the house; and the rest had tailed off in twos and threes some time before most of the guests began to retire for the night. Neighbours always invited to Prior's Park on such occasions went back to their own houses in motors or on foot; the legal and archaeological gentleman had returned to the Inns of Court by a late train, to get a paper called for during his consultation with his client; and most of the other guests were drifting and lingering at various stages on their way up to bed. Horne Fisher, as if to deprive himself of any excuse for his refusal of early rising, had been the first to retire to his room; but, sleepy as he looked, he could not sleep. He had picked up from a table the book of antiquarian

topography, in which Haddow had found his first hints about the
origin of the local name; and being a man with a quiet and quaint
capacity for being interested in anything, he began to read it
steadily, making notes now and then of details on which his
previous reading left him with a certain doubt about his present
conclusions. His room was the one nearest to the lake in the centre
of the woods, and was therefore the quietest; and none of the last
echoes of the evening's festivity could reach him. He had followed
carefully the argument which established the derivation from Mr.
Prior's farm and the hole in the wall, and disposed of any
fashionable fancy about monks and magic wells, when he began to
be conscious of a noise audible in the frozen silence of the night. It
was not a particularly loud noise; but it seemed to consist of a series
of thuds or heavy blows, such as might be struck on a wooden door
by a man seeking to enter. They were followed by something like a
faint creak or crack, as if the obstacle had either been opened or had
given way. He opened his own bedroom door and listened; but as
he heard talk and laughter all over the lower floors, he had no
reason to fear that a summons would be neglected or the house left
without protection. He went to his open window, looking out over
the frozen pond and the moonlit statue in the middle of their circle
of darkling woods, and listened again. But silence had returned to
that silent place; and after straining his ears for a considerable time
he could hear nothing but the solitary hoot of a distant departing
train. Then he reminded himself how many nameless noises can be
heard by the wakeful during the most ordinary night; and, shrug-
ging his shoulders, went wearily to bed.

He awoke suddenly and sat up in bed with his ears filled, as with
thunder, with the throbbing echoes of a rending cry. He remained
rigid for a moment, and then sprang out of bed, throwing on the
loose gown of sacking he had worn all day. He went first to the
window, which was open but covered with a thick curtain, so that
his room was still completely dark; but when he tossed the curtain
aside and put his head out, he saw that a grey and silver daybreak
had already appeared behind the black woods that surrounded the
little lake. And that was all he did see. Though the sound had
certainly come in through the open window from this direction, the
whole scene was still and empty under the morning light as under
the moonlight. Then the long, rather lackadaisical hand he had laid
on a window-sill gripped it tighter as if to master a tremor, and his

peering blue eyes grew bleak with fear. It may seem that his emotion was exaggerated and needless, considering the effort of common sense by which he had conquered his nervousness about the noise on the previous night. But that had been a very different sort of noise. It might have been made by half a hundred things, from the chopping of wood to the breaking of bottles. There was only one thing in nature from which could come the sound that echoed through that dark house at daybreak. It was the awful articulate voice of man; and it was something worse, for he knew what man.

He knew also that it had been a shout for help. It seemed to him that he had heard the very word; but the word, short as it was, had been swallowed up, as if the man had been stifled or snatched away even as he spoke. Only the mocking reverberations of it remained even in his memory; but he had no doubt of the original voice. He had no doubt that the great bull's voice of Francis Bray, Baron Bulmer, had been heard for the last time between the darkness and the lifting dawn.

How long he stood there he never knew; but he was startled into life by the first living thing that he saw stirring in that half-frozen landscape. Along the path beside the lake, and immediately under his window, a figure was walking slowly and softly but with great composure; a stately figure in robes of a splendid scarlet; it was the Italian Prince, still in his Cardinal's costume. Most of the company had indeed lived in their costumes for the last day or two, and Fisher himself had assumed his frock of sacking as a convenient dressing-gown; but there seemed nevertheless something unusually finished and formal, in the way of an early bird, about this magnificent red cockatoo. It was as if the early bird had been up all night.

"What is the matter?" he called sharply, leaning out of the window; and the Italian turned up his great yellow face like a mask of brass.

"We had better discuss it downstairs," said Prince Borodino.

Fisher ran downstairs, and encountered the great red-robed figure entering the doorway and blocking the entrance with his bulk.

"Did you hear that cry?" demanded Fisher.

"I heard a noise and I came out," answered the diplomatist, and his face was too dark in the shadow for its expression to be read.

"It was Bulmer's voice," insisted Fisher. "I'll swear it was Bulmer's voice."

"Did you know him well?" asked the other.

The question seemed irrelevant though it was not illogical; and Fisher could only answer in a random fashion that he only knew Lord Bulmer slightly.

"Nobody seems to have known him well," continued the Italian in level tones. "Nobody except that man Brain. Brain is rather older than Bulmer, but I fancy they shared a good many secrets."

Fisher moved abruptly, as if waking from a momentary trance, and said in a new and more vigorous voice: "But look here, hadn't we better get outside and see if anything has happened?"

"The ice seems to be thawing," said the other, almost with indifference.

When they emerged from the house, dark stains and stars in the grey field of ice did indeed indicate that the frost was breaking up, as their host had prophesied the day before; and the very memory of yesterday brought back the mystery of today.

"He knew there would be a thaw," observed the Prince. "He went out skating quite early on purpose. Did he call out because he landed in the water, do you think?"

Fisher looked puzzled.

"Bulmer was the last man to bellow like that because he got his boots wet. And that's all he could do here; the water would hardly come up to the calf of a man of his size. You can see the flat weeds on the floor of the lake as if it were through a thin pane of glass. No, if Bulmer had only broken the ice he wouldn't have said much at the moment, though possibly a good deal afterwards. We should have found him stamping and damning up and down this path, and calling for clean boots."

"Let us hope we shall find him as happily employed," remarked the diplomatist. "In that case the voice must have come out of the wood."

"I'll swear it didn't come out of the house," said Fisher; and the two disappeared together into the twilight of wintry trees.

The plantation stood dark against the fiery colours of sunrise; a black fringe having that feathery appearance which makes trees when they are bare the very reverse of rugged. Hours and hours afterwards, when the same dense but delicate margin was dark against the cool greenish colours opposite the sunset, the search thus begun at sunrise had not come to an end. By successive stages, and to slowly gathering groups of the company, it became apparent that the most extraordinary of all gaps had appeared in the party; the guests could find no trace of their host anywhere. The servants reported that his bed had been slept in and his skates and his fancy costume were gone, as if he had risen early for the purpose he had himself avowed. But from the top of the house to the bottom, from the walls round the park to the pond in the centre, there was no trace of Lord Bulmer, dead or alive. Horne Fisher realized that a chilling premonition had already prevented him from expecting to find the man alive. But his bald brow was wrinkled over an entirely new and unnatural problem in not finding the man at all.

He considered the possibility of Bulmer having gone off on his own accord, for some reason; but after fully weighing it he finally dismissed it. It was inconsistent with the unmistakable voice heard at daybreak, and with many other practical obstacles. There was only one gateway in the ancient and lofty wall round the small park; the lodge-keeper kept it locked till late in the morning, and the lodge-keeper had seen no one pass. Fisher was fairly sure that he had before him a mathematical problem in an enclosed space. His instinct had been from the first so attuned to the tragedy that it would have been almost a relief to him to find the corpse. He would have been grieved, but not horrified, to come on the nobleman's body dangling from one of his own trees as from a gibbet, or floating in his own pool like a pallid weed. What horrified him was to find nothing.

He soon became conscious that he was not alone even in his most individual and isolated experiments. He often found a figure following him like his shadow, in silent and almost secret clearings in the plantation or outlying nooks and corners of the old wall. The dark-moustachioed mouth was as mute as the deep eyes were mobile, darting incessantly hither and thither, but it was clear that Brain of the Indian police had taken up the trail like an old hunter after a tiger. Seeing that he was the only personal friend of the vanished man, this seemed natural enough; and Fisher resolved to deal frankly with him.

"This silence is rather a social strain," he said. "May I break the ice by talking about the weather; which, by the way, has already broken the ice? I know that breaking the ice might be a rather melancholy metaphor in this case."

"I don't think so," replied Brain shortly. "I don't fancy the ice had much to do with it. I don't see how it could."

"What would you propose doing?" asked Fisher.

"Well, we've sent for the authorities, of course, but I hope to find something out before they come," replied the Anglo-Indian. "I can't say I have much hope from police methods in this country. Too much red tape; Habeas Corpus and that sort of thing. What we want is to see that nobody bolts; the nearest we could get to it would be to collect the company and count them, so to speak. Nobody's left lately, except that lawyer who was poking about for antiquities."

"Oh, he's out of it; he left last night," answered the other. "Eight hours after Bulmer's chauffeur saw his lawyer off by the train, I heard Bulmer's own voice as plain as I hear yours now."

"I suppose you don't believe in spirits?" said the man from India. After a pause he added: "There's somebody else I should like to find, before we go after a fellow with an alibi in the Inner Temple. What's become of that fellow in green; the architect dressed up as a forester? I haven't seen him about."

Mr. Brain managed to secure his assembly of all the distracted company before the arrival of the police. But when he first began to comment once more on the young architect's delay in putting in an appearance, he found himself in the presence of a minor mystery, and a psychological development of an entirely unexpected kind.

Juliet Bray had confronted the catastrophe of her brother's disappearance with a sombre stoicism in which there was perhaps more paralysis than pain; but when the other question came to the surface she was both agitated and angry.

"We don't want to jump to any conclusions about anybody," Brain was saying in his staccato style, "but we should like to know a little more about Mr. Crane. Nobody seems to know much about him or where he comes from. And it seems a sort of coincidence that yesterday he actually crossed swords with poor Bulmer, and could have stuck him too, since he showed himself the better swordsman. Of course, that may be an accident, and couldn't possibly be called a case against anybody; but then we haven't the means to make a real case against anybody. Till the police come we are only a pack of very amateur sleuth-hounds."

"And I think you're a pack of snobs," said Juliet. "Because Mr. Crane is a genius who's made his own way, you try to suggest he's a murderer, without daring to say so. Because he wore a toy sword, and happened to know how to use it, you want us to believe he used it like a blood-thirsty maniac for no reason in the world. And because he could have hit my brother and didn't, you deduce that he did. That's the sort of way you argue. And as for his having disappeared, you're wrong in that as you are in everything else, for here he comes."

And, indeed, the green figure of the fictitious Robin Hood slowly detached itself from the grey background of the trees and came towards them as she spoke.

He approached the group slowly, but with composure; but he was decidedly pale, and the eyes of Brain and Fisher had already taken in one detail of the green-clad figure more clearly than all the rest. The horn still swung from his baldrick, but the sword was gone.

Rather to the surprise of the company, Brain did not follow up the question thus suggested, but, while retaining an air of leading the inquiry, had also an appearance of changing the subject.

"Now we're all assembled," he observed quietly, "there is a question I want to ask to begin with. Did anybody here actually see Lord Bulmer this morning?"

Leonard Crane turned his pale face round the circle of faces till he came to Juliet's; then he compressed his lips a little and said: "Yes, I saw him."

"Was he alive and well?" asked Brain quickly. "How was he dressed?"

"He appeared exceedingly well," replied Crane, with a curious intonation. "He was dressed as he was yesterday, in that purple costume copied from the portrait of his ancestor in the sixteenth century. He had his skates in his hand."

"And his sword at his side, I suppose," added the questioner. "Where is your own sword, Mr. Crane?"

"I threw it away."

In the singular silence that ensued the train of thought in many minds became involuntarily a series of coloured pictures. They had grown used to their fanciful garments looking more gay and gorgeous against the dark grey and streaky silver of the frost, so that the moving figures glowed like stained-glass saints walking. The effect had been more fitting because so many of them had idly parodied pontifical or monastic dress. But the most arresting attitude that remained in their memories had been anything but merely monastic: that of the moment when the figure in bright green and the other in vivid violet had for a moment made a silver cross of their crossing swords. Even when it was a jest it had been something of a drama; and it was a strange and sinister thought that, in the grey daybreak, the same figures in the same posture might have been repeated as a tragedy.

"Did you quarrel with him?" asked Brain suddenly.

"Yes," replied the immovable man in green. "Or he quarrelled with me."

"Why did he quarrel with you?" asked the investigator; and Leonard Crane made no reply.

Horne Fisher, curiously enough, had only given half his attention to this crucial cross-examination. His heavy-lidded eyes had languidly followed the figure of Prince Borodino, who at this stage had strolled away towards the fringe of the wood and, after a pause as of meditation, had disappeared into the darkness of the trees.

He was recalled from his irrelevance by the voice of Juliet Bray, which rang out with an altogether new note of decision:

"If that is the difficulty, it had best be cleared up. I am engaged to Mr. Crane; and when we told my brother, he did not approve of it, that is all."

Neither Brain nor Fisher exhibited any surprise, but the former added quietly:

"Except, I suppose, that he and your brother went off into the wood to discuss it—where Mr. Crane mislaid his sword, not to mention his companion."

"And may I ask," inquired Crane, with a certain flicker of mockery passing over his pallid features, "what I am supposed to have done with either of them? Let us adopt the cheerful thesis that I am a murderer. It has yet to be shown that I am a magician. If I ran your unfortunate friend through the body, what did I do with the body? Did I have it carried away by seven flying dragons, or was it merely a trifling matter of turning it into a milk-white hind?"

"It is no occasion for sneering," said the Anglo-Indian judge with abrupt authority. "It doesn't make it look better for you that you can joke about the loss."

Fisher's dreamy and even dreary eye was still on the edge of the wood behind, and he became conscious of masses of dark red, like a stormy sunset cloud, glowing through the grey network of the thin trees; and the Prince, in his cardinal's robes, re-emerged on to the pathway. Brain had had half a notion that the Prince might have gone to look for the lost rapier, but when he reappeared he was carrying in his hand, not a sword, but an axe.

The incongruity between the masquerade and the mystery had created a curious psychological atmosphere. At first they had all felt horribly ashamed at being caught in the foolish disguises of a festival by an event that had only too much the character of a funeral. Many of them would have already gone back and dressed in clothes that were more funereal, or at least more formal. But somehow at the moment this seemed like a second masquerade, more artificial and frivolous than the first. And as they reconciled themselves to their ridiculous trappings a curious sensation had come over some of them, notably over the more sensitive, like Crane and Fisher and Juliet, but in some degree over everybody except the practical Mr. Brain. It was almost as if they were the ghosts of their own ancestors haunting that dark wood and dismal lake, and playing some old part that they only half remembered. The movements of those coloured figures seemed to mean some-thing that had been settled long before, like a silent heraldry. Acts, attitude, external objects, were accepted as an allegory even without the key; and they knew when a crisis had come, when they did not know what it was. And somehow they knew subconsciously that the whole tale had taken a new and terrible turn when they saw the Prince stand in the gap of the gaunt trees, in his robes of angry crimson and with his lowering face of bronze, bearing in his hand a new shape of death. They could not have named a reason; but the two swords seemed indeed to have become toy swords, and the whole tale of them broken and tossed away like a toy. Borodino looked like the old-world headsman, clad in terrible red, and carrying the axe for the execution of the criminal. And the criminal was not Crane.

Mr. Brain, of the Indian police, was glaring at the new object, and it was a moment or two before he spoke, harshly and almost hoarsely.

"What are you doing with that?" he asked. "Seems to be a woodman's chopper."

"A natural association of ideas," observed Horne Fisher. "If you meet a cat in a wood, you think it's a wild cat, though it may have just strolled from the drawing-room sofa. As a matter of fact, I happen to know that is not the woodman's chopper. It's the kitchen chopper, or meat axe or something like that, that somebody has thrown away in the wood. I saw it in the kitchen myself when I was getting the potato sacks with which I reconstructed a mediaeval hermit."

"All the same, it is not without interest," remarked the Prince, holding out the instrument to Fisher, who took it and examined it carefully. "A butcher's cleaver that has done butcher's work."

"It was certainly the instrument of the crime," assented Fisher in a low voice.

Brain was staring at the dull blue gleam of the axe-head with fierce and fascinated eyes.

"I don't understand you," he said; "there is no—there are no marks on it."

"It has shed no blood," answered Fisher, "but for all that it has committed a crime. This is as near as the criminal came to the crime when he committed it."

"What do you mean?"

"He was not there when he did it," explained Fisher. "It's a poor sort of murderer who can't murder people when he isn't there."

"You seem to be talking merely for the sake of mystification," said Brain. "If you have any practical advice to give, you might as well make it intelligible."

"The only practical advice I can suggest," said Fisher thoughtfully, "is a little research into local topography and nomenclature. They say there used to be a Mr. Prior, who had a farm in this neighbourhood. I think some details about the domestic life of the late Mr. Prior would throw a light on this terrible business."

"And you have nothing more immediate than your topography to offer," said Brain, with a sneer, "to help me to avenge my friend."

"Well," said Fisher, "I shall find out the truth about the Hole in the Wall."

That night, at the close of a stormy twilight and under a strong west wind that followed the breaking of the frost, Leonard Crane was wending his way in a wild rotatory walk round and round the high continuous wall that enclosed the little wood. He was driven by a desperate idea of solving for himself the riddle that had clouded his reputation and already even threatened his liberty. The police authorities, now in charge of the inquiry, had not arrested him; but he knew well enough that if he tried to move far afield he would be instantly arrested. Horne Fisher's fragmentary hints, though he had refused to expand them as yet, had stirred the artistic temperament of the architect to a sort of wild analysis, and he was resolved to read the hieroglyph upside down and every way until it made sense. If it was something connected with a hole in the wall, he would find the hole in the wall; but as a matter of fact he was unable to find the faintest crack in the wall. His professional knowledge told him that the masonry was all of one workmanship and one date; and except for the regular entrance, which threw no light on the mystery, he found nothing suggesting any sort of hiding-place or means of escape. Walking a narrow path between the windy wall and the wild eastward bend and sweep of the grey and feathery trees, seeing shifting gleams of a lost sunset winking almost like lightning as the clouds of tempest scudded across the sky and mingling with the first faint blue light from a slowly strengthened moon behind him, he began to feel his head going round as his heels were going round and round the blind recurrent barrier. He had thoughts on the border of thought, fancies about a fourth dimension which was itself a hole to hide anything, of seeing everything from a new angle out of a new window in the senses, or of some mystical light and transparency, like the new rays of chemistry, in which he could see Bulmer's body, horrible and glaring, floating in a lurid halo over the woods and the wall. He was haunted also with the hint, which somehow seemed to be equally horrifying, that it all had something to do with Mr. Prior. There seemed even to be something creepy in the fact that he was always respectfully referred to as Mr. Prior, and that it was in the domestic life of the dead farmer that he had been bidden to seek the seed of these dreadful things. As a matter of fact, he had found that no local inquiries had revealed anything at all about the Prior family. He dimly imagined Mr. Prior in an old top-hat, perhaps with a chin-beard or whiskers. But he had no face.

The moonlight had broadened and brightened, the wind had driven off the clouds and itself died fitfully away, when he came round again to the artificial lake in front of the house. For some reason it looked a very artificial lake; indeed, the whole scene was like a classical landscape with a touch of Watteau; the Palladian façade of the house pale in the moon, and the same silver touching the very pagan and naked marble nymph in the middle of the pond. Rather to his surprise he found another figure there beside the statue, sitting almost equally motionless; and the same silver pencil traced the wrinkled brow and patient face of Horne Fisher, still dressed as a hermit, and apparently practising something of the solitude of a hermit. Nevertheless he looked up at Leonard Crane and smiled, almost as if he had expected him.

"Look here," said Crane, planting himself in front of him. "Can you tell me anything about this business?"

"I shall soon have to tell everybody everything about it," replied Fisher, "but I've no objection to telling you something first. But, to begin with, will you tell me something? What really happened when you met Bulmer this morning? You did throw away your sword, but you didn't kill him."

"I didn't kill him because I threw away my sword," said the other. "I did it on purpose, or I'm not sure what might have happened."

After a pause he went on quietly:

"The late Lord Bulmer was a very breezy gentleman, extremely breezy. He was very genial with his inferiors and would have his lawyer and his architect staying in his house for all sorts of holidays and amusements. But there was another side to him, which they found out when they tried to be his equals. When I told him that his sister and I were engaged, something happened which I simply can't and won't describe. It seemed to me like some monstrous upheaval of madness. But I suppose the truth is painfully simple. There is such a thing as the coarseness of a gentleman. And it is the most horrible thing in humanity."

"I know," said Fisher. "The Renascence nobles of the Tudor time were like that."

"It is odd that you should say that," Crane went on, "for while we were talking there came on me a curious feeling that we were repeating some scene of the past, and that I was really some outlaw, found in the woods like Robin Hood, and that he had really stepped, in all his plumes and purple, out of the picture-frame of the ancestral portrait. Anyhow, he was the man in possession, and he neither feared God nor regarded man. I defied him, of course, and walked away. I might really have killed him if I had not walked away."

"Yes," said Fisher, nodding, "his ancestor was in possession and he was in possession; and this is the end of the story. It all fits in."

"Fits in with what?" cried his companion, with sudden impatience; "I can't make head or tail of it. You tell me to look for the secret in the hole in the wall, but I can't find any hole in the wall."

"There isn't any," said Fisher. "That's the secret."

After reflecting a moment, he added:

"Unless you call it a hole in the wall of the world. Look here, I'll tell you, if you like, but I'm afraid it involves an introduction. You've got to understand one of the tricks of the modern mind, a tendency that most people obey without noticing it.

"In the village or suburb outside there's an inn with the sign of St. George and the Dragon. Now suppose I went about telling everybody that this was only a corruption of King George and the Dragoon. Scores of people would believe it, without any inquiry, from a vague feeling that it's probable because it's prosaic. It turns something romantic and legendary into something recent and ordinary. And that somehow makes it sound rational, though it is unsupported by reason. Of course, some people would have the sense to remember having seen St. George in old Italian pictures and French romances; but a good many wouldn't think about it at all. They would just swallow the scepticism because it was scepticism. Modern intelligence won't accept anything on authority. But it will accept anything without authority. That's exactly what has happened here.

"When some critic or other chose to say that Prior's Park was not a priory, but was named after some quite modern man named Prior, nobody really tested the theory at all. It never occurred to anybody repeating the story to ask if there *was* any Mr. Prior, if anybody had ever seen him or heard of him. As a matter of fact, it was a priory, and shared the fate of most priories; that is, the Tudor gentleman with the plumes simply stole it by brute force and turned it into his own private house; he did worse things, as you shall hear. But the point here is that this is how the trick works; and the trick works in the same way in the other part of the tale. The name of this district is printed Holinwall in all the best maps produced by the scholars, and they allude lightly, not without a smile, to the fact that it was pronounced Holiwell by the most ignorant and old-fashioned of the poor. But it is spelt wrong and pronounced right."

"Do you mean to say," asked Crane quickly, "that there really was a well?"

"There is a well," said Fisher, "and the truth lies at the bottom of it."

As he spoke he stretched out his hand and pointed towards a sheet of water in front of him.

"The well is under that water somewhere," he said, "and this is not the first tragedy connected with it. The founder of this house did something which his fellow-ruffians very seldom did, something that had to be hushed up even in the anarchy of the pillage of the monasteries. The well was connected with the miracles of some saint, and the last prior that guarded it was something like a saint himself; certainly he was something very like a martyr. He defied the new owner and dared him to pollute the place, till the noble, in a fury, stabbed him and flung his body into the well; whither after four hundred years it has been followed by an heir of the usurper, clad in the same purple and walking the world with the same pride."

"But how did it happen," demanded Crane, "that for the first time Bulmer fell in at that particular spot?"

"Because the ice was only loosened at that particular spot by the only man who knew it," answered Horne Fisher. "It was cracked deliberately with the kitchen chopper at that special place, and I myself heard the hammering and did not understand it. The place had been covered with an artificial lake, if only because the whole truth had to be covered with an artificial legend. But don't you see that it is exactly what those pagan nobles would have done, to desecrate it with a sort of heathen goddess, as the Roman Emperor built a temple to Venus on the Holy Sepulchre? But the truth could still be traced out by any scholarly man determined to trace it. And this man was determined to trace it."

"What man?" asked the other, with a shadow of the answer in his mind.

"The only man who has an alibi," replied Fisher. "James Haddow, the antiquarian lawyer, left the night before the fatality, but he left that black star of death on the ice. He left abruptly, having previously proposed to stay; probably, I think, after an ugly scene with Bulmer at their legal interview. As you know yourself, Bulmer could make a man feel pretty murderous; and I rather fancy the lawyer had himself irregularities to confess, and was in danger of exposure by his client. But it's my reading of human nature that a man will cheat in his trade but not in his hobby. Haddow may have been a dishonest lawyer, but he couldn't help being an honest antiquary. When he got on the track of the truth about the Holy Well, he had to follow it up; he was not to be bamboozled with newspaper anecdotes about Mr. Prior and a hole in the wall; he found out everything, even to the exact location of the well, and he was rewarded, if being a successful assassin can be regarded as a reward."

"And how did you get on the track of all this hidden history?" asked the young architect.

A cloud came across the brow of Horne Fisher.

"I knew only too much about it already," he said, "and, after all, it's shameful for me to be speaking lightly of poor Bulmer, who has paid his penalty, when the rest of us haven't. I dare say every cigar I smoke and every liqueur I drink comes directly or indirectly from the harrying of the holy places and the persecution of the poor. After all, it needs very little poking about in the past to find that hole in the wall; that great breach in the defences of English history. It lies just under the surface of a thin sheet of sham information and instruction, just as the black and bloodstained well lies just under the floor of shallow water and flat weeds. Oh, the ice is thin, but it bears; it is strong enough to support us when we dress up as monks and dance on it in mockery of the dear quaint old Middle Ages. They told me I must put on fancy dress; so I did put on fancy dress, according to my own taste and fancy. You see I do know a little about our national and imperial history, our prosperity and our progress, our commerce and our colonies, our centuries of success or splendour. So I did put on an antiquated sort of costume, when I was asked to do so. I put on the only costume I think fit for a man who has inherited the position of a gentleman and yet has not entirely lost the feelings of one."

In answer to a look of inquiry he rose with a sweeping and downward gesture.

"Sackcloth," he said, "and I would wear the ashes as well, if they would stay on my bald head when I put them there."

HORNE FISHER & CUTHBERT GRAYNE
IN

*The Bottomless
Well*

The Bottomless Well

On an oasis, or green island in the red and yellow seas of sand that
stretch beyond Europe towards the sunrise, there can be found a
rather fantastic contrast which is none the less typical of such a
place, since international treaties have made it an outpost of the
British occupation. The site is famous among archaeologists for
something that is hardly a monument but merely a hole in the
ground. But it is a round shaft like that of a well, and probably a
part of some great irrigation works of remote and disputed date;
perhaps more ancient than anything in that ancient land. There is a
green fringe of palm and prickly pear round the black mouth of the
well; but nothing of the upper masonry remains except two bulky
and battered stones standing like the pillars of a gateway of
nowhere; in which some of the more transcendental archaeologists,
in certain moods at moonrise or sunset, think they can trace the
faint lines of figures or features of more than Babylonian monstrosity; while the more rationalistic archaeologists, in the more rational
hours of daylight, see nothing but two shapeless rocks. It may have
been noticed, however, that all Englishmen are not archaeologists.
Many of those assembled in such a place for official and military
purposes have hobbies other than archaeology. And it is a solemn
fact that the English in this eastern exile have contrived to make a
small golf links out of the green scrub and sand; with a comfortable
club house at one end of it and this primeval monument at the other.
They did not actually use this archaic abyss as a bunker; because it
was by tradition unfathomable, and even for practical purposes
unfathomed. Any sporting projectile sent into it might be counted
most literally as a lost ball. But they often sauntered round it in their
interludes of talking and smoking cigarettes, and one of them had
just come down from the club house to find another gazing
somewhat moodily into the well.

The two Englishmen both wore light clothes and white pith helmets and pugarees, but there for the most part their resemblance ended. And they both almost simultaneously said the same word; but they said it on two totally different notes of the voice.

"Have you heard the news?" asked the man from the club. "Splendid."

'Splendid," replied the man by the well. But the first man pronounced the word as a young man might say it about a woman; and the second as an old man might say it about the weather; not without sincerity but certainly without fervour.

And in this the tone of the two men was sufficiently typical of them. The first, who was a certain Captain Boyle, was of a bold and boyish style, dark and with a sort of native heat in his face that did not belong to the atmosphere of the East, but rather to the ardours and ambitions of the West. The other was an older man and certainly an older resident; a civilian official named Horne Fisher; and his drooping eyelids and drooping light moustaches expressed all the paradox of the Englishman in the East. He was much too hot to be anything but cool.

Neither of them thought it necessary to mention what it was that was splendid. That would indeed have been superfluous conversation about something that everybody knew. The striking victory over a menacing combination of Turks and Arabs in the north, won by troops under the command of Lord Hastings, the veteran of so many striking victories, was already spread by the newspapers all over the Empire, let alone to this small garrison so near to the battlefield.

"Now no other nation in the world could have done a thing like that," cried Captain Boyle emphatically.

Horne Fisher was still looking silently into the well; a moment later he answered:

"We certainly have the art of unmaking mistakes. That's where the poor old Prussians went wrong. They could only make mistakes and stick to them. There is really a certain talent in unmaking mistakes."

"What do you mean?" asked Boyle. "What mistake?"

"Well, everybody knows it looked like biting off more than we could chew," replied Horne Fisher. It was a peculiarity of Mr. Fisher that he always said that everybody knew things that about one person in two million was ever allowed to hear of. "And it was certainly jolly lucky that Travers turned up so well in the nick of time. Odd how often the right thing's been done for us by the second in command, even when a great man was first in command. Like Colborne at Waterloo."

"It ought to add a whole province to the Empire," observed the other.

"Well, I suppose the Zimmerns would have insisted on it as far as the canal," observed Fisher thoughtfully, "though everybody knows adding provinces doesn't always pay much nowadays."

Captain Boyle frowned in a slightly puzzled fashion. Being cloudily conscious of never having heard of the Zimmerns in his life, he could only remark stolidly:

"Well, one can't be a Little Englander."

Horne Fisher smiled; and he had a pleasant smile.

"Every man out here is a Little Englander," he said. "He wishes he were back in Little England."

"I don't know what you're talking about, I'm afraid," said the younger man rather suspiciously. "One would think you didn't really admire Hastings or—or anything."

"I admire him no end," replied Fisher. "He's by far the best man for this post; he understands the Moslems and can do anything with them. That's why I'm all against pushing Travers against him, merely because of this last affair."

"I really don't understand what you're driving at," said the other frankly.

"Perhaps it isn't worth understanding," answered Fisher lightly, "and, anyhow, we needn't talk politics. Do you know the Arab legend about that well?"

"I'm afraid I don't know much about Arab legends," said Boyle rather stiffly.

"That's rather a mistake," replied Fisher, "especially from your point of view. Lord Hastings himself is an Arab legend. That is perhaps the very greatest thing he really is. If his reputation went, it would weaken us all over Asia and Africa. Well, the story about that hole in the ground, that goes down nobody knows where, has always fascinated me rather. It's Mahomedan in form now; but I shouldn't wonder if the tale is a long way older than Mahomet. It's all about somebody they call the Sultan Aladin; not our friend of the lamp, of course, but rather like him in having to do with genii or giants or something of that sort. They say he commanded the giants to build him a sort of pagoda rising higher and higher above all the stars. The Utmost for the Highest, as the people said when they built the Tower of Babel. But the builders of the Tower of Babel were quite modest and domestic people, like mice, compared with old Aladin. They only wanted a tower that would *pass* heaven, and rise above it, and go on rising for ever and ever. And Allah cast him down to earth with a thunderbolt, which sank into the earth, boring a hole deeper and deeper, till it made a well that was without a bottom as the tower was to have been without a top. And down that inverted tower of darkness the soul of the proud Sultan is falling for ever and ever."

"What a queer chap you are," said Boyle, "you talk as if a fellow could believe those fables."

"Perhaps I believe the moral and not the fable," answered Fisher, "but here comes Lady Hastings. You know her, I think?"

The club house on the golf links was used, of course, for many other purposes besides that of golf. It was the only social centre of the garrison besides the strictly military headquarters; it had a billiard-room and a bar, and even an excellent reference library for those officers who were so perverse as to take their profession seriously. Among these was the great general himself, whose head of silver and face of bronze, like that of a brazen eagle, were often to be found bent over the charts and folios of the library. The great Lord Hastings believed in science and study, as in other severe ideals of life; and had given much paternal advice on the point to young Boyle, whose appearances in that place of research were rather more intermittent. It was from one of these snatches of study that the young man had just come out through the glass doors of the library on to the golf links. But above all the club was so appointed as to serve the social conveniences of ladies at least as much as gentlemen; and Lady Hastings was able to play the queen in such a society almost as much as in her own ballroom. She was eminently calculated, and, as some said, eminently inclined to play such a part. She was much younger than her husband; an attractive and some-times dangerously attractive lady; and Mr. Horne Fisher looked after her, a little sardonically, as she swept away with the young soldier. Then his rather dreary eye strayed to the green and prickly growths round the well; growths of that curious cactus formation in which one thick leaf grows directly out of the other without stalk or twig. It gave his fanciful mind a sinister feeling of a blind growth without shape or purpose. A flower or shrub in the West grows to the blossom which is its crown, and is content. But this was as if hands could grow out of hands or legs grow out of legs in a nightmare. "Always adding a province to the Empire," he said with a smile; and then added more sadly: "But I doubt if I was right after all."

A strong but genial voice broke in on his meditations; and he looked up and smiled, seeing the face of an old friend. The voice was indeed rather more genial than the face, which was at the first glance decidedly grim. It was a typically legal face, with angular jaws and heavy grizzled eyebrows: and it belonged to an eminently legal character, though he was now attached in a semi-military capacity to the police of that wild district. Cuthbert Grayne was perhaps more of a criminologist than either a lawyer or a policeman; but in his more barbarous surroundings he had proved successful in turning himself into a practical combination of all three. The discovery of a whole series of strange Oriental crimes stood to his credit; but as few people were acquainted with, or attracted to, such a hobby or branch of knowledge, his intellectual life was somewhat solitary. Among the few exceptions was Horne Fisher, who had a curious capacity for talking to almost anybody about almost anything.

"Studying botany, or is it archaeology?" inquired Grayne. "I shall never come to the end of your interests, Fisher. I should say that what you don't know isn't worth knowing."

"You are wrong," replied Fisher with a very unusual abruptness and even bitterness. "It's what I do know that isn't worth knowing. All the seamy side of things; all the secret reasons and rotten motives and bribery and blackmail they call politics. I needn't be so proud of having been down all these sewers that I should brag about it to the little boys in the street."

"What do you mean? What's the matter with you?" asked his friend. "I never knew you taken like this before."

"I'm ashamed of myself," replied Fisher. "I've just been throwing cold water on the enthusiasms of a boy."

"Even that explanation is hardly exhaustive," observed the criminal expert.

"Damned newspaper nonsense the enthusiasms were, of course," continued Fisher, "but I ought to know that at that age illusions can be ideals. And they're better than the reality, anyhow. But there is one very ugly responsibility about jolting a young man out of the rut of the most rotten ideal."

"And what may that be?"

"It's very apt to set him off with the same energy in a much worse direction," answered Fisher. "A pretty endless sort of direction—a bottomless pit, as deep as the Bottomless Well."

Fisher did not see his friend until a fortnight later, when he found himself in the garden at the back of the club house on the opposite side from the links—a garden heavily coloured and scented with semi-tropical plants in the glow of a desert sunset. Two other men were with him, the third being the now celebrated second in command, familiar to everybody as Tom Travers, a lean, dark man who looked older than his years, with a furrow in his brow and something morose about the very shape of his black moustache. They had just been served with black coffee by the Arab now officiating as the temporary servant of the club, though he was a figure already familiar, and even famous, as the old servant of the General. He went by the name of Said, and was notable among other Semites for that unnatural length of his yellow face and height of his narrow forehead which is sometimes seem among them, and gave an irrational impression of something sinister, in spite of his agreeable smile.

"I never feel as if I could quite trust that fellow," said Grayne, when the man had gone away. "It's very unjust, I take it, for he was certainly devoted to Hastings, and saved his life, they say. But Arabs are often like that—loyal to one man. I can't help feeling he might cut anybody else's throat, and even do it treacherously."

"Well," said Travers, with a rather sour smile, "so long as he leaves Hastings alone the world won't mind much."

There was a rather embarrassing silence, full of memories of the great battle, and then Horne Fisher said quietly:

"The newspapers aren't the world, Tom. Don't you worry about them. Everybody in your world knows the truth well enough."

"I think we'd better not talk about the General just now," remarked Grayne, "for he's just coming out of the club."

"He's not coming here," said Fisher. "He's only seeing his wife to the car."

As he spoke, indeed, the lady came out on the steps of the club, followed by her husband, who then went swiftly in front of her to open the garden gate. As he did so she turned back and spoke for a moment to a solitary man still sitting in a cane chair in the shadow of the doorway, the only man left in the deserted club, save for the three that lingered in the garden. Fisher peered for a moment into the shadow and saw that it was Captain Boyle.

The next moment, rather to their surprise, the General reappeared, and remouting the steps, spoke a word or two to Boyle in his turn. Then he signalled to Said, who hurried up with two cups of coffee, and the two men re-entered the club, each carrying his cup in his hand. The next moment a gleam of white light in the growing darkness showed that the electric lamps had been turned on in the library beyond.

"Coffee and scientific researches," said Travers grimly. "All the luxuries of learning and theoretical research. Well, I must be going, for I have my work to do as well."

And he got up rather stiffly, saluted his companions and strode away into the dusk.

"I only hope Boyle *is* sticking to scientific researches," said Horne Fisher. "I'm not very comfortable about him myself. But let's talk about something else."

They talked about something else longer than they probably imagined, until the tropical night had come and a splendid moon painted the whole scene with silver; but before it was bright enough to see by, Fisher had already noted that the lights in the library had been abruptly extinguished. He waited for the two men to come out by the garden entrance, but nobody came.

"They must have gone for a stroll on the links," he said.

"Very possibly," replied Grayne. "It's going to be a beautiful night."

A moment or two after he had spoken they heard a voice hailing them out of the shadow of the club-house, and were astonished to perceive Travers hurrying towards them, calling out as he came:

"I shall want your help, you fellows," he cried. "There's something pretty bad out on the links."

They found themselves plunging through the club smoking-room and the library beyond in complete darkness, mental as well as material. But Horne Fisher, in spite of his affectation of indifference, was a person of a curious and almost transcendental sensibility to atmospheres, and he already felt the presence of something more than an accident. He collided with a piece of furniture in the library and almost shuddered with the shock; for the thing moved as he could never have fancied a piece of furniture moving. It seemed to move like a living thing, yielding and yet striking back. The next moment Grayne had turned on the lights; and he saw he had only stumbled against one of the revolving bookstands that had swung round and struck him; but his own involuntary recoil had revealed to him his own subconsciousness of something mysterious and monstrous. There were several of these revolving bookcases here and there about the library; on one of them stood the two cups of coffee, and on another a large open book. It was Budge's book on Egyptian hieroglyphics, with coloured plates of strange birds and gods; and even as he rushed past, he was conscious of something odd about the fact that this, and not any work of military science, should be open in that place at that moment. He was even conscious of the gap in the well-lined bookshelf from which it had been taken; and it seemed almost to gape at him in an ugly fashion, like a gap in the teeth of some sinister face.

A run brought them in a few minutes to the other side of the ground in front of the Bottomless Well; and a few yards from it, in a moonlight almost as broad as daylight, they saw what they had come to see.

The great Lord Hastings lay prone on his face, in a posture in which there was a touch of something strange and stiff, with one elbow erect above his body, the arm being doubled, and his big bony hand clutching the rank and ragged grass. A few feet away was Boyle, almost as motionless, but supported on his hands and knees, and staring at the body. It might have been no more than shock and accident; but there was something ungainly and unnatural about the quadrupedal posture and the gaping face. It was as if his reason had fled him. Behind there was nothing but the clear blue southern sky and the beginning of the desert, except for the two great broken stones in front of the well. And it was in such a light and atmosphere that men could fancy they traced in them enormous and evil faces, looking down.

Horne Fisher stooped and touched the strong hand that was still clutching the grass; and it was as cold as a stone. He knelt by the body and was busy for a moment applying other tests; then he rose again and said with a sort of confident despair: "Lord Hastings is dead."

There was a stony silence; and then Travers remarked gruffly: "This is your department, Grayne; I will leave you to question

Captain Boyle. I can make no sense of what he says."

Boyle had pulled himself together and risen to his feet, but his face still wore an awful expression, making it like a new mask or the face of another man.

"I was looking at the well," he said "and when I turned he had fallen down."

Grayne's face was very dark.

"As you say, this is my affair," he said. "I must first ask you to help me carry him to the library, and let me examine things thoroughly."

When they had deposited the body in the library, Grayne turned to Fisher, and said in a voice that had recovered its fullness and confidence: "I am going to lock myself in and make a thorough examination first. I look to you to keep in touch with the others, and make a preliminary examination of Boyle. I will talk to him later. And just telephone to headquarters for a policeman; and let him come here at once and stand by till I want him."

Without more words, the great criminal investigator went into the lighted library, shutting the door behind him; and Fisher, without replying, turned and began to talk quietly to Travers.

"It is curious," he said, "that the thing should happen just in front of that place."

"It would certainly be very curious," replied Travers, "if the place played any part in it."

"I think," replied Fisher, "that the part it didn't play is more curious still."

And with these apparently meaningless words he turned to the shaken Boyle, and, taking his arm, began to walk him up and down in the moonlight, talking in low tones.

Dawn had begun to break abrupt and white when Cuthbert Grayne turned out the lights in the library and came out on to the links. Fisher was lounging about alone in his listless fashion; but the police messenger for whom he had sent was standing at attention in the background.

"I sent Boyle off with Travers," observed Fisher carelessly, "he'll look after him; and he'd better have some sleep, anyhow."

"Did you get anything out of him?" asked Grayne. "Did he tell you what he and Hastings were doing?"

"Yes," answered Fisher, "he gave me a pretty clear account after all. He said that after Lady Hastings went off in the car, the General asked him to take coffee with him in the library, and look up a point about local antiquities. He himself was beginning to look for Budge's book in one of the revolving bookstands, when the General found it in one of the book-shelves on the wall. After looking at some of the plates they went out, it would seem rather abruptly, on to the links and walked towards the old well; and while Boyle was looking into it, he heard a thud behind him and turned round to find the General lying as we found him. He himself dropped on his knees to examine the body, and then was paralysed with a sort of terror and could not come nearer to it or touch it. But I think very little of that; people caught in a shock of surprise are sometimes found in the queerest postures."

Grayne wore a grim smile of attention, and said after a short silence:

"Well, he hasn't told you many lies. It's really a creditably clear and consistent account of what happened, with everything of importance left out."

"Have you discovered anything in there?" asked Fisher.

"I have discovered everything," answered Grayne.

Fisher maintained a somewhat gloomy silence, as the other resumed his explanation in quiet and assured tones.

"You were quite right, Fisher, when you said that young fellow was in danger of going down dark ways towards the pit. Whether or no, as you fancied, the jolt you gave to his view of the General had anything to do with it, he has not been treating the General well for some time. It's an unpleasant business, and I don't want to dwell on it, but it's pretty plain that his wife was not treating him well either. I don't know how far it went, but it went as far as concealment anyhow; for when Lady Hastings spoke to Boyle, it was to tell him she had hidden a note in the Budge book in the library. The General overheard, or came somehow to know, and he went straight to the book and found it. He confronted Boyle with it, and they had a scene, of course. And Boyle was confronted with something else; he was confronted with an awful alternative; in which the life of one old man meant ruin, and his death meant triumph and even happiness."

"Well," observed Fisher at last. "I don't blame him for not telling you the woman's part of the story. But how do you know about the letter?"

"I found it on the General's body," answered Grayne, "but I

found worse things than that. The body had stiffened in the way rather peculiar to poisons of a certain Asiatic sort. Then I examined the coffee cups, and I knew enough chemistry to find poison in the dregs of one of them. Now the General went straight to the bookcase, leaving his cup of coffee on the book-stand in the middle of the room. While his back was turned and Boyle was pretending to examine the book-stand, he was left alone with the coffee cups. The poison takes about ten minutes to act; and ten minutes' walk would bring them to the Bottomless Well."

"Yes," remarked Horne Fisher, "and what about the Bottomless Well?"

"What has the Bottomless Well got to do with it?" asked his friend.

"It has nothing to do with it," replied Fisher. "That is what I find utterly confounding and incredible."

"And why should that particular hole in the ground have anything to do with it?"

"It is a particular hole in your case," said Fisher. "But I won't insist on that just now. By the way, there is another thing I ought to tell you. I said I sent Boyle away in charge of Travers. It would be just as true to say I sent Travers in charge of Boyle."

"You don't mean to say you suspect Tom Travers?" cried the other.

"He was a deal bitterer against the General than Boyle ever was," observed Horne Fisher with a curious indifference.

"Man, you're not saying what you mean," cried Grayne. "I tell you I found the poison in one of the coffee cups."

"There was always Said, of course," added Fisher, "either for hatred or for hire. We agreed he was capable of almost anything."

"And we agreed he was incapable of hurting his master," retorted Grayne.

"Well, well," said Fisher amiably, "I dare say you are right, but I should just like to have a look at the library and the coffee cups."

He passed inside, while Grayne turned to the policeman in attendance and handed him a scribbled note to be telegraphed from headquarters. The man saluted and hurried off; and Grayne, following his friend into the library, found him beside the book-stand in the middle of the room, on which were the empty cups.

"This is where Boyle looked for Budge, or pretended to look for him, according to your account," he said.

As Fisher spoke he bent down in a half crouching attitude, to look at the volumes in the low revolving shelf; for the whole book-stand was not much higher than an ordinary table. The next moment he sprang up as if he had been stung.

"Oh, my God!" he cried.

Very few people, if any, had ever seen Mr. Horne Fisher behave as he behaved just then. He flashed a glance at the door, saw that the open window was nearer, went out of it with a flying leap as if over a hurdle, and went racing across the turf in the track of the disappearing policeman. Grayne, who stood staring after him, soon saw his tall, loose figure returning, restored to all its normal limpness and air of leisure. He was fanning himself slowly with a piece of paper: the telegram he had so violently intercepted.

"Lucky I stopped that," he observed. "We must keep this affair as quiet as death. Hastings must die of apoplexy or heart disease."

"What on earth is the trouble?" demanded the other investigator.

"The trouble is," said Fisher, "that in a few days we should have a very agreeable alternative: of hanging an innocent man or knocking the British Empire to hell."

"Do you mean to say," asked Grayne, "that this infernal crime is not to be punished?"

Fisher looked at him steadily.

"It is already punished," he said.

After a moment's pause he went on.

"You reconstructed the crime with admirable skill, old chap, and nearly all you said was true. Two men with two coffee cups did go into the library and did put their cups on the book-stand and did go together to the well, and one of them was a murderer and had put poison in the other's cup. But it was not done while Boyle was looking at the revolving bookcase. He did look at it, though, searching for the Budge book with the note in it; but I fancy that Hastings had already moved it to the shelves on the wall. It was part of that grim game that he should find it first.

"Now how does a man search a revolving bookcase? He does not generally hop all round it in a squatting attitude, like a frog. He simply gives it a touch and makes it revolve."

He was frowning at the floor as he spoke, and there was a light under his heavy lids that was not often seen there. The mysticism that was buried deep under all the cynicism of his experience was awake and moving in the depths. His voice took unexpected turns and inflexions, almost as if two men were speaking.

"That was what Boyle did; he barely touched the thing, and it went round as easily as the world goes round. Yes, very much as the world goes round; for the hand that turned it was not his. God, who turns the wheel of all the stars, touched that wheel and brought it full circle, that his dreadful justice might return."

"I am beginning," said Grayne slowly, "to have some hazy and horrible idea of what you mean."

"It is very simple," said Fisher. "When Boyle straightened himself from his stooping posture, something had happened which he had not noticed, which his enemy had not noticed, which nobody had noticed. The two coffee cups had exactly changed places."

The rocky face of Grayne seemed to have sustained a shock in silence; not a line of it altered, but his voice when it came was unexpectedly weakened.

"I see what you mean," he said, "and, as you say, the less said about it the better. It was not the lover who tried to get rid of the husband, but—the other thing. And a tale like that about a man like that would ruin us here. Had you any guess of this at the start?"

"The Bottomless Well, as I told you," answered Fisher quietly, "that was what stumped me from the start. Not because it had anything to do with it. Because it had nothing to do with it."

He paused a moment, as if choosing an approach, and then went on: "When a murderer knows his enemy will be dead in ten minutes, and takes him to the edge of an unfathomable pit, he means to throw his body into it. What else should he do? A born fool would have the sense to do it; and Boyle is not a born fool. Well, why did not Boyle do it? The more I thought of it the more I suspected there was some mistake in the murder, so to speak. Somebody had taken somebody there to throw him in; and yet he was not thrown in. I had already an ugly unformed idea of some substitution or reversal of parts; then I stooped to turn the bookstand myself, by accident, and I instantly knew everything; for I saw the two cups revolve once more, like moons in the sky."

After a pause Cuthbert Grayne said: "And what are we to say to the newspapers?"

"My friend Harold March is coming along from Cairo today," said Fisher. "He is a very brilliant and successful journalist. But for all that he's a thoroughly honourable man; so you must not tell him the truth."

Half an hour later Fisher was again walking to and fro in front of the club house with Captain Boyle, the latter by this time with a very buffeted and bewildered air; perhaps a sadder and a wiser man.

"What about me, then?" he was saying. "Am I cleared? Aren't I going to be cleared?"

"I believe and hope," answered Fisher, "that you are not going to be suspected. But you are certainly not going to be cleared. There must be no suspicion against him, and therefore no suspicion against you. Any suspicion against him, let alone such a story against him, would knock us endways from Malta to Mandalay. He was a hero as well as a holy terror among the Moslems. Indeed, you might almost call him a Moslem hero in the English service. Of course he got on with them partly because of his own little dose of Eastern blood; he got it from his mother, the dancer from Damascus; everybody knows that."

"Oh," repeated Boyle mechanically, staring at him with round eyes. "Everybody knows that."

"I dare say there was a touch of it in his jealousy and ferocious vengeance," went on Fisher. "But for all that the crime would ruin us among the Arabs, all the more because it was something like a crime against hospitality. It's been hateful for you, and it's pretty horrid for me. But there are some things that damned well can't be done, and while I'm alive that's one of them."

"What do you mean?" asked Boyle, glancing at him curiously. "Why should you, of all people, be so passionate about it?"

Horne Fisher looked at the young man with a baffling expression.

"I suppose," he said, "it's because I'm a Little Englander."

"I can never make out what you mean by that sort of thing," answered Boyle doubtfully.

"Do you think England is so little as all that," said Fisher, with a warmth in his cold voice; "that it can't hold a man across a few thousand miles? You lectured me with a lot of ideal patriotism, my young friend; but it's practical patriotism now for you and me, and with no lie to help it. You talked as if everything went right with us, all over the world, in a triumphant crescendo culminating in Hastings. I tell you everything has gone wrong with us here, except Hastings. His was the one name we had left to conjure with; and that mustn't go as well; no, by God! It's bad enough that a gang of infernal Jews should plant us here, where there's no earthly English interest to serve, and all hell beating up against us, simply because Nosey Zimmern has lent money to half the Cabinet. It's bad enough that an old pawnbroker from Bagdad should make us fight his battles; we can't fight with our right hand cut off. Our one score was Hastings and his victory; which was really somebody else's victory. Tom Travers has to suffer, and so have you."

Then, after a moment's silence, he pointed towards the Bottomless Well and said in a quieter tone:

"I told you," he said, "that I didn't believe in the philosophy of the Tower of Aladin. I don't believe in the Empire growing until it reaches the sky; I don't believe in the Union Jack going up and up eternally like the Tower. But if you think I am going to let the Union Jack go down and down eternally like the Bottomless Well, down into the blackness of the Bottomless Pit, down in defeat and derision amid the jeers of the very Jews who have sucked us dry—no, I won't, and that's flat; not if the Chancellor were blackmailed by twenty millionaires with their gutter rags, not if the Prime Minister married twenty Yankee Jewesses, not if Woodville and Carstairs had shares in twenty swindling mines. If the thing is really tottering, God help it, it mustn't be we who tip it over."

Boyle was regarding him with a bewilderment that was almost fear, and had even a touch of distaste.

"Somehow," he said, "there seems to be something rather horrid about the things you know."

"There is," replied Horne Fisher. "I am not at all pleased with my small stock of knowledge and reflection. But as it is partly responsible for your not being hanged, I don't know that you need complain of it."

And as if a little ashamed of his first boast, he turned and strolled away towards the Bottomless Well.

MR. POND
IN

*The Three Horsemen
of the Apocalypse*

The Three Horsemen
of the Apocalypse

The curious and sometimes creepy effect which Mr. Pond produced upon me, despite his commonplace courtesy and dapper decorum, was possibly connected with some memories of childhood; and the vague verbal association of his name. He was a Government official who was an old friend of my father; and I fancy my infantile imagination had somehow mixed up the name of Mr. Pond with the pond in the garden. When one came to think of it, he was curiously like the pond in the garden. He was so quiet at all normal times, so neat in shape and so shiny, so to speak, in his ordinary reflections of earth and sky and the common daylight. And yet I knew there were some queer things in the pond in the garden. Once in a hundred times, on one or two days during the whole year, the pond would look oddly different; or there would come a flitting shadow or a flash in its flat serenity; and a fish or a frog or some more grotesque creature would show itself to the sky. And I knew there were monsters in Mr. Pond also: monsters in his mind which rose only for a moment to the surface and sank again. They took the form of monstrous remarks, in the middle of all his mild and rational remarks. Some people thought he had suddenly gone mad in the midst of his sanest conversation. But even they had to admit that he must have suddenly gone sane again.

Perhaps, again, this foolish fantasy was fixed in the youthful mind because, at certain moments, Mr. Pond looked rather like a fish himself. His manners were not only quite polite but quite conventional; his very gestures were conventional, with the exception of one occasional trick of plucking at his pointed beard, which seemed to come on him chiefly when he was at last forced to be serious about one of his strange and random statements. At such moments he would stare owlishly in front of him and pull his beard, which had a comic effect of pulling his mouth open, as if it were the mouth of a puppet with hairs for wires. This odd, occasional opening and shutting of his mouth, without speech, had quite a startling similarity to the slow gaping and gulping of a fish. But it never lasted for more than a few seconds, during which, I suppose, he swallowed the unwelcome proposal of explaining what on earth he meant.

He was talking quite quietly one day to Sir Hubert Wotton, the well-known diplomatist; they were seated under gaily-striped tents or giant parasols in our own garden, and gazing towards the pond which I had perversely associated with him. They happened to be talking about a part of the world that both of them knew well, and very few people in Western Europe at all: the vast flats fading into fens and swamps that stretch across Pomerania and Poland and Russia and the rest; right away, for all I know, into the Siberian deserts. And Mr. Pond recalled that, across a region where the swamps are deepest and intersected by pools and sluggish rivers, there runs a single road raised on a high causeway with steep and sloping sides: a straight path safe enough for the ordinary pedestrian, but barely broad enough for two horsemen to ride abreast. That is the beginning of the story.

It concerned a time not very long ago, but a time in which horsemen were still used much more than they are at present, though already rather less as fighters than as couriers. Suffice it to say that it was in one of the many wars that have laid waste that part of the world—in so far as it is possible to lay waste such a wilderness. Inevitably it involved the pressure of the Prussian system on the nation of the Poles, but beyond that it is not necessary to expound the politics of the matter, or discuss its rights and wrongs here. Let us merely say, more lightly, that Mr. Pond amused the company with a riddle.

"I expect you remember hearing," said Pond, "of all the excitement there was about Paul Petrowski, the poet from Cracow, who did two things rather dangerous in those days: moving from Cracow and going to live in Poznan; and trying to combine being a poet with being a patriot. The town he was living in was held at the moment by the Prussians; it was situated exactly at the eastern end of the long causeway; the Prussian command having naturally taken care to hold the bridgehead of such a solitary bridge across such a sea of swamps. But their base for that particular operation was at the western end of the causeway; the celebrated Marshal Von Grock was in general command; and, as it happened, his own old regiment, which was still his favourite regiment, the White Hussars, was posted nearest to the beginning of the great embanked road. Of course, everything was spick and span, down to every detail of the wonderful white uniforms, with the flame-coloured baldrick slung across them; for this was just before the universal use of colours like mud and clay for all the uniforms in the world. I don't blame them for that; I sometimes feel the old epoch of heraldry was a finer thing than all that epoch of imitative colouring, that came in with natural history and the worship of chameleons and beetles. Anyhow, this crack regiment of cavalry in the Prussian service still wore its own uniform; and, as you will see, that was another element in the fiasco. But it wasn't only the uniforms; it was the uniformity. The whole thing went wrong because the discipline was too good. Grock's soldiers obeyed him too well; so he simply couldn't do a thing he wanted."

"I suppose that's a paradox," said Wotton, heaving a sigh. "Of course it's very clever and all that; but really, it's all nonsense, isn't it? Oh, I know people say in a general way that there's too much discipline in the German army. But you can't have too much discipline in an army."

"But I don't say it in a general way," said Pond plaintively. "I say it in a particular way, about this particular case. Grock failed because his soldiers obeyed him. Of course, if *one* of his soldiers had obeyed him, it wouldn't have been so bad. But when *two* of his soldiers obeyed him—why, really, the poor old devil had no chance."

Wotton laughed in a guttural fashion. "I'm glad to hear your new military theory. You'd allow one soldier in a regiment to obey orders; but two soldiers obeying orders strikes you as carrying Prussian discipline a bit too far."

"I haven't got any military theory. I'm talking about a military fact," replied Mr. Pond placidly. "It is a military fact that Grock failed, because two of his soldiers obeyed him. It is a military fact that he might have succeeded, if one of them had disobeyed him. You can make up what theories you like about it afterwards."

"I don't go in much for theories myself," said Wotton rather stiffly, as if he had been touched by a trivial insult.

At this moment could be seen, striding across the sun-chequered lawn, the large and swaggering figure of Captain Gahagan, the highly incongruous friend and admirer of little Mr. Pond. He had a flaming flower in his buttonhole and a grey top-hat slightly slanted upon his ginger-haired head; and he walked with a swagger that seemed to come out of an older period of dandies and duellists, though he himself was comparatively young. So long as his tall, broad-shouldered figure was merely framed against the sunlight, he looked like the embodiment of all arrogance. When he came and sat down, with the sun on his face, there was a sudden contradiction of all this in his very soft brown eyes, which looked sad and even a little anxious.

Mr. Pond, interrupting his monologue, was almost in a twitter of apologies: "I'm afraid I'm talking too much, as usual; the truth is I was talking about that poet, Petrowski, who was nearly executed in Poznan—quite a long time ago. The military authorities on the spot hesitated and were going to let him go, unless they had direct orders from Marshal Von Grock or higher; but Marshal Von Grock was quite determined on the poet's death; and sent orders for his execution that very evening. A reprieve was sent afterwards to save him; but as the man carrying the reprieve died on the way, the prisoner was released, after all."

"But as——" repeated Wotton mechanically.

"The man carrying the *reprieve*," added Gahagan somewhat sarcastically.

"Died on the way," muttered Wotton.

"Why then, of course, the prisoner was released," observed Gahagan in a loud and cheerful voice. "All as clear as clear can be. Tell us another of those stories, Grandpapa."

"It's a perfectly true story," protested Pond, "and it happened exactly as I say. It isn't any paradox or anything like that. Only, of course, you have to know the story to see how simple it is."

"Yes," agreed Gahagan. "I think I should have to know the story, before realising how simple it is."

"Better tell us the story and have done with it," said Wotton shortly.

Paul Petrowski was one of those utterly unpractical men who are of prodigious importance in practical politics. His power lay in the fact that he was a national poet but an international singer. That is, he happened to have a very fine and powerful voice, with which he sang his own patriotic songs in half the concert halls of the world. At home, of course, he was a torch and trumpet of revolutionary

hopes, especially then, in the sort of international crisis in which
practical politicians disappear, and their place is taken by men either
more or less practical than themselves. For the true idealist and the
real realist have at least the love of action in common. And the
practical politician thrives by offering practical objections to any
action. What the idealist does may be unworkable, and what the
man of action does may be unscrupulous; but in neither trade can a
man win a reputation by doing nothing. It is odd that these two
extreme types stood at the two extreme ends of that one ridge and
road among the marshes—the Polish poet a prisoner in the town at
one end, the Prussian soldier a commander in the camp at the
other.

For Marshal Von Grock was a true Prussian, not only entirely
practical but entirely prosaic. He had never read a line of poetry
himself; but he was no fool. He had the sense of reality which
belongs to soldiers; and it prevented him from falling into the
asinine error of the practical politician. He did not scoff at visions;
he only hated them. He knew that a poet or a prophet could be as
dangerous as an army. And he was resolved that the poet should die.
It was his one compliment to poetry; and it was sincere.

He was at the moment sitting at a table in his tent; the spiked
helmet that he always wore in public was lying in front of him; and
his massive head looked quite bald, though it was only closely
shaven. His whole face was also shaven; and had no covering but a
pair of very strong spectacles, which alone gave an enigmatic look to
his heavy and sagging visage. He turned to a Lieutenant standing
by, a German of the pale-haired and rather pudding-faced variety,
whose blue saucer-eyes were staring vacantly.

"Lieutenant Von Hocheimer," he said, "did you say His Highness would reach the camp to-night?"

"Seven forty-five, Marshal," replied the Lieutenant, who seemed
rather reluctant to speak at all, like a large animal learning a new
trick of talking.

"Then there is just time," said Grock, "to send you with that
order for execution, before he arrives. We must serve His Highness
in every way, but especially in saving him needless trouble. He will
be occupied enough reviewing the troops; see that everything is
placed at His Highness's disposàl. He will be leaving again for the
next outpost in an hour."

The large Lieutenant seemed partially to come to life and made a shadowy salute. "Of course, Marshal, we must all obey His Highness."

"I said we must all serve His Highness," said the Marshal.

With a sharper movement than usual, he unhooked his heavy spectacles and rapped them down upon the table. If the pale blue eyes of the Lieutenant could have seen anything of the sort, or if they could have opened any wider even if they had, they might as well have opened wide enough at the transformation made by the gesture. It was like the removal of an iron mask. An instant before, Marshal Von Grock had looked uncommonly like a rhinoceros, with his heavy folds of leathery cheek and jaw. Now he was a new kind of monster: a rhinoceros with the eyes of an eagle. The bleak blaze of his old eyes would have told almost anybody that he had something within that was not merely heavy; at least, that there was a part of him made of steel and not only of iron. For all men live by a spirit, though it were an evil spirit, or one so strange to the commonalty of Christian men that they hardly know whether it be good or evil.

"I said we must all serve His Highness," repeated Grock. "I will speak more plainly, and say we must all save His Highness. Is it not enough for our kings that they should be our gods? Is it not enough for them to be served and saved? It is we who must do the serving and saving."

Marshal Von Grock seldom talked, or even thought, as more theoretical people would count thinking. And it will generally be found that men of his type, when they do happen to think aloud, very much prefer to talk to the dog. They have even a certain patronising relish in using long words and elaborate arguments before the dog. It would be unjust to compare Lieutenant Von Hocheimer to a dog. It would be unjust to the dog, who is a much more sensitive and vigilant creature. It would be truer to say that Grock in one of his rare moments of reflection, had the comfort and safety of feeling that he was reflecting aloud in the presence of a cow or a cabbage.

"Again and again, in the history of our Royal House, the servant has saved the master," went on Grock, "and often got little but kicks for it, from the outer world at least, which always whines sentimentalism against the successful and the strong. But at least we were successful and we were strong. They cursed Bismark for deceiving even his own master over the Ems telegram; but it made that master the master of the world. Paris was taken; Austria dethroned; and we were safe. Tonight Paul Petrowski will be dead; and we shall again be safe. That is why I am sending you with his death-warrant at once. You understand that you are bearing the order for Petrowski's instant execution—and that you must remain to see it obeyed?"

The inarticulate Hocheimer saluted; he could understand that all right. And he had some qualities of a dog, after all: he was as brave as a bulldog; and he could be faithful to the death.

"You must mount and ride at once," went on Grock, "and see that nothing delays or thwarts you. I know for a fact that fool Arnheim is going to release Petrowski tonight, if no message comes. Make all speed."

And the Lieutenant again saluted and went out into the night; and mounting one of the superb white chargers that were part of the splendour of that splendid corps, began to ride along the high, narrow road along the ridge, almost like the top of a wall, which overlooked the dark horizon, the dim patterns and decaying colours of those mighty marshes.

Almost as the last echoes of his horse's hoofs died away along the causeway, Von Grock rose and put on his helmet and his spectacles and came to the door of his tent; but for another reason.

The chief men of his staff, in full dress, were already approaching him; and all along the more distant lines there were the sounds of ritual salutation and the shouting of orders. His Highness the Prince had come.

His Highness the Prince was something of a contrast, at least in externals, to the men around him; and, even in other things, something of an exception in his world. He also wore a spiked helmet, but that of another regiment, black with glints of blue steel; and there was something half incongruous and half imaginatively appropriate, in some antiquated way, in the combination of that helmet with the long, dark, flowing beard, amid all those shaven Prussians. As if in keeping with the long, dark, flowing beard, he wore a long, dark, flowing cloak, blue with one blazing star on it of the highest Royal Order; and under the blue cloak he wore a black uniform. Though as German as any man, he was a very different kind of German; and something in his proud but abstracted face was consonant with the legend that the one true passion of his life was music.

In truth, the grumbling Grock was inclined to connect with that

remote eccentricity the, to him, highly irritating and exasperating
fact that the Prince did not immediately proceed to the proper
review and reception by the troops, already drawn out in all the
labyrinthine parade of the military etiquette of their nation; but
plunged at once impatiently into the subject which Grock most
desired to see left alone: the subject of this infernal Pole, his
popularity and his peril; for the Prince had heard some of the man's
songs sung in half the opera-houses of Europe.

"To talk of executing a man like this is madness," said the Prince,
scowling under his black helmet. "He is not a common Pole. He is a
European institution. He would be deplored and deified by our
allies, by our friends, even by our fellow-Germans. Do you want to
be the mad women who murdered Orpheus?"

"Highness," said the Marshal, "he would be deplored; but he
would be dead. He would be deified; but he would be dead.
Whatever he means to do, he would never do it. Whatever he is
doing, he would do no more. Death is the fact of all facts; and I am
rather fond of facts."

"Do you know nothing of the world?" demanded the Prince.

"I care nothing for the world," answered Grock, "beyond the
last black and white post of the Fatherland."

"God in heaven," cried His Highness, "you would have hanged
Goethe for a quarrel with Weimar!"

"For the safety of your Royal House," answered Grock, "without one instant's hesitation."

There was a short silence and the Prince said sharply and
suddenly: "What does this mean?"

"It means that I had not an instant's hesitation," replied the
Marshall steadily. "I have already myself sent orders for the
execution of Petrowski."

The Prince rose like a great dark eagle, the swirl of his cloak like
the sweep of mighty wings; and all men knew that a wrath beyond
mere speech had made him a man of action. He did not even speak
to Von Grock; but talking across him, at the top of his voice, called
out to the second in command, General Von Voglen, a stocky man
with a square head, who had stood in the background as motionless
as a stone.

"Who has the best horse in your cavalry division, General? Who
is the best rider?"

"Arnold Von Schacht has a horse that might beat a racehorse," replied the General promptly. "And rides it as well as a jockey. He is of the White Hussars."

"Very well," said the Prince, with the same new ring in his voice. "Let him ride at once after the man with this mad message and stop him. I will give him authority, which I think the distinguished Marshal will not dispute. Bring me pen and ink."

He sat down, shaking out the cloak, and they brought him writing materials; and he wrote firmly and with a flourish the order, overriding all other orders, for the reprieve and release of Petrowski the Pole.

Then amid a dead silence, in the midst of which old Grock stood with an unblinking stare like a stone idol of prehistoric times, he swept out of the room, trailing his mantle and sabre. He was so violently displeased that no man dared to remind him of the formal reviewing of the troops. But Arnold Von Schacht, a curly-haired active youth, looking like a boy, but wearing more than one medal on the white uniform of the Hussars, clicked his heels, and received the folded paper from the Prince; then, striding out, he sprang on his horse and flew along the high, narrow road like a silver arrow or a shooting star.

The old Marshal went back slowly and calmly to his tent, slowly and calmly removed his spiked helmet and his spectacles, and laid them on the table as before. Then he called out to an orderly just outside the tent; and bade him fetch Sergeant Schwartz of the White Hussars immediately.

A minute later, there presented himself before the Marshal a gaunt and wiry man, with a great scar across his jaw, rather dark for a German, unless all his colours had been changed by years of smoke and storm and bad weather. He saluted and stood stiffly at attention, as the Marshal slowly raised his eyes to him. And vast as was the abyss between the Imperial Marshall, with Generals under him, and that one battered non-commissioned officer, it is true that of all the men who have talked in this tale, these two men alone looked and understood each other without words.

"Sergeant," said the Marshall, curtly, "I have seen you twice before. Once, I think, when you won the prize of the whole army for marksmanship with the carbine."

The sergeant saluted and said nothing.

"And once again," went on Von Grock, "when you were questioned for shooting that damned old woman who would not give us information about the ambush. The incident caused considerable comment at the time, even in some of our own circles. Influence, however, was exerted on your side. My influence."

The sergeant saluted again; and was still silent. The Marshal continued to speak in a colourless but curiously candid way.

"His Highness the Prince has been misinformed and deceived on a point essential to his own safety and that of the Fatherland. Under this error, he has rashly sent a reprieve to the Pole Petrowski, who is to be executed tonight. I repeat: who is to be executed tonight. You must immediately ride after Von Schacht, who carried the reprieve, and stop him."

"I can hardly hope to overtake him, Marshal," said Sergeant Schwartz. "He has the swiftest horse in the regiment and is the finest rider."

"I did not tell you to overtake him. I told you to stop him," said Grock. Then he spoke more slowly: "A man may often be stopped or recalled by various signals: by shouting or shooting." His voice dragged still more ponderously, but without a pause. "The discharge of a carbine might attract his attention."

And then the dark sergeant saluted for the third time; and his grim mouth was again shut tight.

"The world is changed," said Grock, "not by what is said, or what is blamed or praised, but by what is done. The world never recovers from what is done. At this moment the killing of a man is a thing that must be done." He suddenly flashed his brilliant eyes of steel at the other, and added: "I mean, of course, Petrowski."

And Sergeant Schwartz smiled still more grimly; and he also, lifting the flap of the tent, went out into the darkness and mounted his horse and rode.

The last of the three riders was even less likely than the first to indulge in imaginative ideas for their own sake. But because he also was in some imperfect manner human, he could not but feel, on such a night and such an errand, the oppressiveness of that inhuman landscape. While he rode along that one abrupt bridge, there spread out to infinity all round him something a myriad times more inhuman than the sea. For a man could not swim in it, nor sail boats on it, nor do anything human with it; he could only sink in it and practically without a struggle. The sergeant felt vaguely the presence of some primordial slime that was neither solid nor liquid nor capable of any form; and he felt its presence behind the forms of all things.

He was atheist, like so many thousands of dull, clever men in Northern Germany; but he was not that happier sort of pagan who can see in human progress a natural flowering of the earth. That world before him was not a field in which green or living things evolved and developed and bore fruit; it was only an abyss in which all living things would sink for ever as in a bottomless pit; and the thought hardened him for all the strange duties he had to do in so hateful a world. The grey-green blotches of flattened vegetation, seen from above like a sprawling map, seemed more like the chart of a disease than a development; and the land-locked pools might have been of poison rather than water. He remembered some humanitarian fuss or other about the poisoning of pools.

But the reflections of the sergeant, like most reflections of men not normally reflective, had a root in some subconscious strain on his nerves and his practical intelligence. The truth was that the straight road before him was not only dreary, but seemed interminably long. He would never have believed he could have ridden so far without catching some distant glimpse of the man he followed. Van Schacht must indeed have the fleetest of horses to have got so far ahead already; for, after all, he had only started, at whatever speed, within a comparatively short time. As Schwartz had said, he hardly expected to overtake him; but a very realistic sense of the distances involved had told him that he must very soon come in sight of him. And then, just as despair was beginning to descend and spread itself vaguely over the desolate landscape, he saw him at last.

A white spot, which slightly, slowly, enlarged into something like a white figure, appeared far ahead, riding furiously. It enlarged to that extent because Schwartz managed a spurt of riding furiously himself; but it was large enough to show the faint streak of orange across the white uniform that marked the regiment of the Hussars. The winner of the prize for shooting, in the whole army, had hit the white of smaller targets than that.

He unslung his carbine; and a shock of unnatural noise shook up all the wild fowl for miles upon the silent marshes. But Sergeant Schwartz did not trouble about them. What interested him was that, even at such a distance, he could see the straight, white figure turn crooked and alter in shape, as if the man had suddenly grown deformed. He was hanging like a humpback over the saddle; and Schwartz, with his exact eye and long experience was certain that his victim was shot through the body; and almost certain that he was shot through the heart. Then he brought the horse down with a second shot; and the whole equestrian groups heeled over and slipped and slid and vanished in one white flash into the dark fenland below.

The hard-headed sergeant was certain that his work was done. Hard-headed men of his sort are generally very precise about what they are doing; that is why they are so often quite wrong about what they do. He had outraged the comradeship that is the soul of armies; he had killed a gallant officer who was in the performance of his duty; he had deceived and defied his sovereign and committed a common murder without excuse of personal quarrel; but he had obeyed his superior officer and he had helped to kill a Pole. These two last facts for the moment filled his mind; and he rode thoughtfully back again to make his report to Marshal Von Grock. He had no doubts about the thoroughness of the work he had done. The man carrying the reprieve was certainly dead; and even if by some miracle he were only dying, he could not conceivably have ridden his dead or dying horse to the town in time to prevent the execution. No; on the whole it was much more practical and prudent to get back under the wing of his protector, the author of the desperate project. With his whole strength he leaned on the strength of the great Marshal.

And truly the great Marshal had this greatness about him: that after the monstrous thing he had done, or caused to be done, he disdained to show any fear of facing the facts on the spot or the compromising possibilities of keeping in touch with his tool. He and the sergeant, indeed, an hour or so later, actually rode along the ridge together, till they came to a particular place where the Marshal dismounted, but bade the other ride on. He wished the sergeant to go forward to the original goal of the riders, and see if all was quiet in the town after the execution, or whether there remained some danger from popular resentment.

"Is it here then, Marshal?" asked the sergeant in a low voice. "I fancied it was further on; but it's a fact the infernal road seemed to lengthen out like a nightmare."

"It is here," answered Grock, and swung himself heavily from saddle and stirrup, and then went to the edge of the long parapet and looked down.

The moon had risen over the marshes and gone up strengthening in splendour and gleaming on dark waters and green scum; and in the nearest clump of reeds, at the foot of the slope, there lay, as in a sort of luminous and radiant ruin, all that was left of one of those superb white horses and white horsemen of his old brigade. Nor was the identity doubtful; the moon made a sort of aureole of the curled golden hair of young Arnold, the second rider and the bearer of the reprieve; and the same mystical moonshire glittered not only on baldrick and buttons, but on the special medals of the young soldier and the stripes and signs of his degree. Under such a glamorous veil of light, he might almost have been in the white armour of Sir Galahad; and there could scarcely have been a more horrible contrast than that between such fallen grace and youth below and the rocky and grotesque figure looking down from above. Grock had taken off his helmet again; and though it is possible that this was the vague shadow of some funereal form of respect, its visible effect was that the queer naked head and neck like that of a pachyderm glittered stonily in the moon, like the hairless head and neck of some monster of the Age of Stone. Rops, or some such etcher of the black fantastic German schools, might have drawn such a picture: of a huge beast as inhuman as a beetle looking down on the broken wings and white and golden armour of some defeated champion of the Cherubim.

Grock said no prayer and uttered no pity; but in some dark way his mind was moved, as even the dark and mighty swamp will sometimes move like a living thing; and as such men will, when feeling for the first time faintly on their defence before they know not what, he tried to formulate his only faith and confront it with the stark universe and the staring moon.

"After and before the deed the German Will is the same. It cannot be broken by changes and by time, like that of those others who repent. It stands outside time like a thing of stone, looking forward and backward with the same face."

The silence that followed lasted long enough to please his cold vanity with a certain sense of portent; as if a stone figure had spoken in a valley of silence. But the silence began to thrill once more with a distant whisper which was the faint throb of horsehoofs; and a moment later the sergeant came galloping, or rather racing, back along the uplifted road, and his scarred and swarthy visage was no longer merely grim but ghastly in the moon.

"Marshal," he said, saluting with a strange stiffness, "I have seen Petrowski the Pole!"

"Haven't they buried him yet?" asked the Marshal, still staring down and in some abstraction.

"If they have," said Schwartz, "he has rolled the stone away and risen from the dead."

He stared in front of him at the moon and marshes; but, indeed, though he was far from being a visionary character, it was not these things that he saw, but rather the things he had just seen. He had, indeed, seen Paul Petrowski walking alive and alert down the brilliantly illuminated main avenue of that Polish town to the very beginning of the causeway; there was no mistaking the slim figure with plumes of hair and tuft of Frenchified beard which figured in so many private albums and illustrated magazines. And behind him he had seen that Polish town aflame with flags and firebrands and a population boiling with triumphant hero-worship, though perhaps less hostile to the government than it might have been, since it was rejoicing at the release of its popular hero.

"Do you mean," cried Grock with a sudden croaking stridency of voice, "that they have dared to release him in defiance of my message?"

Schwartz saluted again and said:

"They had already released him and they have received no message."

"Do you ask me, after all this," said Grock, "to believe that no messenger came from our camp at all?"

"No messenger at all," said the sergeant.

There was a much longer silence, and then Grock said, hoarsely: "What in the name of hell has happened? Can you think of anything to explain it all?"

"I have seen something," said the sergeant, "which I think does explain it all."

When Mr. Pond had told the story up to this point, he paused with an irritating blankness of expression.

"Well," said Gahagan impatiently, "and do *you* know anything that would explain it all?"

"Well, I think I do," said Mr. Pond meekly. "You see, I had to worry it out for myself, when the report came round to my department. It really did arise from an excess of Prussian obedience.

It also arose from an excess of another Prussian weakness: contempt. And of all the passions that blind and madden and mislead men, the worst is the coldest: contempt.

"Grock had talked much too comfortably before the cow, and much too confidently before the cabbage. He despised stupid men even on his own staff; and treated Von Hocheimer, the first messenger, as a piece of furniture merely because he looked like a fool; but the lieutenant was not such a fool as he looked. He also understood what the great Marshal meant, quite as well as the cynical sergeant, who had done such dirty work all his life. Hocheimer also understood the Marshal's peculiar moral philosophy: that an act is unanswerable even when it is indefensible. He knew that what his commander wanted was simply the corpse of Petrowski; that he wanted it anyhow, at the expense of any deception of princes or destruction of soldiers. And when he heard a swifter horseman behind him, riding to overtake him, he knew as well as Grock himself that the new messenger must be carrying with him the message of the mercy of the Prince. Von Schacht, that very young but very gallant officer, looking like the very embodiment of all that more generous tradition of Germany that has been too much neglected in this tale, was worthy of the accident that made him the herald of a more generous policy. He came with the speed of that noble horsemanship that has left behind it in Europe the very name of chivalry, calling out to the other in a tone like a herald's trumpet to stop and stand and turn. And Von Hocheimer obeyed. He stopped, he reined in his horse, he turned in his saddle; but his hand held the carbine levelled like a pistol, and he shot the boy between the eyes.

"Then he turned again and rode on, carrying the death-warrant of the Pole. Behind him horse and man had crashed over the edge of the embankment, so that the whole road was clear. And along that clear and open road toiled in his turn the third messenger, marvelling at the interminable length of his journey; till he saw at last the unmistakable uniform of a hussar like a white star disappearing in the distance, and he shot also. Only he did not kill the second messenger, but the first.

"That was why no messenger came alive to the Polish town that night. That was why the prisoner walked out of his prison alive. Do you think I was quite wrong in saying that Von Grock had two faithful servants, and one too many?"

MR. POND

IN

When Doctors Agree

When Doctors Agree

Mr. Pond's paradoxes were of a very peculiar kind. They were indeed paradoxical defiances even of the law of paradox. Paradox has been defined as "Truth standing on her head to attract attention." Paradox has been defended; on the ground that so many fashionable fallacies still stand firmly on their feet, because they have no heads to stand on. But it must be admitted that writers, like other mendicants and mountebanks, frequently do try to attract attention. They set out conspicuously, in a single line in a play, or at the head or tail of a paragraph, remarks of this challenging kind; as when Mr. Bernard Shaw wrote: "The Golden Rule is that there is no Golden Rule"; or Oscar Wilde observed: "I can resist everything except temptation"; or a duller scribe (not to be named with these and now doing penance for his earlier vices in the nobler toil of celebrating the virtues of Mr. Pond) said in the defence of hobbies and amateurs and general duffers like himself: "If a thing is worth doing, it is worth doing badly." To these things do writers sink; and then the critics tell them that they "talk for effect"; and then the writers answer: "What the devil else should we talk for? Ineffectualness?" It is a sordid scene.

But Mr. Pond belonged to a more polite world and his paradoxes were quite different. It was quite impossible to imagine Mr. Pond standing on his head. But it was quite as easy to imagine him standing on his head as to imagine him trying to attract attention. He was the quietest man in the world to be a man of the world; he was a small, neat Civil Servant; with nothing notable about him except a beard that looked not only old-fashioned but vaguely foreign, and perhaps a little French, though he was as English as any man alive. But, for that matter, French respectability is far more respectable than English; and Mr. Pond though in some ways cosmopolitan, was completely respectable. Another thing that was

161

faintly French about him was the level ripple of his speech: a tripping monotone that never tripped over a single vowel. For the French carry their sense of equality even to the equality of syllables. With this equable flow, full of genteel gossip on Vienna, he was once entertaining a lady; and five minutes later she rejoined her friends with a very white face; and whispered to them the shocking secret that the mild little man was mad.

The peculiarity of his conversation was this: in the middle of a steady stream of sense, there would suddenly appear two or three words which seemed simply to be nonsense. It was as if something had suddenly gone wrong with the works of a gramophone. It was nonsense which the speaker never seemed to notice himself; so that sometimes his hearers also hardly noticed that speech so natural was nonsensical. But to those who did notice, he seemed to be saying something like, "Naturally, having no legs, he won the walking-race easily," or "As there was nothing to drink, they all got tipsy at once." Broadly speaking, two kinds of people stopped him with stares or questions: the very stupid and the very clever. The stupid because the absurdity alone stuck out from a level of intelligence that baffled them; it was indeed in itself an example of the truth in paradox. The only part of his conversation they could understand was the part they could not understand. And the clever stopped him because they knew that, behind each of these queer compact contradictions, there was a very queer story—like the queer story to be narrated here.

His friend Gahagan, that ginger-haired giant and somewhat flippant Irish dandy, declared that Pond put in these senseless phrases merely to find out whether his listeners were listening. Pond never said so; and his motive remained rather a mystery. But Gahagan declared that there is a whole tribe of modern intellectual ladies, who have learned nothing except the art of turning on a talker a face of ardour and attention, while their minds are so very absent that some little phrase like, "Finding himself in India, he naturally visited Toronto," will pass harmlessly in at one ear and out at the other, without disturbing the cultured mind within.

It was at a little dinner given by old Wotton to Gahagan and Pond and others, that we first got a glimpse of the real meaning of these wild parentheses of so tame a talker. The truth was, to begin with, that Mr. Pond, in spite of his French beard, was very English in his habit of assuming that he ought to be a little dull, in deference to other people. He disliked telling long and largely fantastic stories about himself, such as his friend Gahagan told, though Pond thoroughly enjoyed them when Gahagan told them. Pond himself had had some very curious experiences; but, as he would not turn them into long stories, they appeared only as short stories; and the short stories were so very short as to be quite unintelligible. In trying to explain the eccentricity, it is best to begin with the simplest example, like a diagram in a primer of logic. And I will begin with the short story, which was concealed in the shorter phrase, which puzzled poor old Wotton so completely on that particular evening. Wotton was an old-fashioned diplomatist, of the sort that seemed to grow more national by trying to be international. Though far from militarist, he was very military. He kept the peace by staccato sentences under a stiff grey moustache. He had more chin than forehead.

"They tell me," Wotton was saying, "that the Poles and Lithuanians have come to an agreement about Wilno. It was an old row, of course; and I expect it was six to one and half a dozen to the other."

"You are a real Englishman, Wotton," said Gahagan, "and you say in your heart, 'All these foreigners are alike.' You're right enough if you mean that we're all unlike you. The English are the lunatics of the earth, who know that everybody else is mad. But we do sometimes differ a little from each other, you know. Even we in Ireland have been known to differ from each other. But you see the Pope denouncing the Bolshevists, or the French Revolution rending the Holy Roman Empire, and you still say in your hearts, 'What can the difference be betwixt Tweedledum and Tweedledee?'"

"There was no difference," said Pond, "between Tweedledum and Tweedledee. You will remember that it is distinctly recorded that they agreed. But remember what they agreed about."

Wotton looked a little baffled and finally grunted: "Well, if these fellows have agreed, I suppose there will be a little peace."

"Funny things, agreements," said Pond. "Fortunately people generally go on disagreeing, till they die peacefully in their beds. Men very seldom do fully and finally agree. I did know two men who came to agree so completely that one of them naturally murdered the other; but as a rule. ... ."

"'Agreed so completely,'" said Wotton thoughtfully. "Don't you—are you quite sure you don't mean: 'Disagreed so completely'?"

Gahagan uttered a sort of low whoop of laughter. "Oh, no," he said, "he doesn't mean that. I don't know what the devil he does mean; but he doesn't mean anything so sensible as that."

But Wotton, in his ponderous way, still attempted to pin down the narrator to a more responsible statement; and the upshot of it was that Mr. Pond was reluctantly induced to explain what he really meant and let us hear the whole story.

The mystery was involved at first in another mystery: the strange murder of Mr. James Haggis, of Glasgow, which filled the Scottish and English newspapers not many years ago. On the face of it, the thing was a curious story; to introduce a yet more curious sequel. Haggis had been a prominent and wealthy citizen, a bailie of the city and an elder of the kirk. Nobody denied that even in these capacities he had sometimes been rather unpopular; but, to do him justice, he had often been unpopular through his loyalty to unpopular causes. He was the sort of old Radical who is more rigid and antiquated than any Tory; and, maintaining in theory the cause of Retrenchment and Reform, he managed to suggest that almost any Reform was too expensive for the needs of Retrenchment. Thus he had stood alone in opposition to the universal support given to old Dr. Campbell's admirable campaign for fighting the epidemic in the slums during the slump. But to deduce from his economics that he was a demon delighting in the sight of poor children dying of typhoid was perhaps an exaggerated inference. Similarly, he was prominent in the Presbyterian councils as refusing all modern compromise with the logic of Calvinism; but to infer that he actually hoped all his neighbours were damned before they were born is too personal an interpretation of theological theory.

On the other side, he was admittedly honest in business and faithful to his wife and family; so that there was a general reaction in favour of his memory when he was found stabbed to the heart in the meagre grass of the grim little churchyard that adjoined his favourite place of worship. It was impossible to imagine Mr. Haggis as involved in any romantic Highland feud falling for the dirk, or any romantic assignation interrupted with the stiletto; and it was generally felt that to be knifed and left unburied among the buried dead was an exaggerated penalty for being a rather narrow Scottish merchant of the old school.

It happened that Mr. Pond himself had been present at a little party where there was high debate about the murder as a mystery. His host, Lord Glenorchy, had a hobby of reading books on criminology; his hostess, Lady Glenorchy, had the less harmful hobby of reading those much more solid and scientific books which are called detective stories. There were present, as the society papers say, Major MacNabb, the Chief Constable, and Mr. Launcelot Browne, a brilliant London barrister who found it much more of a bore to be a lawyer than to pretend to be a detective; also, among those present, was the venerable and venerated Dr. Campbell, whose work among the poor has already been inadequately commended, and a young friend of his named Angus, whom he was understood to be coaching and instructing generally for his medical examinations and his scientific career.

Responsible people naturally love to be irresponsible. All these persons delighted to throw theories about in private which they need not answer for in public. The barrister, being a humane man, was delighted to prosecute somebody whom he would not have to hang. The criminologist was enchanted to analyse the lunacy of somebody he could never have proved to be a lunatic. And Lady Glenorchy was charmed at the chance of considering poor Mr. Haggis (of all people) as the principal character in a shocker. Hilarious attempts were made to fix the crime on the United Presbyterian minister, a notorious Sublapsarian, naturally, nay inevitably, impelled to stick a dirk in a Supralapsarian. Lord Glenorchy was more serious, not to say monotonous. Having learnt from his books of criminology the one great discovery of that science, that mental and moral deformity are found only among poor people, he suspected a plot of local Communists (all with the wrong-shaped thumb and ear) and picked for his fancy a Socialist agitator of the city. Mr. Angus made bold to differ; his choice was an old lag, or professional criminal, known to be in the place, who had been almost everything that is alarming except a Socialist agitator. Then it was that the point was referred, not with a certain reverence, to the white-haired and wise old physician, who had now behind him a whole lifetime of charity and good works. One of the many ways in which Dr. Campbell seemed to have emerged from an older and perhaps honester world was the fact that he not only spoke with a Scottish accent but he spoke Scottish. His speech will, therefore, be rendered here with difficulty and in doubt and trembling.

"Weel, ye will a' be asking wha dirked Jamie Haggis? And I'll tell ye fair at the start that I winna gie a bawbee to ken wha dirked Jamie Haggis. Gin I kent, I wadna' say. It's a sair thing, na doot, that the freens and benefactors o' puir humanity should no be named and fitly celebrated; but like the masons that built our gran' cathedral and the gran' poets that wrote our ballads of Otterburn and Sir Patrick Spens, the man that achieved the virtuous act o' killing Jamie Haggis will ha'e nae pairsonal credit for't in this world; it is even possible he might be a wee bit inconvenienced. So ye'll get nae guesses out of me; beyond saying I've lang been seekin' a man of sic prudence and public spirit."

There followed that sort of silence in which people are not certain whether to laugh at a deliberate stroke of wit; but before they could do so, young Angus, who kept his eyes fixed on his venerable preceptor, had spoken with the eagerness of the ardent student.

"But you'll not say, Dr. Campbell, that murder is right because some acts or opinions of the murdered man are wrong?"

"Aye, if they're wrang enough," replied the benevolent Dr. Campbell blandly. "After all, we've nae ither test o' richt and wrang. *Salus populi suprema lex.*"

"Aren't the Ten Commandments a bit of a test?" asked the young man, with a rather heated countenance, emphasized by his red hair, that stood up on his head like stiff flames.

The silver-haired saint of sociology continued to regard him with a wholly benevolent smile; but there was an odd gleam in his eye as he answered:

"Aye, the Ten Commandments are a test. What we doctors are beginning to ca' an Intelligence Test."

Whether it was an accident, or whether the intuitions of Lady Glenorchy were a little alarmed by the seriousness of the subject, it was at this point that she struck in.

"Well, if Dr. Campbell won't pronounce for us, I suppose we must all stick to our own suspicions. I don't know whether you like cigarettes in the middle of dinner; it's a fashion I can't get used to myself."

At this point in his narrative, Mr. Pond threw himself back in his chair with a more impatient movement than he commonly permitted himself.

"Of course, they will do it," he said, with a mild explosiveness. "They're admired and thought very tactful when they do it."

"When who do what?" said Wotton. "What on earth are you talking about now?"

"I'm talking about hostesses," said Pond, with an air of pain. "Good hostesses. Really successful hostesses. They will cut into conversation, on the theory that it can be broken off anywhere. Just as it's quite the definition of a good hostess to make two people talk when they hate it, and part them when they are beginning to like it. But they sometimes do the most deadly and awful damage. You see, they stop conversations that are not worth starting again. And that's horrible, like murder."

"But if the conversation's not worth starting again, why is it horrible to stop it?" asked the conscientious Wotton, still laboriously in pursuit.

"Why, *that's* why it's horrible to stop it," answered Pond, almost snappishly for so polite a person. "Talk ought to be sacred because it is so light, so tenuous, so trivial, if you will; anyhow, so frail and easy to destroy. Cutting short its life is worse than murder; it's infanticide. It's like killing a baby that's trying to come to life. It can never be restored to life, though one rose from the dead. A good light conversation can never be put together again when it's broken to pieces; because you can't get all the pieces. I remember a splendid talk at Trefusis's place, that began because there was a crack of thunder over the house and a cat howled in the garden, and somebody made a rather crude joke about a catastrophe. And then Gahagan here had a perfectly lovely theory that sprang straight out of cats and catastrophes and everything, and would have started a splendid talk about a political question on the Continent."

"The Catalonian question, I suppose," said Gahagan, laughing, "but I fear I've quite forgotten my lovely theory."

"That's just what I say," said Pond, gloomily. "It could only have been started then; it ought to have been sacred because it wasn't worth starting again. The hostess swept it all out of our heads, and then had the cheek to say afterwards that we could talk about it some other time. Could we? Could we make a contract with a cloud to break just over the roof, and tie a cat up in the garden and pull its tail at the right moment, and give Gahagan just enough champagne to inspire him with a theory so silly that he's forgotten it already? It was then or never with that debate being started; and yet bad results enough followed from it being stopped. But that, as they say, is another story."

"You must tell it to us another time," said Gahagan. "At present I am still curious about the man who murdered another man because he agreed with him."

"Yes," assented Wotton, "we've rather strayed from the subject, haven't we?"

"So Mrs. Trefusis said," murmured Mr. Pond sadly. "I suppose we can't all feel the sanctity of really futile conversation. But if you're really interested in the other matter, I don't mind telling you all about it; though I'd rather not tell you exactly how I came to know all about it. That was rather a confidential matter—what they call a confession. Pardon my little interlude on the tactful hostess; it had something to do with what followed and I have a reason for mentioning it.

"Lady Glenorchy quite calmly changed the subject from murder to cigarettes; and everybody's first feeling was that we had been done out of a very entertaining little tiff about the Ten Commandments. A mere trifle, too light and airy to recur to our minds at any other time. But there was another trifle that did recur to my own mind afterwards; and kept my attention on a murder of which I might have thought little enough at the time, as De Quincey says. I remembered once looking up Glenorchy in *Who's Who*, and seeing that he had married the daughter of a very wealthy squire near Lowestoft in Suffolk."

"Lowestoft, Suffolk. These are dark hints," said Gahagan. "Do these in themselves point to some awful and suspicious fact?"

"They point," said Pond, "to the awful fact that Lady Glenorchy is not Scottish. If she had introduced the cigarettes at her father's dinner-table in Suffolk, such trifles as the Ten Commandments would instantly have been tossed away from everyone's mind and memory. But I knew I was in Scotland and that the story had only just begun. I have told you that old Campbell was tutoring or coaching young Angus for his medical degree. It was a great honour for a lad like Angus to have Campbell for a coach; but it must have been quite agreeable even to an authority like Campbell to have Angus for a pupil. For he had always been a most industrious and ambitious and intelligent pupil, and one likely to do the old man credit; and after the time I speak of, he seemed to grow more industrious and ambitious than ever. In fact, he shut himself up so exclusively with his coach that he failed in his examination. That was what first convinced me that my guess was right."

"And very lucid, too," said Gahagan with a grin. "He worked so hard with his coach that he failed in his examination. Another statement that might seem to some to require expansion."

"It's very simple, really," said Mr. Pond innocently. "But in order to expand it, we must go back for a moment to the mystery of Mr. Haggis's murder. It had already spread a sort of detective fever in the neighbourhood; for all the Scots love arguing and it really was rather a fascinating riddle. One great point in the mystery was the wound, which seemed at first to have been made by a dirk or dagger of some kind but was afterwards found by the experts to demand a different instrument of rather peculiar shape. Moreover, the district had been combed for knives and daggers; and temporary suspicion fixed on any wild youths from beyond the Highland line, who might retain an historic tenderness for the possession of dirks. All the medical authorities agreed that the instrument had been something more subtle than a dirk, though no medical authorities would consent even to guess what it was. People were perpetually ransacking the churchyard and the church in search of clues. And just about this time young Angus, who had been a strict supporter of this particular church, and had even once induced his old tutor and friend to sit under its minister for one evening service, suddenly left off going there; indeed, he left off going to any church at all. So I realized that I was still on the right track."

"Oh," said Wotton blankly, "so you realized that you were still on the right track."

"I fear I did not realize that you were on any track," said Gahagan. "To speak with candour, my dear Pond, I should say that of all the trackless and aimless and rambling human statements I have ever heard, the most rambling was the narrative we have just been privileged to hear from you. First you tell us that two Scotsmen began a conversation about the morality of murder and never finished it; then you go off on a tirade against society hostesses; then you reveal the horrid fact that one of them came from Lowestoft; then you go back to one of the Scotsmen and say he failed to pass his examination because he worked so hard with his tutor; then, pausing for a moment upon the peculiar shape of an undiscovered dagger, you tell us that the Scotsman has left off going to church and you are on the right track. Frankly, if you really do find something sacred about futile conversation, I should say that you were on the track of that all right."

"I know," said Mr. Pond patiently, "all I've said is quite relevant to what really happened; but, of course, you don't know what really happened. A story always does seem rambling and futile if you leave out what really happened. That's why newspapers are so dull. All the political news, and much of the police news (though rather higher in tone than the other), is made quite bewildering and pointless by the necessity of telling stories without telling the story."

"Well, then," said Gahagan, "let us try to get some sense out of all this nonsense, which has not even the excuses of newspaper nonsense. To take one of your nonsense remarks as a test, why do you say that Angus failed to pass because he worked so much with his coach?"

"Because he didn't work with his coach," replied Pond. "Because I didn't say he worked with his coach. At least I didn't say he worked for the examination. I said he was with his coach. I said he spent days and nights with his coach; but they weren't preparing for any examination."

"Well, what were they doing?" asked Wotton gruffly.

"They were going on with the argument," cried Pond, in a squeak that was almost shrill. "They hardly stopped to sleep or eat; but they went on with the argument; the argument interrupted at the dinner table. Have you never known any Scotsmen? Do you suppose that a woman from Suffolk with a handful of cigarettes, and a mouthful of irrelevance, can stop two Scotsmen from going on with an argument when they've started it? They began it again when they were getting their hats and coats; they were at it hammer and tongs as they went out of the gate, and only a Scottish poet can describe what they did then:

> And the tane went hame with the ither; and then,
> The tither went hame with the ither again.

"And for hours and weeks and months they never turned aside from the same interminable debate on the thesis first propounded by Dr. Campbell: that when a good man is well and truly convinced that a bad man is actively bad for the community, and is doing evil on a large scale which cannot be checked by law or any other action, the good man has a moral right to murder the bad man, and thereby only increases his own goodness."

Pond paused a moment, pulling his beard and staring at the table; then he began again:

"For reasons I've already mentioned but not explained——"

"That's what's the matter with you, my boy," said Gahagan genially. "There are always such a damned lot of things you have mentioned but not explained."

"For those reasons," went on Pond deliberately, "I happen to know a great deal about the stages of that stubborn and forcible controversy, about which nobody else knew anything at all. For Angus was a genuine truth-seeker who wished to satisfy his soul and not merely to make his name; and Campbell was enough of a great man to be quite as anxious to convince a pupil as to convince a crowd in a lecture-rooom. But I am not going to tell you about those stages of the controversy at any great length. To tell the truth, I am not what people call impartial on this controversy. How any man can form any conviction, and remain what they call impartial on any controversy, is more than I have ever understood. But I suppose they would say I couldn't describe the debate fairly; because the side I sympathize with was not the side that won.

"Society hostesses, especially when they come from near Lowestoft, do not know where an argument is tending. They will drop not only bricks but bombshells; and then expect them not to explode. Anyhow, I knew where that argument at Glenorchy's table was tending. When Angus made a test of the Ten Commandments, and Campbell said they were an intelligence test, I knew what would come next. In another minute, he would be saying that nobody of intelligence now troubles about the Ten Commandments.

"What a disguise there is in snowy hair and the paternal stoop of age! Dickens somewhere describes a patriarch who needed no virtue except his white hair. As Dr. Campbell smiled across the table at Angus, most people saw nothing in that smile but patriarchal and parental kindness. But I happened to see also a glint in the eye, which told me that the old man was quite as much of a fighter as the red-haired boy who had rashly challenged him. In some odd way, indeed, I seemed suddenly to see old age itself as a masquerade. The white hair had turned into a white wig, the powder of the eighteenth century; and the smiling face underneath it was the face of Voltaire.

"Dr. Andrew Glenlyon Campbell was a real philanthropist; so was Voltaire. It is not always certain whether philanthropy means a love of men, or of man, or of mankind. There is a difference. I think he cared less about the individual than about the public or the race; hence doubtless his gentle eccentricity of defending an act of private execution. But anyhow, I knew he was one of the grim line of Scottish sceptics, from Hume down to Ross or Robertson. And, whatever else they are, they are stubborn and stick to their point. Angus also was stubborn, and as I have already said, he was a devout worshipper in the same dingy kirk as the late James Haggis; that is, one of the extreme irreconcilable sectaries of the seventeenth-century Puritanism. And so the Scottish atheist and the Scottish Calvinist argued and argued and argued, until milder races might have expected them to drop down dead with fatigue. But it was not of disagreement that either of them died.

"But the advantage was with the older and more learned man in his attack; and you must remember that the younger man had only a rather narrow and provincial version of the creed to defend. As I say, I will not bore you with the arguments; I confess they rather bore me. Doubtless Dr. Campbell said that the Ten Commandments could not be of divine origin, because two of them are mentioned by the virtuous Emperor Foo Chi, in the Second Dynasty; or one of them is paraphrased by Synesius of Samothrace and attributed to the lost code of Lycurgus."

"Who was Synesius of Samothrace?" inquired Gahagan, with an appearance of sudden and eager curiosity.

"He was a mythical character of the Minoan Age first discovered in the twentieth century A.D.," replied the unruffled Pond. "I made him up just now; but you know the sort of thing I mean—the mythical nature of Mount Sinai proved from the parallel myth that the ark rested on Mount Ararat, and the mountain that would not come to Mahomet. But all this textual criticism really affects a religion only founded on texts. I knew how the fight was going; and I knew when it ended. I knew when Robert Angus left off going to kirk on the Sabbath."

The end of the debate may best be described more directly; for, indeed, Mr. Pond described it himself with a strange sort of directness; almost as if he had unaccountably been present, or had seen it in a vision. Anyhow, it appears that the operating-theatre of the medical schools was the scene of the final phase of disagreement and agreement. They had gone back there very late at night, when the schools were closed and the theatre deserted, because Angus fancied he had left some of his instruments there, which it would be more neat and proper to lock up. There was no sound in that hollow place but the echo of their own footsteps, and very little light save a faint moonshine that trickled through the cracks between the curtained windows. Angus had retrieved his operating-tool, and was turning again towards the steep stairs that climbed through the semi-circular rows of seats, when Campbell said to him casually:

"Ye'll find the facts I mentioned aboot the Aztec hymns in the——"

Angus tossed the tool on the table like a man throwing down his sword, and turned on his companion with a new and transfigured air of candour and finality.

"You needn't trouble about hymns any more; I may as well tell you that I've done with them, for one. You're too strong for me— or, rather, the truth is too strong for me. I've defended my own nursery nightmare as long as I could; but you've woken me up at last. You are right, you must be right; I don't see any way out of it."

After a silence, Campbell answered very softly: "I'll no mak' apologies for fighting for the truth; but, man, ye made a real bonny fight for the falsehood."

It might well have seemed that the old blasphemer had never spoken on the topic in a tone so delicate and respectful; and it seemed strange that his new convert did not respond to the appeal. Looking up, Campbell saw that his new convert's attention had been abruptly abstracted; he was standing staring at the implement in his hand: a surgical knife made upon an odd pattern for special purposes. At last he said in a hoarse and almost inaudible voice:

"A knife of an unusual shape."

"See report o' inquest on Jamie Haggis," said the old man, nodding benevolently. "Aye, ye've guessed richt, I'm thinking." Then, after a pause, he added, with equal calm:

"Noo that we are agreed, and a' of one mind, aboot the need for sic social surgery, it's as weel ye should know the hale truth. Aye, lad, I did it mysel'; and with a blade like yon. That nicht ye took me to the kirk—weel, it's the fairst time, I hope, I've ever been hypocreetical; but I stayed behind to pray, and I think ye had hopes of my convairsion. But I prayed because Jamie prayed; and when he rose from his prayers, I followed him and killed him i' the kirkyard."

Angus was still looking at the knife in silence; then he said suddenly: "Why did you kill him?"

"Ye needna ask, noo we are agreed in moral philosophy," replied the old doctor simply. "It was just plain surgery. As we sacrifice a finger to save the body, so we maun sacrifice a man to save the body politic. I killed him because he was doing evil, and inhumanly preventing what was guid for humanity: the scheme for the slums and the lave. And I understand that, upon reflection, ye tak the same view."

Angus nodded grimly.

The proverb asks: "Who shall decide when doctors disagree?" But in that dark and ominous theatre of doctoring the doctors agreed.

"Yes," said Angus, "I take the same view. Also, I have had the same experience."

"And what's that?" inquired the other.

"I have had daily dealings with a man I thought was doing nothing but evil," answered Angus. "I still think you were doing evil; even though you were serving truth. You have convinced me that my beliefs were dreams; but not that dreaming is worse than waking up. You brutally broke the dreams of the humble, sneered at the weak hopes of the bereaved. You seem cruel and inhuman to me, just as Haggis seemed cruel and inhuman to you. You are a good man by your own code, but so was Haggis a good man by his code. He did not pretend to believe in salvation by good works, any more than you pretended to believe in the Ten Commandments. He was good to individuals, but the crowd suffered; you are good to the crowd and an individual suffered. But, after all, you also are only an individual."

Something in the last words, that were said very softly, made the old doctor stiffen suddenly and then start backwards towards the steps behind. Angus sprang like a wildcat and pinned him to his place with a choking violence; still talking, but now at the top of his voice.

"Day after day, I have itched and tingled to kill you; and been held back only by the superstition you have destroyed tonight. Day after day, you have been battering down the scruples which alone defended you from death. You wise thinker; you wary reasoner; you fool! It would be better for you tonight if I still believed in God and in his Commandment against murder."

The old man twisted speechlessly in the throttling grip; but he was too feeble, and Angus flung him with a crash across the operating-table, where he lay as if fainting. Round them and above them the empty tiers of concentric seats glimmered in the faint and frigid moonlight as desolate as the Colosseum under the moon; a deserted amphitheatre where there was no human voice to cry *"Habet!"* The red-haired slayer stood with the knife uplifted, as strange in shape as the flint knife of some prehistoric sacrifice; and still he talked on in the high tones of madness.

"One thing alone protected you and kept the peace between us: that we disagreed. Now we agree, now we are at one in thought—and deed, I can do as you would do. I can do as you have done. We are at peace."

And with the sound of that word he struck; and Andrew Campbell moved for the last time. In his own cold temple, upon his own godless altar . . . he stirred and then lay still; and the murderer bent and fled from the building and from the city and across the Highland line at night, to hide himself in the hills.

When Pond had told this story, Gahagan rose slowly to his gigantic height and knocked out his cigar in an ashtray: "I darkly suspect, Pond," he said, "that you are not quite so irrelevant as you sound. Not quite irrelevant, I mean, even to our opening talk about European affairs."

"Tweedledum and Tweedledee agreed—to have a battle," said Pond. "We are rather easily satisfied with saying that some people like Poles or Prussians or other foreigners have agreed. We don't often ask what they've agreed on. But agreements can be rather risky, unless it's agreement with the truth."

Wotton looked at him with a smouldering suspicion; but finally decided, with a sigh of relief, that it was only metaphysics.

GABRIEL GALE
IN

The Shadow
of the Shark

The Shadow
of the Shark

It is notable that the late Mr. Sherlock Holmes, in the course of those inspiring investigations for which we can never be sufficiently grateful to their ingenious author, seems only twice to have ruled out an explanation as intrinsically impossible. And it is curious to notice that in both cases the distinguished author himself has since come to regard that impossible thing as possible, and even as positively true. In the first case the great detective declared that he never knew a crime committed by a flying creature. Since the development of aviation, and especially the development of German aviation, Sir Arthur Conan Doyle, patriot and war historian, has seen a good many crimes committed by flying creatures. And in the other case the detective implied that no deed need be attributed to spirits or supernatural beings; in short, to any of the agencies to which Sir Arthur is now the most positive and even passionate witness. Presumably, in his present mood and philosophy the Hound of the Baskervilles might well have been a really ghostly hound; at least, if the optimism which seems to go with spiritualism would permit him to believe in such a thing as a hell-hound. It may be worth while to note this coincidence, however, in telling a tale in which both these explanations necessarily played a part. The scientists were anxious to attribute it to aviation, and the spiritualists to attribute it to spirits; though it might be questioned whether either the spirit or the flying-man should be congratulated on his utility as an assassin.

A mystery which may yet linger as a memory, but which was in its time a sensation, revolved round the death of a certain Sir Owen Cram, a wealthy eccentric, chiefly known as a patron of learning and the arts. And the peculiarity of the case was that he was found stabbed in the middle of a great stretch of yielding sand by the sea-shore, on which there was absolutely no trace of any foot-prints

but his own. It was admitted that the wound could not have been
self-inflicted; and it grew more and more difficult even to suggest
how it could have been inflicted at all. Many theories were
suggested, ranging, as we have said, from that of the enthusiasts for
aviation to that of the enthusiasts for psychical research; it being
evidently regarded as a feather in the cap either of science or
spiritualism to have effected so neat an operation. The true story of
this strange business has never been told; it certainly contained
elements which, if not supernatural, were at least supernormal. But
to make it clear, we must go back to the scene with which it began;
the scene on the lawn of Sir Owen's seaside residence, where the old
gentleman acted as a sort of affable umpire in the disputes of the
young students who were his favourite company; the scene which
led up to the singular silence and isolation, and ultimately to the
rather eccentric exit of Mr. Amos Boon.

Mr. Amos Boon had been a missionary, and still dressed like one; at
any rate, he dressed like nothing else. His sturdy, full-bearded
figure carried a broad-brimmed hat combined with a frock-coat;
which gave him an air at once outlandish and dowdy. Though he
was no longer a missionary, he was still a traveller. His face was
brown and his long beard was black; there was a furrow of thought
in his brow and a rather strained look in his eyes, one of which
sometimes looked a little larger than the other, giving a sinister
touch to what was in some ways so commonplace. He had ceased to
be a missionary through what he himself would have called the
broadening of his mind. Some said there had been a broadening of
his morals as well as of his mind; and that the South Sea Islands,
where he had lived, had seen not a little of such ethical emancipa-
tion. But this was possibly a malicious misrepresentation of his very
human curiosity and sympathy in the matter of the customs of the
savages; which to the ordinary prejudice was indistinguishable from
a white man going *fantee*. Anyhow, travelling about alone with
nothing but a big Bible, he had learned to study it minutely, first for
oracles and commandments, and afterwards for errors and contradictions; for the Bible-smasher is only the Bible-worshipper turned
upside down. He pursued the not very arduous task of proving that
David and Saul did not on all occasions merit the Divine favour; and
always concluded by roundly declaring that he preferred the

Philistines. Boon and his Philistines were already a byword of some levity among the young men who, at that moment, were arguing and joking around him.

At that moment Sir Owen Cram was playfully presiding over a dispute between two or three of his young friends about science and poetry. Sir Owen was a little restless man, with a large head, a bristly grey moustache, and a grey fan of hair like the crest of a cockatoo. There was something sprawling and splayfooted about his continuous movement which was compared by thoughtless youth to that of a crab; and it corresponded to a certain universal eagerness which was really ready to turn in all directions. He was a typical amateur, taking up hobby after hobby with equal inconsistency and intensity. He had impetuously left all his money to a museum of natural history, only to become immediately swallowed up in the single pursuit of landscape painting; and the groups around him largely represented the stages of his varied career. At the moment a young painter, who was also by way of being a poet, was defending some highly poetical notions against the smiling resistance of a rising doctor, whose hobby was biology. The data of agreement would have been difficult to find, and few save Sir Owen could have claimed any common basis of sympathy; but the important matter just then was the curious effect of the young men's controversy upon Mr. Boon.

"The subject of flowers is hackneyed, but the flowers are not," the poet was insisting. "Tennyson was right about the flower in the crannied wall; but most people don't look at flowers in a wall, but only in a wall-paper. If you generalize them, they are dull, but if you simply see them they are always startling. If there's a special providence in a falling star, there's more in a rising star; and a live star at that."

"Well, I can't see it," said the man of science, good-humouredly; he was a red-haired, keen-faced youth in pince-nez, by the name of Wilkes. "I'm afraid we fellows grow out of the way of seeing it like that. You see, a flower is only a growth like any other, with organs and all that; and its inside isn't any prettier or uglier than an animal's. An insect is much the same pattern of rings and radiations. I'm interested in it as I am in an octopus or any sea-beast you would think a monster."

"But why should you put it that way round?" retorted the poet. "Why isn't it quite as logical the other way round? Why not say the octopus is as wonderful as the flower, instead of the flower as ordinary as the octopus? Why not say that crackens and cuttles and all the sea-monsters are themselves flowers; fearful and wonderful flowers in that terrible twilight garden of God. I do not doubt that God can be as fond of a shark as I am of a buttercup."

"As to God, my dear Gale," began the other quietly, and then he seemed to change his form of words. "Well, I am only a man—nay, only a scientific man, which you may think lower than a sea-beast. And the only interest I have in a shark is to cut him up; always on the preliminary supposition that I have prevented him from cutting me up."

"Have you ever met a shark?" asked Amos Boon, intervening suddenly.

"Not in society," replied the poet with a certain polite discomposure, looking round with something like a flush under his fair hair; he was a long, loose-limbed man named Gabriel Gale, whose pictures were more widely known than his poems.

"You've seen them in the tanks, I suppose," said Boon; "but I've seen them in the sea. I've seen them where they are lords of the sea, and worshipped by the people as great gods. I'd as soon worship those gods as any other."

Gale the poet was silent, for his mind always moved in a sort of sympathy with merely imaginative pictures; and he instantly saw, as in a vision, boiling purple seas and plunging monsters. But another young man standing near him, who had hitherto been rather primly silent, cut in quietly; a theological student, named Simon, the deposit of some epoch of faith in Sir Owen's stratified past. He was a slim man with sleek, dark hair and darting, mobile eyes, in spite of his compressed lips. Whether in caution or contempt, he had left the attack on medical materialism to the poet, who was always ready to plunge into an endless argument with anybody. Now he intervened merely to say:

"Do they only worship a shark? It seems rather a limited sort of religion."

"Religion!" repeated Amos Boon, rudely; "what do you people know about religion? You pass the plate round, and when Sir Owen puts a penny in it, you put up a shed where a curate can talk to a congregation of maiden aunts. These people have got something like a religion. They sacrifice things to it—their beasts, their babies, their lives. I reckon you'd turn green with fear if you'd ever so much as caught a glimpse of Religion. Oh, it's not just a fish in the sea; rather it's the sea round a fish. The sea is the blue cloud he moves in, or the green veil or curtain hung about him, the skirts of which trail with thunder."

All faces were turned towards him, for there was something about him beyond his speech. Twilight was spreading over the garden, which lay near the edge of a chalk cliff above the shore, but the last light of sunset still lay on a part of the lawn, painting it yellow rather than green, and glowing almost like gold against the last line of the sea, which was a sombre indigo and violet, changing nearer land to a lurid, pale green. A long cloud of a jagged shape happened to be trailing across the sun; and the broad-hatted, hairy man from the South Seas suddenly pointed at it.

"I know where the shape of that cloud would be called the shadow of the shark," he cried, "and a thousand men would fall on their faces ready to fast or fight, or die. Don't you see the great black dorsal fin, like the peak of a moving mountain? And then you lads discuss him as if he were a stroke at golf; and one of you says he would cut him up like birthday cake; and the other says your Jewish Jehovah would condescend to pat him like a pet rabbit."

"Come, come," said Sir Owen, with a rather nervous waggishness, "we mustn't have any of your broad-minded blasphemies."

Boon turned on him a baneful eye; literally an eye, for one of his eyes grew larger till it glowed like the eye of the Cyclops. His figure was black against the fiery turf, and they could almost hear his beard bristling.

"Blasphemy!" he cried in a new voice, with a crack in it. "Take care it is not you who blaspheme."

And then, before anyone could move, the black figure against the patch of gold had swung round and was walking away from the house, so impetuously that they had a momentary fear that he would walk over the cliff. However, he found the little wooden gate that led to a flight of wooden steps; and they heard him stumbling down the path to the fishing village below.

Sir Owen seemed suddenly to shake off a paralysis like a fit of slumber. "My old friend is a little eccentric," he said. "Don't go, gentlemen; don't let him break up the party. It is early yet."

But growing darkness and a certain social discomfort had already begun to dissolve the group on the lawn; and the host was soon left with a few of the most intimate of his guests. Simon and Gale, and his late antagonist, Dr. Wilkes, were staying to dinner; the darkness drove them indoors, and eventually found them sitting round a flask of green Chartreuse on the table; for Sir Owen had his expensive conventions as well as his expensive-eccentricities. The talkative poet, however, had fallen silent, and was staring at the green liquid in his glass as if it were the green depth of the sea. His host attacked with animation the other ordinary topics of the day.

"I bet I'm the most industrious of the lot of you," he said. "I've been at my easel on the beach all day, trying to paint this blessed cliff, and make it look like chalk and not cheese."

"I saw you, but I didn't like to disturb you," said Wilkes. "I generally try to put in an hour or so looking for specimens at high tide: I suppose most people think I'm shrimping or only paddling and doing it for my health. But I've got a pretty good nucleus of that museum we were talking about, or at least the aquarium part of it. I put in most of the rest of the time arranging the exhibits; so I deny the implication of idleness. Gale was on the sea-shore too. He was doing nothing as usual; and now he's saying nothing, which is much more uncommon."

"I have been writing letters," said Simon, in his precise way, "but letters are not always trivial. Sometimes they are rather tremendous."

Sir Owen glanced at him for a moment, and a silence followed, which was broken by a thud and a rattle of glasses as Gale brought his fist down on the table like a man who had thought of something suddenly.

"Dagon!" he cried, in a sort of ecstasy.

Most of the company seemed but little enlightened; perhaps they thought that saying "Dagon" was his poetical and professional fashion of saying "Damn." But the dark eyes of Simon brightened, and he nodded quickly.

"Why, of course you're right," he said. "That must be why Mr. Boon is so fond of the Philistines."

In answer to a general stare of inquiry, he said smoothly: "The Philistines were a people from Crete, probably of Hellenic origin, who settled on the coast of Palestine, carrying with them a worship which may very well have been that of Poseidon, but which their enemies, the Israelites, described as that of Dagon. The relevant matter here is that the carved or painted symbol of the god seems always to have been a fish."

The mention of the new matter seemed to reawaken the tendency of the talk to turn into a wrangle between the poet and the professional scientist.

"From my point of view," said the latter, "I must confess myself somewhat disappointed with your friend Mr. Boon. He represented himself as a rationalist like myself, and seemed to have made some scientific studies of folklore in the South Seas. But he seemed a little unbalanced; and surely he made a curious fuss about some sort of a fetish, considering it was only a fish."

"No, no, no!" cried Gale, almost with passion. "Better make a fetish of the fish. Better sacrifice yourself and everybody else on the horrible huge altar of the fish. Better do anything than utter the star-blasting blasphemy of saying it is *only* a fish. It's as bad as saying the other thing is only a flower."

"All the same, it *is* only a flower," answered Wilkes, "and the advantage of looking at these things in a cool and rational way from the outside is that you can——"

He stopped a moment and remained quite still, as if he were watching something. Some even fancied that his pale, aquiline face looked paler as well as sharper.

"What was that at the window?" he asked. "Is anybody outside this house?"

"What's the matter? What did you see?" asked his host, in abrupt agitation.

"Only a face," replied the doctor, "but it was not—it was not like a man's face. Let's get outside and look into this."

Gabriel Gale was only a moment behind the doctor, who had impetuously dashed out of the room. Despite his lounging demeanour, the poet had already leapt to his feet with his hand on the back of the chair, when he stiffened where he stood; for he had seen it. The faces of the others showed that they had seen it too.

Pressed against the dark window-pane, but only wanly luminous as it protruded out of the darkness, was a large face looking at first rather like a green goblin mask in a pantomime. Yet it was in no sense human; its eyes were set in large circles, rather in the fashion of an owl. But the glimmering covering that faintly showed on it was not of feathers, but of scales.

The next moment it had vanished. The mind of the poet, which made images as rapidly as a cinema, even in a crisis of action, had already imagined a string of fancies about the sort of creature he saw it to be. He had thought involuntarily of some great flying fish winging its way across the foam, and the flat sand and the spire and roofs of the fishing village. He had half-imagined the moist sea air thickening in some strange way to a greener and more liquid atmosphere in which the marine monsters could swim about in the streets. He had entertained the fancy that the house itself stood in the depths of the sea, and that the great goblin-headed fishes were nosing round it, as round the cabin windows of a wreck.

At that moment a loud voice was heard outside crying in distinct accents:

"The fish has legs."

For that instant, it seemed to give the last touch to the monstrosity. But the meaning of it came back to them, a returning reality, with the laughing face of Dr. Wilkes as he reappeared in the doorway, panting.

"Our fish had two legs, and used them," he said. "He ran like a hare when he saw me coming; but I could see plainly enough it was a man, playing you a trick of some sort. So much for that psychic phenomenon."

He paused and looked at Sir Owen Cram with a smile that was keen and almost suspicious.

"One thing is very clear to me," he said. "You have an enemy."

The mystery of the human fish, however, did not long remain even a primary topic of conversation in a social group that had so many topics of conversation. They continued to pursue their hobbies and pelt each other with their opinions; even the smooth and silent Simon being gradually drawn into the discussions, in which he showed a dry and somewhat cynical dexterity. Sir Owen continued to paint with all the passion of an amateur. Gale continued to neglect to paint, with all the nonchalance of a painter. Mr. Boon was presumably still as busy with his wicked Bible and his good Philistines as Dr. Wilkes with his museum and his microscopic marine animals, when the little seaside town was shaken as by an earthquake with the incomprehensible calamity which spread its name over all the newspapers of the country.

Gabriel Gale was scaling the splendid swell of turf that terminated in the great chalk cliff above the shore, in a mood consonant to the sunrise that was storming the skies above him. Clouds haloed with sunshine were already sailing over his head as if sent flying from a flaming wheel; and when he came to the brow of the cliff he saw one of those rare revelations when the sun does not seem to be merely the most luminous object in a luminous landscape, but itself the solitary focus and streaming fountain of all light. The tide was at the ebb, and the sea was only a strip of delicate turquoise over which rose the tremendous irradiation. Next to the strip of turquoise was a strip of orange sand, still wet, and nearer the sand was a desert of a more dead yellow or brown, growing paler in the increasing light. And as he looked down from the precipice upon that plain of pale gold, he saw two black objects lying in the middle of it. One was a small easel, still standing, with a camp-stool fallen beside it; the other was the flat and sprawling figure of a man.

The figure did not move, but as he stared he became conscious that another human figure was moving, was walking over the flat sands towards it from under the shadow of the cliff. Looking at it steadily, he saw that it was the man called Simon; and in an instant he seemed to realize that the motionless figure was that of Sir Owen Cram. He hastened to the stairway down the cliff and so to the sands; and soon stood face to face with Simon; for they both looked at each other for a moment before they both looked down at the body. The conviction was already cold in his heart that it was a dead body. Nevertheless, he said sharply: "We must have a doctor; where is Dr. Wilkes?"

"It is no good, I fear," said Simon, looking away at the sea.

"Wilkes may only confirm our fears that he is dead," said Gale, "but he may have something to say about how he died."

"True," said the other, "I will go for him myself." And he walked back rapidly towards the cliff in the track of his own foot-prints.

Indeed, it was at the foot-prints that Gale was gazing in a bemused fashion at that moment. The tracks of his own coming were clear enough, and the tracks of Simon's coming and going; and the third rather more rambling track of the unmistakable boots of the unfortunate Sir Owen, leading up to the spot where his easel was planted. And that was all. The sand was soft, so that the lightest foot would disturb it; it was well above the tides; and there was not the faintest trace of any other human being having been near the body. Yet the body had a deep wound under the angle of the jaw; and there was no sign of any weapon of suicide.

Gabriel Gale was a believer in commonsense, in theory if not always in practice. He told himself repeatedly that these things were the practical clues in such a case; the wound, the weapon or absence of weapon, the foot-prints or absence of foot-prints. But there was also a part of his mind which was always escaping from his control and playing tricks; fixing on his memory meaningless things as if they were symbols, and then haunting him with them as mysteries. He made no point of it; it was rather sub-conscious than self-conscious; but the parts of any living picture that he saw were seldom those that others saw, or that it seemed sensible to see. And there were one or two details in the tragedy before him that haunted him then and long afterwards. Cram had fallen backwards in a rather twisted fashion, with his feet towards the shore; and a few inches from the left foot lay a star-fish. He could not say whether it was merely the bright orange colour of the creature that irrationally rivetted his eye, or merely some obscure fancy of repetition, in that the human figure was itself spread and sprawling flat like a star-fish, with four limbs instead of five. Nor did he attempt to analyse this aesthetic antic of his psychology; it was a suppressed part of his mind which still repeated that the mystery of the untrodden sands would turn out to be something quite simple; but that the star-fish possessed the secret.

He looked up to see Simon returning with the doctor, indeed with two doctors; for there was more than one medical representative in the mob of Sir Owen's varied interests. The other was a Dr. Garth, a little man with an angular and humorous face; he was an old friend of Gale's, but the poet's greeting was rather *distrait*. Garth and his colleagues, however, got to work on a preliminary examination, which made further talk needless. It could not be a full examination till the arrival of the police, but it was sufficient to extinguish any hope of life, if any such had lingered. Garth, who was bent over the body in a crouching posture, spoke to his fellow physician without raising his head.

"There seems to be something rather odd about this wound. It goes almost straight upwards, as if it was struck from below. But Sir Owen was a very small man; and it seems queer that he should be stabbed by somebody smaller still."

Gale's sub-consciousness exploded with a strange note of harsh mockery.

"What," he cried, "you don't think the starfish jumped up and killed him?"

"No, of course not," said Garth, with his gruff good humour. "What on earth is the matter with you?"

"Lunacy, I think," said the poet, and began to walk slowly towards the shore.

As time went on he almost felt disposed to fancy that he had correctly diagnosed his own complaint. The image began to figure even in his dreams, but not merely as a natural nightmare about the body on the sea-shore. The significant sea creature seemed more vivid even than the body. As he had originally seen the corpse from above, spread flat out beneath him, he saw it in his visions as something standing, as if propped against a wall or even merely drawn or graven on a wall. Sometimes the sandy ground had become a ground of old gold in some decoration of the Dark Ages, with the figure in the stiff agonies of a martyr, but the red star always showed like a lamp by his feet. Sometimes it was a hieroglyphic of a more Eastern sort, as of some stone god rigidly dancing; but the five-pointed star was always in the same place below. Sometimes it seemed a rude, red-sandstone sort of drawing; yet more archaic; but the star was always the reddest spot in it. Now and again, while the human figure was as dry and dark as a mummy, the star would seem to be literally alive, waving its flaming fingers as if it were trying to tell him something. Now and then even the whole figure was upside down, as if to restore the star to its proper place in the skies.

"I told Wilkes that a flower was a living star," he said to himself. "A starfish is more literally a living star. But this is like going crazy. And if there is one thing I strongly object to, it is going crazy. What use should I be to all my brother lunatics, if I once really lost my balance on the tight-rope over the abyss?"

He sat staring into vacancy for some time, trying to fit in this small and stubborn fancy with a much steadier stream of much deeper thoughts that were already driving in a certain direction. At last, the light of a possibility began to dawn in his eyes; and it was evidently something very simple when it was realized; something which he felt he ought to have thought of before; for he laughed shortly and scornfully at himself as he rose to his feet.

"If Boon goes about everywhere introducing his shark and I go into society always attended by my starfish," he murmured to himself, "we shall turn the world into an aquarium bigger and better than Dr. Wilkes is fixing up. I'm going down to make some inquiries in the village."

Returning thence across the sands at evening, after several conversations with skippers and fishermen, he wore a more satisfied expression.

"I always did believe," he reflected, "that the foot-print business would be the simplest thing in the affair. But there are some things in it that are by no means simple."

Then he looked up, and saw far off on the sands, lonely and dark against the level evening light, the strange hat and stumpy figure of Amos Boon.

He seemed to consider for a moment the advisability of a meeting; then he turned away and moved towards the stairway up the cliff. Mr. Boon was apparently occupied in idly drawing lines on the sand with his shabby umbrella; like one drawing plans for a child's sand-castle, but apparently without any such intelligent object or excuse. Gale had often seen the man mooning about with equally meaningless and automatic gestures; but as the poet mounted the rocky steps, climbing higher and higher, he had a return of the irrational feeling of a visionary vertigo. He told himself again, as if in warning, that it was his whole duty in life to walk on a tight-rope above a void in which many imaginative men were swallowed up. Then he looked down again at the drop of the dizzy cliffs to the flats that seemed to be swimming below him like a sea. And he saw the long, loose lines drawn in the sand unified into a shape, as flat as a picture on a wall. He had often seen a child, in the same fashion, draw on the sand a pig as large as a house. But in this case he could not shake off his former feeling of something archaic, like a palaeolithic drawing, about the scratching of the brown sand. And Mr. Boon had not drawn a pig, but a shark; conspicuous with its jagged teeth and fin like a horn exalted.

But he was not the only person overlooking this singular decorative scheme. When he came to the short railings along the brow of the cliff in which the stairway terminated, he found three figures leaning on it and looking down; and instantly realized how the case was closing in. For even in their outlines against the sky he had recognized the two doctors and an inspector of police.

"Hullo, Gale," observed Wilkes, "may I present you to Inspector Davies; a very active and successful officer."

Garth nodded. "I understand the inspector will soon make an arrest," he said.

"The inspector must be getting back to his work and not talking about it," said that official good-humouredly. "I'm going down to the village. Anybody coming my way?"

Dr. Wilkes assented and followed him, but Dr. Garth stopped a moment, being detained by the poet, who caught hold of his sleeve with unusual earnestness.

"Garth," he said, "I want to apologize. I'm afraid I was wool-gathering when we met the other day, and didn't hail you as I ought to hail an old friend. You and I have been in one or two queer affairs together, and I want to talk to you about this one. Shall we sit down on that seat over there?"

They seated themselves on an iron seat set up on the picturesque headland; and Gale added, "I wish you could tell me roughly how you got as far as you seem to have got."

Garth gazed silently out to sea, and said at last:

"Do you know that man Simon?"

"Yes," replied the poet, "that's the way it works, is it?"

"Well, the investigation soon began to show that Simon knew rather more than he said. He was on the spot before you; and for some time he wouldn't admit what it was he saw before you turned up. We guessed it was because he was afraid to tell the truth; and in one sense he was."

"Simon doesn't talk enough," said Gale thoughtfully. "He doesn't talk about himself enough; so he thinks about himself too much. A man like that always gets secretive; not necessarily in the sense of being criminal, or even of being malicious, but merely of being morbid. He is the sort that is ill-treated at school and never says so. As long as a thing terrified him, he couldn't talk about it."

"I don't know how you guessed it," said Garth, "but that is something like the line of discoveries. At first they thought that Simon's silence was guilt, but it was only a fear of something more than guilt; of some diabolic destiny and entanglement. The truth is, that when he went up before you to the cliff-head at day-break, he saw something that hag-rode his morbid spirit ever since. He saw the figure of this man Boon poised on the brink of the precipice, black against the dawn, and waving his arms in some unearthly fashion as if he were going to fly. Simon thought the man was talking to himself, and perhaps even singing. Then the strange creature passed on towards the village and was lost in the twilight; but when Simon came to the edge of the cliff he saw Sir Owen lying dead far out on the sands below, beside his easel."

"And ever since, I suppose," observed Gale, "Simon has seen sharks everywhere."

"You are right again," said the doctor. "He has admitted since that a shadow on the blind or a cloud on the moon would have the unmistakable shape of the fish with the fin erect. But, in fact, it is a very mistakable shape; anything with a triangular top to it would suggest it to a man in his state of nerves. But the truth is that so long as he thought Boon had dealt death from a distance by some sort of curse or spell, we could get nothing out of him. Our only chance was to show him that Boon might have done it even by natural means. And we did show it, after all."

"What is your theory, then?" asked the other.

"It is too general to be called a theory yet," replied the doctor; "but, honestly, I do not think it at all impossible that Boon might have killed a man on the sands from the top of a cliff, without falling back on any supernatural stuff. You've got to consider it like this: Boon has been very deep in the secrets of savages, especially in that litter of islands that lie away towards Australia. Now, we now that such savages, for all they are called ignorant, have developed many dexterities and many unique tools. They have blow-pipes that kill at a considerable distance; they harpoon and lasso things, and draw them in on a line. Above all, the Australian savages have discovered the boomerang, that actually returns to the hand. Is it quite so inconceivable that Boon might know some way of sending a penetrating projectile from a distance, and even possibly of recovering it in some way? Dr. Wilkes and I, on examining the wound, found it a very curious one: it was made by some tapering, pointed tool, with a slight curve; and it not only curved upwards, but even slightly outwards, as if the curve were returning on itself. Does not that suggest to you some outlandish weapon of a strange shape, and possibly with strange properties? And always remember that such an explanation would explain something else as well, which is generally regarded as the riddle. It would explain why the murderer left no foot-prints round the body."

Gale gazed out to sea in silence, as if considering; then he said simply:

"An extremely shrewd argument. But I know why he left no

foot-prints. It is a much simpler explanation than that."

Garth stared at him for a few moments; and then observed gravely:

"May I then ask, in return, what is your theory?"

"My theory will seem a maze of theories, and nothing else," said Gale. "It is, as many would say, of such stuff as dreams are made of. Most modern people have a curious contradiction; they abound in theories, yet they never see the part that theories play in practical life. They are always talking about temperament and circumstances and accident; but most men are what their theories make them; most men go in for murder or marriage, or mere lounging because of some theory of life, asserted or assumed. So I can never manage to begin my explanations in that brisk, pointed, practical way that you doctors and detectives do. I see a man's mind first, sometimes almost without any particular man attached to it. I could only begin this business by describing a mental state—which can't be described. Our murderer or maniac, or whatever you call him, is certainly affected by some of the elements attributed to him. His view has reached an insane degree of simplicity, and in that sense of savagery. But I doubt whether he would necessarily transfer the savagery from the end to the means. In one sense, indeed, his view might be compared to the barbaric. He saw every creature and even every object naked. He did not understand that what clothes a thing is sometimes the most real part of it. Have you ever noticed how true is that old phrase, 'clothed and in his right mind'? Man is not in his right mind when he is not clothed with the symbols of his social dignity. Humanity is not even human when it is naked. But in a lower sense it is so of lesser things, even of lifeless things. A lot of nonsense is talked about auras; but this is the truth behind it. Everything has a halo. Everything has a sort of atmosphere of what it signifies, which makes it sacred. Even the little creatures he studied had each of them its halo; but he would not see it."

"But what little creatures did Boon study?" asked Garth in some wonder. "Do you mean the cannibals?"

"I was not thinking about Boon," replied Gabriel Gale.

"What do you mean?" cried the other, in sudden excitement. "Why, Boon is almost in the hands of the police."

"Boon is a good man," said Gale, calmly; "he is very stupid; that is why he is an atheist. There are intelligent atheists, as we shall see presently; but that stunted, stupid sort is much commoner, and much nicer. But he is a good man; his motive is good; he originally talked all that tosh of the superiority of the savage because he thought he was the underdog. He may be a trifle cracked, by now, about sharks and other things; but that's only because his travels have been too much for his intellect. They say travel broadens the mind; but you must have the mind. He had a mind for a suburban chapel, and there passed before it all the panorama of gilded nature-worship and purple sacrifice. He doesn't know if he's on his head or his heels, any more than a good many others. But I shouldn't wonder if heaven is largely populated with atheists of that sort, scratching their heads and wondering where they are.

"But Boon is a parenthesis; that is all he is. The man I am talking about is very much the point, and a sharp one at that. He dealt in something very different from muddled mysticism about human sacrifice. Human sacrifice is quite a human weakness. He dealt in assassination; direct, secret, straight from a head as inhuman as hell. And I knew it when I first talked to him over the tea-cups and he said he saw nothing pretty in a flower."

"My dear fellow!" remonstrated Dr. Garth.

"I don't mean that a man merely dissecting a daisy must be on the road to the gallows," conceded the poet, magnanimously, "but I do say that to mean it as he meant it is to be on a straight road of logic that leads there if he chooses to follow it. God is inside everything. But this man wanted to be outside everything; to see everything hung in a vacuum, simply its own dead self. It's not only not the same, it's almost the opposite of scepticism in the sense of Boon or the Book of Job. That's a man overwhelmed by the mysteries; but this man denies that there are any mysteries. It's not, in the ordinary sense, a matter of theology, but psychology. Most good pagans and pantheists might talk of the miracles of nature; but this man denies that there are any miracles, even in the sense of marvels. Don't you see that dreadful dry light shed on things must at last wither up the moral mysteries as illusions, respect for age, respect for property, and that the sanctity of life will be a superstition? The men in the street are only organisms, with their organs more or less displayed. For such a one there is no longer any terror in the touch of human flesh, nor does he see God watching him out of the eyes of a man."

"He may not believe in miracles, but he seems to work them," remarked the doctor. What else was he doing, when he struck a man down on the sand without leaving a mark to show where he stood?"

"He was paddling," answered Gale.

"As high up on the shore as that?" inquired the other.

Gale nodded. "That was what puzzled me; till something I saw on the sand started a train of thought that led to my asking the seafaring people about the tides. It's very simple; the night before we found the body was a flood-tide, and the sea came up higher than usual; not quite to where Cram was sitting, but pretty near. So that was the way that the real human fish came out of the sea. That was the way the divine shark really devoured the sacrifice. The man came paddling in the foam, like a child on a holiday."

"Who came?" asked Garth; but he shuddered.

"Who did go dredging for sea-beasts with a sort of shrimping-net along the shore every evening? Who did inherit the money of the old man for his ambitious museum and his scientific career? Who did tell me in the garden that a cowslip was only a growth like a cancer?"

"I am compelled to understand you," said the doctor gloomily. "You mean that very able young man named Wilkes?"

"To understand Wilkes you must understand a good deal," continued his friend. "You must reconstruct the crime, as they say. Look out over that long line of darkening sea and sand, where the last light runs red as blood; that is where he came dredging every day, in the same bloodshot dusk, looking for big beasts and small; and in a true sense everything was fish that came to his net. He was constructing his museum as a sort of cosmos; with everything traced from the fossil to the flying fish. He had spent enormous sums on it, and had got quite disinterestedly into debt; for instance he had had magnificent models made, in wax or papier maché, of small fish magnified, or extinct fish restored; things that South Kensington cannot afford, and certainly Wilkes could not afford. But he had persuaded Cram to leave his money to the museum, as you know; and for him Cram was simply a silly old fool, who painted pictures he couldn't paint, and talked of sciences he didn't understand; and whose only natural function was to die and save the museum. Well, when every morning Wilkes had done polishing the glass cases of his masks and models, he came round by the cliff and took a turn at the fossils in the chalk with his geological hammer; then he put it back in that great canvas bag of his, and unslung his long shrimping net and began to wade. This is where I want you to look at that dark red sand and see the picture; one never understands anything till one sees the picture. He went for miles along the shallows of that desolate shore, long inured to seeing one queer creature or another stranded on the sand; here a sea-hedgehog, and there a starfish, and then a crab, and then another creature. I have told you he had reached a stage when he would have looked at an angel with the eye of an ornithologist. What would he think of a man, and a man looking like that? Don't you see that poor Cram must have looked like a crab or a sea-urchin; his dwarfed, hunched figure seen from behind, with his fan of bristling whiskers, his straggling bow legs and restless twisting feet all tangled up with the three legs of his stool; making him look as if he had five limbs like a starfish? Don't you see he looked like a Common Object of the Seashore? And Wilkes had only to collect this specimen, and all his other specimens were safe. Everything was fish that came to his net, and . . .

"He stretched out the long pole in his hand to its full extent, and drew the net over the old man's head as if he were catching a great grey moth. He plucked him backwards off his stool so that he lay kicking on his back on the sand; and doubtless looking more like a large insect than ever. Then the murderer bent forward, propped by one hand upon his pole, and the other armed with his geological hammer. With the pick at the back of that instrument he struck in what he well knew to be a vital spot. The curve you noticed in the wound is due to that sharp side of the hammer being shaped like a pickaxe. But the unusual position of it, and the puzzle of how such a blow could be struck upwards, was due to the queer posture of the two figures. The murderer struck at a head that was upside down. It could only occur as a rule if the victim were standing on his head, a posture in which few persons await the assassin. But with the flourish and sweep of the great net, I fancy a starfish caught in it fell out of it, just beyond the dead man's foot. At any rate, it was that starfish and the accident of its flying so high on the shore, that set my mind drifting in the general direction of tides; and the possibility of the murderer having been moving about in the water. If he made any prints the breakers washed them out; and I should never have begun to think of it but for that red-fingered little monster."

"Then do you mean to tell me," demanded Garth, "that all this business about the shadow of the shark had nothing to do with it?"

"The shadow of the shark had everything to do with it," replied Gale. "The murderer hid in the shadow of the shark, and struck from under the shadow of the shark. I doubt if he would have struck at all, if he had not had the shadow of that fantastic fin in which to hide. And the proof is that he himself took the trouble to emphasize and exaggerate the legend of poor Boon dancing before Dagon. Do you remember that queer incident of the fish's face at the window? How did anybody merely playing a practical joke get hold of a fish's face? It was very life-like; for it was one of the masks modelled for the Wilkes museum; and Wilkes had left it in the hall in his great canvas bag. It seems simple, doesn't it, for a man to raise an alarm inside a house, walk out to see, and instantly put on a mask and look in at a window? That's all he did; and you can see his idea, from the fact that he proceeded to warn Sir Owen of an enemy. He wanted all this idolatrous and mystical murder business worked for all it was worth, that his own highly reasonable murder might not be noticed. And you see he has succeeded. You tell me that Boon is in the hands of the police."

Garth sprang to his feet. "What is to be done?" he said.

"You will know what to do," said the poet. "You are a good and just man, and a practical man too. I am not a practical man." He rose with a certain air of apology. "You see, you want an unpractical man for finding out this sort of thing."

And once more he gazed down from the precipice into the abysses below.

GABRIEL GALE & BERTRAND
IN

*The Finger of
Stone*

The Finger of
Stone

Three young men on a walking tour came to a halt outside the little
town of Carillon, in the south of France; which is doubtless
described in the guide books as famous for its fine old Byzantine
monastery, now the seat of a university; and for having been the
scene of the labours of Boyg. At that name, at least, the reader will
be reasonably thrilled; for he must have seen it in any number of
newspapers and novels. Boyg and the Bible are periodically reconciled at religious conferences; Boyg broadens and slightly bewilders
the minds of numberless heroes of long psychological stories, which
begin in the nursery and nearly end in the madhouse. The journalist,
writing rapidly his recurrent reference to the treatment meted out to
pioneers like Galileo, pauses in the effort to think of another
example, and always rounds off the sentence either with Bruno or
with Boyg. But the mildly orthodox are equally fascinated, and feel
a glow of agnosticism while they continue to say that, since the
discoveries of Boyg, the doctrine of the Homoousian or of the
human conscience does not stand where it did; wherever that was. It
is needless to say that Boyg was a great discoverer, for the public has
long regarded him with the warmest reverence and gratitude on that
ground. It is also unnecessary to say what he discovered; for the
public will never display the faintest curiosity about that. It is
vaguely understood that it was something about fossils, or the long
period required for petrification; and that it generally implied those
anarchic or anonymous forces of evolution supposed to be hostile
to religion. But certainly none of the discoveries he made while he
was alive was so sensational, in the newspaper sense, as the
discovery that was made about him when he was dead. And this, the
more private and personal matter, is what concerns us here.

The three tourists had just agreed to separate for an hour, and
meet again for luncheon at the little café opposite; and the different

ways in which they occupied their time and indulged their tastes will serve for a sufficient working summary of their personalities. Arthur Armitage was a dark and grave young man, with a great deal of money, which he spent on a conscientious and continuous course of self-culture, especially in the matter of art and architecture; and his earnest aquiline profile was already set towards the Byzantine monastery, for the exhaustive examination of which he had already prepared himself, as if he were going to pass an examination rather than to make one. The man next him, though himself an artist, betrayed no such artistic ardour. He was a painter who wasted most of his time as a poet; but Armitage, who was always picking up geniuses, had become in some sense his patron in both departments. His name was Gabriel Gale; a long, loose, rather listless man with yellow hair; but a man not easy for any patron to patronize.

He generally did as he liked in an abstracted fashion; and what he very often liked to do was nothing. On this occasion he showed a lamentable disposition to drift towards the café first; and having drunk a glass or two of wine, he drifted not into the town but out of it, roaming about the steep bare slope above, with a rolling eye on the rolling clouds; and talking to himself until he found somebody else to talk to, which happened when he put his foot through the glass roof of a studio just below him on the steep incline. As it was an artist's studio, however, their quarrel fortunately ended in an argument about the future of realistic art; and when he turned up to lunch, that was the extent of his acquaintance with the quaint and historic town of Carillon.

The name of the third man was Garth; he was shorter and uglier and somewhat older than the others, but with a much livelier eye in his hatchet face; he stepped much more briskly, and in the matter of a knowledge of the world, the other two were babies under his charge. He was a very able medical practitioner, with a hobby of more fundamental scientific inquiry; and for him the whole town, university and studio, monastery and café, was only the temple of the presiding genius of Boyg. But in this case the practical instinct of Dr. Garth would seem to have guided him rightly: for he discovered things considerably more startling than anything the antiquarian found in the Romanesque arches or the poet in the rolling clouds. And it is his adventures, in that single hour before lunch, upon which this tale must turn.

The café tables stood on the pavement under a row of trees

opposite the old round gate in the wall, through which could be seen the white gleam of the road up which they had just been walking. But the steep hills were so high round the town that they rose clear above the wall, in a more enormous wall of smooth and slanting rock, bare except for occasional clumps of cactus. There was no crack in that sloping wilderness of stone except the rather shallow and stony bed of a little stream. Lower down, where the stream reached the level of the valley, rose the dark domes of the basilica of the old monastery; and from this a curious stairway of rude stones ran some way up the hill beside the watercourse, and stopped at a small and solitary building looking little more than a shed made of stones. Some little way higher the gleam of the glass roof of the studio, with which Gale had collided in his unconscious wanderings, marked the last spot of human habitation in all those rocky wastes that rose about the little town.

Armitage and Gale were already seated at the table when Dr. Garth walked up briskly and sat down somewhat abruptly.

"Have you fellows heard the news?" he asked.

He spoke somewhat sharply, for he was faintly annoyed by the attitudes of the antiquarian and the artist, who were deep in their own dreamier and less practical tastes and topics. Armitage was saying at the moment:

"Yes, I suppose I've seen today some of the very oldest sculpture of the veritable Dark Ages. And it's not stiff like some Byzantine work; there's a touch of the true grotesque you generally get in Gothic."

"Well, I've seen today some of the newest sculpture of the Modern Ages," replied Gale, "and I fancy they are the veritable Dark Ages. Quite enough of the true grotesque up in that studio, I can tell you."

"Have you heard the news, I say?" rapped out the doctor. "Boyg is dead."

Gale stopped in a sentence about Gothic architecture, and said seriously, with a sort of hazy reverence:

"*Requiescat in pace.* Who was Boyg?"

"Well, really," replied the doctor, "I did think every baby had heard of Boyg."

"Well, I daresay you've never heard of Paradou," answered Gale. "Each of us lives in his little cosmos with its classes and degrees. Probably you haven't heard of the most advanced sculptor, or perhaps of the latest lacrosse expert or champion chess player."

It was characteristic of the two men, that while Gale went on talking in the air about an abstract subject, till he had finished his own train of thought, Armitage had a sufficient proper sense of the presence of something more urgent to relapse into silence. Nevertheless, he unconsciously looked down at his notes; at the name of the advanced sculptor he looked up.

"Who is Paradou?" he asked.

"Why, the man I've been talking to this morning," replied Gale. "His sculpture's advanced enough for anybody. He's no end of a chap; talks more than I do, and talks very well. Thinks too; I should think he could do everything except sculpt. There his theories get in his way. As I told him, this notion of the new realism—"

"Perhaps we might drop realism and attend to reality," said Dr. Garth grimly. "I tell you Boyg is dead. And that's not the worst either."

Armitage looked up from his notes with something of the vagueness of his friend the poet. "If I remember right," he said, "Professor Boyg's discovery was concerned with fossils."

"Professor Boyg's discovery involved the extension of the period required for petrification as distinct from fossilization," replied the doctor stiffly, "and thereby relegated biological origins to a period which permits the chronology necessary to the hypothesis of natural selection. It may affect you as humorous to interject the observation 'loud cheers,' but I assure you the scientific world, which happens to be competent to judge, was really moved with amazement as well as admiration."

"In fact it was petrified to hear it couldn't be petrified," suggested the poet.

"I have really no time for your flippancy," said Garth. "I am up against a great ugly fact."

Armitage interposed in the benevolent manner of a chairman. "We must really let Garth speak; come, doctor, what is it all about? Begin at the beginning."

"Very well," said the doctor, in his staccato way. "I'll begin at the beginning. I came to this town with a letter of introduction to Boyg himself; and as I particularly wanted to visit the geological museum, which his own munificence provided for this town, I went there first. I found all the windows of the Boyg Museum were broken;

and the stones thrown by the rioters were actually lying about the room within a foot or two of the glass cases, one of which was smashed."

"Donations to the geological museum, no doubt," remarked Gale. "A munificent patron happens to pass by, and just heaves in a valuable exhibit through the window. I don't see why that shouldn't be done in what you call the world of science; I'm sure it's done all right in the world of art. Old Paradou's busts and bas-reliefs are just great rocks chucked at the public and—"

"Paradou may go to—Paradise, shall we say?" said Garth, with pardonable impatience. "Will nothing make you understand that something has really happened that isn't any of your ideas and isms? It wasn't only the geological museum; it was the same everywhere. I passed by the house Boyg first lived in, where they very properly put up a medallion; and the medallion was all splashed with mud. I crossed the market-place, where they put up a statue to him just recently. It was still hung with wreaths of laurel by his pupils and the party that appreciates him; but they were half torn away, as if there had been a struggle, and stones had evidently been thrown, for a piece of the hand was chipped off."

"Paradou's statue, no doubt," observed Gale. "No wonder they threw things at it."

"I think not," replied the doctor, in the same hard voice. "It wasn't because it was Paradou's statue, but because it was Boyg's statue. It was the same business as the museum and the medallion. No, there's been something like a French Revolution here on the subject; the French are like that. You remember the riot in the Breton village where Renan was born, against having a statue of him. You know, I suppose, that Boyg was a Norwegian by birth, and only settled here because the geological formation, and the supposed mineral properties of that stream there, offered the best field for his investigations. Well, besides the fits the parsons were in at his theories in general, it seems he bumped into some barbarous local superstition as well; about it being a sacred stream that froze snakes into ammonites at a wink; a common myth, of course, for the same was told about St. Hilda at Whitby. But there are peculiar conditions that made it pretty hot in this place. The theological students fight with the medical students, one for Rome and the other for Reason; and they say there's a sort of raving lunatic of a Peter the Hermit, who lives in that hermitage on the hill over there, and every now and then comes out waving his arms and setting the place on fire."

"I heard something about that," remarked Armitage. "The priest who showed me over the monastery; I think he was the head man there—anyhow, he was a most learned and eloquent gentleman—told me about a holy man on the hill who was almost canonized already."

"One is tempted to wish he were martyred already; but the martyrdom, if any, was not his," said Garth darkly. "Allow me to continue my story in order. I had crossed the market-place to find Professor Boyg's private house, which stood at the corner of it. I found the shutters up and the house apparently empty, except for one old servant, who refused at first to tell me anything; indeed, I found a good deal of rustic reluctance on both sides to tell a foreigner anything. But when I had managed to make the nature of my introduction quite plain to him, he finally broke down; and told me his master was dead."

There was a pause, and then Gale, who seemed for the first time somewhat impressed, asked abstractedly: "Where is his tomb? Your tale is really rather strange and dramatic, and obviously it must go on to his tomb. Your pilgrimage ought to end in finding a magnificent monument of marble and gold, like the tomb of Napoleon, and then finding that even the grave had been desecrated."

"He has no tomb," replied Garth sternly, "though he will have many monuments. I hope to see the day when he will have a statue in every town, he whose statue is now insulted in his own town. But he will have no tomb."

"And why not?" asked the staring Armitage.

"His body cannot be found," answered the doctor; "no trace of him can be found anywhere."

"Then how do you know he is dead?" asked the other.

There was an instant of silence, and then the doctor spoke out in a voice fuller and stronger than before:

"Why, as to that," he said, "I think he is dead because I am sure he is murdered."

Armitage shut his note book, but continued to look down steadily at the table. "Go on with your story," he said.

"Boyg's old servant," resumed the doctor, "who is a queer, silent, yellow-faced old card, was at last induced to tell me of the existence of Boyg's assistant, of whom I think he was rather jealous.

The Professor's scientific helper and right-hand man is a man of the name of Bertrand, and a very able man, too, eminently worthy of the great man's confidence, and intensely devoted to his cause. He is carrying on Boyg's work so far as it can be carried on; and about Boyg's death or disappearance he knows the little that can be known. It was when I finally ran him to earth in a little house full of Boyg's books and instruments, at the bottom of the hill just beyond the town, that I first began to realize the nature of this sinister and mysterious business. Bertrand is a quiet man, though he has a little of the pardonable vanity which is not uncommon in assistants. One would sometimes fancy the great discovery was almost as much his as his master's; but that does no harm, since it only makes him fight for his master's fame almost as if it were his. But in fact he is not only concerned about the discovery; or rather, he is not only concerned about that discovery. I had not looked for long at the dark bright eyes and keen face of that quiet young man before I realized that there was something else that he is trying to discover. As a matter of fact, he is no longer merely a scientific assistant, or even a scientific student. Unless I am much mistaken, he is playing the part of an amateur detective.

"Your artistic training, my friends, may be an excellent thing for discovering a poet, or even a sculptor; but you will forgive me for thinking a scientific training rather better for discovering a murderer. Bertrand has gone to work in a very workmanlike way, I consider, and I can tell you in outline what he has discovered so far. Boyg was last seen by Bertrand descending the hillside by the water-course, having just come away from the studio of Gale's friend the sculptor, where he was sitting for an hour every morning. I may say here, rather for the sake of logical method than because it is needed by the logical argument, that the sculptor at any rate had no quarrel with Boyg, but was, on the contrary, an ardent admirer of him as an advanced and revolutionary character."

"I know," said Gale, seeming to take his head suddenly out of the clouds. "Paradou says realistic art must be founded on the modern energy of science; but the fallacy of that—"

"Let me finish with the facts first before you retire into your theories," said the doctor firmly. "Bertrand saw Boyg sit down on the bare hillside for a smoke; and you can see from here how bare a hillside it is; a man walking for hours on it would still be as visible as a fly crawling on a ceiling. Bertrand says he was called away to the crisis of an experiment in the laboratory; when he looked again he could not see his master, and he has never seen him from that day to this.

"At the foot of the hill, and at the bottom of the flight of steps which runs up to the hermitage, is the entrance to the great monastic buildings on the very edge of the town. The very first thing you come to on that side is the great quadrangle, which is enclosed by cloisters, and by the rooms or cells of the clerical or semi-clerical students. I need not trouble you with the tale of the political compromise by which this part of the institution has remained clerical, while the scientific and other schools beyond it are now entirely secular. But it is important to fix in your mind the fact itself: that the monastic part is on the very edge of the town, and the other part bars its way, so to speak, to the inside of the town. Boyg could not possibly have gone past that secular barrier, dead or alive, without being under the eyes of crowds who were more excited about him than about anything else in the world. For the whole place was in a fuss, and even a riot for him as well as against him. Something happened to him on the hillside, or anyhow before he came to the internal barrier. My friend the amateur detective set to work to examine the hillside, or all of it that could seriously count; an enormous undertaking, but he did it as if with a microscope. Well, he found that rocky field, when examined closely, very much what it looks even from here. There are no caves or even holes, there are no chasms or even cracks in that surface of blank stone for miles and miles. A rat could not be hidden in those few tufts of prickly pear. He could not find a hiding-place; but for all that, he found a hint. The hint was nothing more than a faded scrap of paper, damp and draggled from the shallow bed of the brook, but faintly decipherable on it were words in the writing of the Master. They were but part of a sentence, but they included the words, 'will call on you to-morrow to tell you something you ought to know."

"My friend Bertrand sat down and thought it out. the letter had been in the water, so it had not been thrown away in the town, for the highly scientific reason that the river does not flow uphill. There only remained on the higher ground the sculptor's studio and the hermitage. But Boyg would not write to the sculptor to warn him that he was going to call, since he went to his studio every morning. Presumably the person he was going to call on was the hermit; and a guess might well be made about the nature of what he had to say.

Bertrand knew better than anybody that Boyg had just brought his great discovery to a crushing completeness, with fresh facts and ratifications; and it seems likely enough that he went to announce it to his most fanatical opponent, to warn him to give up the struggle."

Gale, who was gazing up into the sky with his eye on a bird, again abruptly intervened.

"In these attacks on Boyg," he said, "were there any attacks on his private character?"

"Even these madmen couldn't attack that," replied Garth with some heat. "He was the best sort of Scandinavian, as simple as a child, and I really believe as innocent. But they hated him for all that; and you can see for yourself that their hatred begins to appear on the horizon of our inquiry. He went to tell the truth in the hour of triumph; and he never reappeared to the light of the sun."

Armitage's far-away gaze was fixed on the solitary cell half-way up the hill. "You don't mean seriously," he said, "that the man they talk about as a saint, the friend of my friend the abbot, or whatever he is, is neither more nor less than an assassin?"

"You talked to your friend the abbot about Romanesque sculpture," replied Garth. "If you had talked to him about fossils, you might have seen another side to his character. These Latin priests are often polished enough, but you bet they're pointed as well. As for the other man on the hill, he's allowed by his superiors to live what they call the eremitical life; but he's jolly well allowed to do other things, too. On great occasions he's allowed to come down here and preach, and I can tell you there is Bedlam let loose when he does. I might be ready to excuse the man as a sort of a maniac; but I haven't the slightest difficulty in believing that he is a homicidal maniac."

"Did your friend Bertrand take any legal steps on his suspicions?" asked Armitage, after a pause.

"Ah, that's where the mystery begins," replied the doctor.

After a moment of frowning silence, he resumed, "Yes, he did make a formal charge to the police, and the Juge d'Instruction examined a good many people and so on, and said the charge had broken down. It broke down over the difficulty of disposing of the body; the chief difficulty in most murders. Now the hermit, who is called Hyacinth, I believe, was summoned in due course; but he had no difficulty in showing that his hermitage was as bare and as hard as the hill-side. It seemed as if nobody could possibly have

concealed a corpse in those stone walls, or dug a grave in that rocky
floor. Then it was the turn of the abbot, as you call him, Father
Bernard of the Catholic College. And he managed to convince the
magistrate that the same was true of the cells surrounding the
college quadrangle, and all the other rooms under his control. They
were all like empty boxes, with barely a stick or two of furniture;
less than usual, in fact, for some of the sticks had been broken up for
the bonfire demonstration I told you of. Anyhow, that was the line
of defence, and I daresay it was well conducted, for Bernard is a
very able man, and knows about many other things besides
Romanesque architecture; and Hyacinth, fanatic as he is, is famous
as a persuasive orator. Anyhow, it was successful, the case broke
down; but I am sure my friend Bertrand is only biding his time, and
means to bring it up again. These difficulties about the concealment
of a corpse—Hullo! why here he is in person."

He broke off in surprise as a young man walking rapidly down
the street paused a moment, and then approached the café table at
which they sat. He was dressed with all the funereal French
respectability: his black stove-pipe hat, his high and stiff black
neckcloth resembling a stock, and the curious corners of dark beard
at the edges of his chin, gave him an antiquated air like a character
out of Gaboriau. But if he was out of Gaboriau, he was nobody less
than Lecocq; the dark eyes in his pale face might indeed be called
the eyes of a born detective. At this moment, the pale face was paler
than usual with excitement, and as he stopped a moment behind the
doctor's chair, he said to him in a low voice:

"I have found out."

Dr. Garth sprang to his feet, his eyes brilliant with curiosity;
then, recovering his conventional manner, he presented M. Bertrand
to his friends, saying to the former, "You may speak freely with us,
I think; we have no interest except an interest in the truth."

"I have found the truth," said the Frenchman, with compressed
lips. "I know now what these murderous monks have done with the
body of Boyg."

"Are we to be allowed to hear it?" asked Armitage gravely.

"Everyone will hear it in three days' time," replied the pale
Frenchman. "As the authorities refuse to reopen the question, we
are holding a public meeting in the market-place to demand that
they do so. The assassins will be there, doubtless, and I shall not
only denounce but convict them to their faces. Be there yourself,

monsieur, on Thursday at half-past two, and you will learn how one of the world's greatest men was done to death by his enemies. For the moment I will only say one word. As the great Edgar Poe said in your own language, 'Truth is not always in a well.' I believe it is sometimes too obvious to be seen."

Gabriel Gale, who had rather the appearance of having gone to sleep, seemed to rouse himself with an unusual animation.

"That's true," he said, "and that's the truth about the whole business."

Armitage turned to him with an expression of quiet amusement.

"Surely you're not playing the detective, Gale," he said, "I never pictured such a thing as your coming out of fairyland to assist Scotland Yard."

"Perhaps Gale thinks he can find the body," suggested Dr. Garth, laughing.

Gale lifted himself slowly and loosely from his seat, and answered in his dazed fashion:

"Why, yes, in a way," he said; "in fact, I'm pretty sure I can find the body. In fact, in a manner of speaking, I've found it."

Those with any intimations of the personality of Mr. Arthur Armitage will not need to be told that he kept a diary; and endeavoured to note down his impressions of foreign travel with atmospheric sympathy and the *mot juste*. But the pen dropped from his hand, so to speak, or at least wandered over the page in a mazy desperation, in the attempt to describe the great mob meeting, or rather the meeting of two mobs, which took place in the picturesque market-place in which he had wandered alone a few days before, criticizing the style of the statue, or admiring the sky-line of the basilica. He had read and written about democracy all his life; and when first he met it, it swallowed him like an earthquake. One actual and appalling difference divided this French mob in a provincial market from all the English mobs he had ever seen in Hyde Park or Trafalgar Square. These Frenchmen had not come there to get rid of their feelings, but to get rid of their enemies. Something would be done as a result of this sort of public meeting; it might be murder, but it would be something.

And although, or rather because, it had this militant ferocity, it had also a sort of military discipline. The clusters of men voluntarily deployed into cordons, and in some rough fashion followed the command of leaders. Father Bernard was there, with a face of bronze, like the mask of a Roman emperor, eagerly obeyed by his crowd of crusading devotees, and beside him the wild preacher, Hyacinth, who looked himself like a dead man brought out of the grave, with a face built out of bones, and cavernous eye-sockets deep and dark enough to hide the eyes. On the other side were the grim pallor of Bertrand and the rat-like activity of the red-haired Dr. Garth; their own anti-clerical mob was roaring behind them, and their eyes were alight with triumph. Before Armitage could collect himself sufficiently to make proper notes of any of these things, Bertrand had sprung upon a chair placed near the pedestal of the statue, and announced almost without words, by one dramatic gesture, that he had come to avenge the dead.

Then the words came, and they came thick and fast, telling and terrible; but Armitage heard them as in a dream till they reached the point for which he was waiting; the point that would awaken any dreamer. He heard the prose poems of laudation, the hymn to Boyg the hero, the tale of his tragedy so far as he knew it already. He heard the official decision about the impossibility of the clerics concealing the corpse, as he had heard it already. And then he and the whole crowd leapt together at something they did not know before; or rather, as in all such riddles, something they did know and did not understand.

"They plead that their cells are bare and their lives simple," Bertrand was saying, "and it is true that these slaves of superstition are cut off from the natural joys of men. But they have their joys; oh, believe me, they have their festivities. If they cannot rejoice in love, they can rejoice in hatred. And everybody seems to have forgotten that on the very day the Master vanished, the theological students in their own quadrangle burnt him. In effigy.

A thrill that was hardly a whisper, but was wilder than a cry, went through the whole crowd; and men had taken in the whole meaning before they could keep pace with the words that followed.

"Did they burn Bruno in effigy? Did they burn Dolet in effigy?" Bertrand was saying, with a white, fanatical face. "Those martyrs of the truth were burned alive for the good of their Church and for the glory of their God. Oh, yes, progress has improved them; and they did not burn Boyg alive. But they burned him dead; and that is how they obliterated the traces of the way they had done him to death. I have said that truth is not always hidden in a well, but rather high on a tower. And while I have searched every crevice and cactus bush for the bones of my master, it was in truth in public, under the open sky, before a roaring crowd in the quadrangle, that his body vanished from the sight of men."

When the last cheer and howl of a whole hell of such noises had died away, Father Bernard succeeded in making his voice heard.

"It is enough to say in answer to this maniac charge that the atheists who bring it against us cannot induce their own atheistic Government to support them. But as the charge is against Father Hyacinth rather than against me, I will ask him to reply to it."

There was another tornado of conflicting noises when the eremitical preacher opened his mouth; but his very tones had a certain power of piercing, and quelling it. There was something strange in such a voice coming out of such a skull-and-cross-bones of a countenance; for it was unmistakably the musical and moving voice that had stirred so many congregations and pilgrimages. Only in this crisis it had an awful accent of reality, which was beyond any arts of oratory. But before the tumult had yet died away Armitage, moved by some odd nervous instinct, had turned abruptly to Garth and said, "What's become of Gale? He said he was going to be here. Didn't he talk some nonsense about bringing the body himself?"

Dr. Garth shrugged his shoulders. "I imagine he's talking some other nonsense at the top of the hill somewhere else. You mustn't ask poets to remember all the nonsense they talk."

"My friends," Father Hyacinth was saying, in quiet but penetrating tones, "I have no answer to give to this charge. I have no proofs with which to refute it. If a man can be sent to the guillotine on such evidence, to the guillotine I will go. Do you fancy I do not know that innocent men have been guillotined? M. Bertrand spoke of the burning of Bruno, as if it is only the enemies of the Church that have been burned. Does any Frenchman forget that Joan of Arc was burned; and was she guilty? The first Christians were tortured for being cannibals, a charge as probable as the charge against me. Do you imagine because you kill men now by modern machinery and modern law, that we do not know that you are as likely to kill unjustly as Herod or Heliogabalus? Do you think we do not know that the powers of the world are what they always were, that your lawyers who oppress the poor for hire will shed innocent blood for gold? If I were here to bandy such lawyer's talk, I could use it against you more reasonably than you against me. For what reason am I supposed to have imperilled my soul by such a monstrous crime? For a theory about a theory; for a hypothesis about a hypothesis, for some thin fantastic notion that a discovery about fossils threatened the everlasting truth. I could point to others who had better reasons for murder than that. I could point to a man who by the death of Boyg has inherited the whole power and position of Boyg. I could point to one who is truly the heir and the man whom the crime benefits; who is known to claim much of the discovery as his own; who has been not so much the assistant as the rival of the dead. He alone has given evidence that Boyg was seen on the hill at all on that fatal day. He alone inherits by the death anything solid, from the largest ambitions in the scientific world, to the smallest magnifying glass in his collection. The man lives, and I could stretch out my hand and touch him."

Hundreds of faces were turned upon Bertrand with a frightful expression of inhuman eagerness; the turn of the debate had been too dramatic to raise a cry. Bertrand's very lips were pale, but they smiled as they formed the words:

"And what did I do with the body?"

"God grant you did nothing with it, dead or alive," answered the other. "I do not charge you; but if ever you are charged as I am unjustly, you may need a God on that day. Though I were ten times guillotined, God could testify to my innocence; if it were by bidding me walk these streets, like St. Denis, with my head in my hand. I have no other proof. I can call no other witness. He can deliver me if He will."

There was a sudden silence, which was somehow stronger than a pause; and in it Armitage could be heard saying sharply, and almost querulously:

"Why, here's Gale again, after all. Have you dropped from the sky?"

Gale was indeed sauntering in a clear space round the corner of the statue with all the appearance of having just arrived at a crowded At Home; and Bertrand was quick to seize the chance of an anti-climax to the hermit's oratory.

"This," he cried, "is a gentleman who thinks he can find the body himself. Have you brought it with you, monsieur?"

The joke about the poet as detective had already been passed round among many people, and the suggestion received a new kind of applause. Somebody called out in a high, piping voice, "He's got it in his pocket"; and another, in deep sepulchral tones, "His waistcoat pocket."

Mr. Gale certainly had his hands in his pockets, whether or no he had anything else in them; and it was with great nonchalance that he replied:

"Well, in that sense, I suppose I haven't got it. But you have."

The next moment he had astonished his friends, who were not used to seeing him so alert, by leaping on the chair, and himself addressing the crowd in clear tones, and in excellent French:

"Well, my friends," he said, "the first thing I have to do is to associate myself with everything said by my honourable friend, if he will allow me to call him so, about the merits and high moral qualities of the late Professor Boyg. Boyg, at any rate, is in every way worthy of all the honour you can pay to him. Whatever else is doubtful, whatever else we differ about, we can all salute in him that search for truth which is the most disinterested of all our duties to God. I agree with my friend Dr. Garth that he deserves to have a statue, not only in his own town, but in every town in the world."

The anti-clericals began to cheer warmly, while their opponents watched in silence, wondering where this last eccentric development might lead. The poet seemed to realize their mystification, and smiled as he continued:

"Perhaps you wonder why I should say that so emphatically. Well, I suppose you all have your own reasons for recognizing this genuine love of truth in the late Professor. But I say it because I happen to know something that perhaps you don't know, which makes me specially certain about his honesty."

"And what is that?" asked Father Bernard, in the pause that followed.

"Because," said Gale, "he was going to see Father Hyacinth to own himself wrong."

Bertrand made a swift movement forward that seemed almost to threaten an assault: but Garth arrested it, and Gale went on, without noticing it.

"Professor Boyg had discovered that his theory was wrong after all. That was the sensational discovery he had made in those last days and with those last experiments. I suspected it when I compared the current tale with his reputation as a simple and kindly man. I did not believe he would have gone merely to triumph over his worst enemy; it was far more probable that he thought it a point of honour to acknowledge his mistake. For, without professing to know much about these things, I am sure it was a mistake. Things do not, after all, need all those thousand years to petrify in that particular fashion. Under certain conditions, which chemists could explain better than I, they do not need more than one year, or even one day. Something in the properties of the local water, applied or intensified by special methods, can really in a few hours turn an animal organism into a fossil. The scientific experiment has been made; and the proof is before you."

He made a gesture with his hand, and went on, with something more like excitement:

"M. Bertrand is right in saying that truth is not in a well, but on a tower. It is on a pedestal. You have looked at it every day. There is the body of Boyg!"

And he pointed to the statue in the middle of the market-place, wreathed with laurel and defaced with stones, as it had stood so long in that quiet square, and looked down at so many casual passers-by.

"Somebody suggested just now," he went on, glancing over a sea of gaping faces, "that I carried the statue in my waistcoat pocket. Well, I don't carry all of it, of course, but this is a part of it," and he took out a small object like a stick of grey chalk; "this is a finger of it knocked off by a stone. I picked it up by the pedestal. If anybody who understands these things likes to look at it, he will agree that the consistency is precisely the same as the admitted fossils in the geological museum."

He held it out to them, but the whole mob stood still as if it also was a mob of men turned to stone.

"Perhaps you think I'm mad," he said pleasantly. "Well, I'm not exactly mad, but I have an odd sort of sympathy with madmen. I can manage them better than most people can, because I can fancy somehow the wild way their minds will work. I understand the man who did this. I know he did, because I talked to him for half the morning; and it's exactly the sort of thing he would do. And when first I heard talk of fossil shells and petrified insects and so on, I did the same thing that such men always do. I exaggerated it into a sort of extravagant vision, a vision of fossil forests, and fossil cattle, and fossil elephants and camels; and so, naturally, to another thought: a coincidence that somehow turned me cold. A Fossil Man.

"It was then that I looked up at the statue; and knew it was not a statue. It was a corpse petrified by the curious chemistry of your strange mountain-stream. I call it a fossil as a loose popular term; of course I know enough geology to know it is not the correct term. But I was not exactly concerned with a problem of geology. I was concerned with what some prefer to call criminology and I prefer to call crime. If that extraordinary erection was the corpse, who and where was the criminal? Who was the assassin who had set up the dead man to be at once obvious and invisible; and had, so to speak, hidden him in the broad daylight? Well, you have all heard the arguments about the stream and the scrap of paper, and up to a point I have entirely followed them. Everyone agreed that the secret was somewhere hidden on that bare hill where there was nothing but the glass-roofed studio and the lonely hermitage; and suspicion centred entirely upon the hermitage. For the man in the studio was a fervent friend of the man who was murdered, and one of those rejoicing most heartily at what he had discovered. But perhaps you have rather forgotten what he really had discovered. His real discovery was of the sort that infuriates friends and not foes. The man who has the courage to say he is wrong has to face the worst hatred; the hatred of those who think he is right. Boyg's final discovery, like our final discovery, rather reverses the relations of those two little houses on the hill. Even if Father Hyacinth had been a fiend instead of a saint, he had no possible motive to prevent his enemy from offering him a public apology. It was a believer in Boygism who struck down Boyg. It was his follower who became his pursuer and persecutor; who at least turned in unreasonable fury upon him. It was Paradou the sculptor who snatched up a chisel and struck his philosophical teacher, at the end of some furious argument about the theory which the artist had valued only as a wild inspiration, being quite indifferent to the tame question of its truth. I don't think he meant to kill Boyg; I doubt whether anybody could possibly prove he did; and even if he did, I rather doubt whether he can be held responsible for that or for anything else. But though Paradou may be a lunatic, he is also a logician; and there is one more interesting logical step in this story.

"I met Paradou myself this morning; owing to my good luck in putting my leg through his skylight. He also has his theories and controversies; and this morning he was very controversial. As I say, I had a long argument with him, all about realism in sculpture. I know many people will tell you that nothing has ever come out of arguments; and I tell you that everything has always come out of arguments; and anyhow, if you want to know what has come out of this, you've got to understand this argument. Everybody was always jeering at poor old Paradou as a sculptor and saying he turned men into monsters; that his figures had flat heads like snakes, or sagging knees like elephants, or humps like human camels. And he was always shouting back at them, 'Yes, and eyes like blind-worms when it comes to seeing your own hideous selves! This is what you *do* look like, you ugly brutes! These are the crooked, clownish, lumpish attitudes in which you really do stand; only a lot of lying fashionable portrait-painters have persuaded you that you look like Graces and Greek gods.' He was at it hammer and tongs with me this morning; and I dare say I was lucky he didn't finish that argument with a chisel. But anyhow the argument wasn't started then. It all came upon him with a rush, when he had committed his real though probably unintentional killing. As he stood staring at the corpse, there arose out of the very abyss of his disappointment the vision of a strange vengeance or reparation. He began to see the vast outlines of a joke as gigantic as the Great Pyramid. He would set up that grim granite jest in the market-place, to grin for ever at his critics and detractors. The dead man himself had just been explaining to him the process by which the water of that place would rapidly petrify organic substances. The notes and documents of his proof lay scattered about the studio where he had fallen. His own proof should be applied to his own body, for a purpose of which he had never dreamed. If the sculptor simply lifted the body in the ungainly attitude in which it had actually fallen, if he froze or fixed it in the stream, or set it upon the public pedestal, it would be the very thing about which he had so bitterly debated; a real man, in a real posture, held up to the scorn of men.

"That insane genius promised himself a lonely laughter, and a secret superiority to all his enemies, in hearing the critics discuss it as the crazy creation of a crank sculptor. He looked forward to the groups that would stand before the statue, and prove the anatomy to be wrong, and clearly demonstrate the posture to be impossible. And he would listen, and laugh inwardly like a true lunatic, knowing that they were proving the utter unreality of a real man. That being his dream, he had no difficulty in carrying it out. He had no need to hide the body; he had it brought down from his studio, not secretly but publicly and even pompously, the finished work of a great sculptor escorted by the devotees of a great discoverer. But indeed, Boyg was something more than a man who made a discovery; and there is, in comparison, a sort of cant even in the talk of a man having the courage to discover it. What other man would have had the courage to undiscover it? That monument that hides a strange sin, hides a much stranger and much rarer virtue. Yes, you do well to hail it as a true scientific trophy. That is the statue of Boyg the Undiscoverer. That cold chimera of the rock is not only the abortion born of some horrible chemical change; it is the outcome of a nobler experiment, which attests for ever the honour and probity of science. You may well praise him as a man of science; for he, at least, in an affair of science, acted like a man. You may well set up statues to him as a hero of science; for he was more of a hero in being wrong than he could ever have been in being right. And though the stars have seen rise, from the soils and substance of our native star, no such monstrosity as that man of stone, heaven may look down with more wonder at the man than at the monster. And we of all schools and of all philosophies can pass it like a funeral procession taking leave of an illustrious grave and, like soldiers, salute it as we pass."

MAX PEMBERTON
PRESENTS THE PUZZLE OF

The Donnington Affair

The Donnington Affair

The following statement of the Donnington affair has been written from the original notes by the Priest-in-charge of the Parish of Borrow-in-the-Vale.

John Barrington Cope came to Sussex from King's College, Cambridge, at a time when the aged vicar could no longer undertake single-handed even the pleasant duties of that rural charge.

He had been nearly two years at Borrow when the tragedy occurred. A man of considerable scholastic attainment, he appears immediately to have realised the magnitude of the mystery and to have set down, without loss of time, an orderly statement of the facts as they presented themselves to him.

The accepted lover of Evelyn Donnington's sister Harriet, he enjoyed the liberties of Borrow Close, and was almost daily at the house. It was at his suggestion that "another" was summoned from London to investigate a case which promised at an early moment to baffle alike the vigilance of the police and the curiosity of the public.

Mr. Cope's notes were written primarily for Father Brown's perusal. An amplification of them seems to be the swiftest method of putting the reading public in possession of the salient features of this amazing occurrence.

I

My name is John Barrington Cope, and I had been priest-in-charge of the parish of Borrow-in-the-Vale for twenty-one months.

I last saw Evelyn Donnington alive on Sunday evening at a quarter past ten o'clock. I had supped at Borrow Close as it has been my privilege to do almost every Sunday evening since I came to the parish. The fact that my fiancée, Harriet Donnington, was and is at Bath made no difference.

Sir Borrow Donnington has few friends. He is not a man who

loves the society of other men, nor, for that matter, of women. It may be that I understand him a little better than his fellows. I am welcome at Borrow Close, and there is no other house which has a prior claim upon me.

I saw Evelyn Donnington alive and well at a quarter past ten on the evening of Sunday last, the 24th day of July. She came to the porch with me to tell me of a letter she had received from Harriet on the previous day, and there I said "good-night" to her.

The rectory stands perhaps a third part of a mile across the park, and is best reached by a bridle-path through what is known as Adam's Thicket. The way is dark and shut in by the magnificent beeches for which Borrow is famous. I saw no living thing as I returned to the rectory, nor heard any sound that was ominous.

Two hours later a footman from the Close awakened me to say that Evelyn was dead. "Murdered, sir!" he gasped, and without another word he ran on headlong towards the doctor's house.

I had fallen into a light sleep when this man's ring awakened me. There had been much trouble at Borrow Close since I came to the parish. The world is well acquainted with the nature of this, and knows much of the shame which has overtaken the Donnington family. Whatever sympathy it may have withheld from Sir Borrow Donnington himself, it has lavished freely upon his daughters.

To me Evelyn was already as a sister. I was to have married Harriet in September, though God knows what may be in store for us now.

Men deride omens, though often they are but the mind's logic waging a war upon our optimism. Though the affair of Southby Donnington would appear to have been settled by his conviction and imprisonment, I dreaded from the first that such could not be the end of it; and it was of Southby Donnington, Sir Borrow's only son, that I had been dreaming in my sleep when the footman awakened me.

What a sardonic chapter in the history of human nature! An only son—a wealthy father! Upon the one side a profligacy almost without parallel, upon the other side a parsimony stupendous in its ironic selfishness.

Southby Donnington was sent to Eton and to Trinity (Cambridge) as an Army candidate. A disgraceful affair at a gambling den in London, with a subsequent appearance at a police-court, finished his university career in his first term. He could not even pass the trivial examination now demanded for Sandhurst. He would suggest no other vocation. The man became a derelict in the dangerous seas of London's underworld. In vain his sisters pleaded with Sir Borrow. The baronet had finished with his son. A man of iron resolution which nothing could bend, he swore that Southby should never enter his house again. There followed the cataclysm.

We heard of the boy's arrest in London upon a charge of forgery. He was committed for trial, defended with what money his sisters could supply him, sent to the Old Bailey, convicted. The sentence was one of three years' penal servitude. We learned that he had been taken to Wormwood Scrubs, and nine months later that he was at Parkhurst.

It is no place here to dwell upon the secrets of the stricken house or of the aftermath of this terrible downfall.

Borrow Close is an old mansion lying between Ashdown Forest and Crowborough. It has always been remote from men and affairs, and there is no domain in the south of England so wonderful in its solitudes.

All about it is the forest. The very park is primeval woodland; here abounding in undergrowth so thick that the foot of man might never have been set therein; there characterised by marshy pools and groves where noonday is but a shimmer of reluctant light. Few were admitted to the house even in the days when Lady Donnington was its mistress. Since her death it has become medieval in its isolation. The old baronet had nothing in common with his neighbours; his daughters were always afraid of him, and they go through life as it were on tiptoe, fearing that if they speak above a whisper they will awake the curiosity of the world beyond their gates.

It is true that Southby flouted the sanctities of this retreat, despite the baronet's displeasure. Parties of wild undergraduates made the "welkin ring" during the vacations; the story of Evelyn and Harriet's beauty was not unknown in the courts at Cambridge. Few of the boys, however, had the courage to persist, and I think that even Southby himself was astonished when Captain Willy Kennington appeared suddenly upon the scene as a suitor for Evelyn's hand, and was not to be repulsed even by Sir Borrow's savage discouragement.

Captain Kennington had met Evelyn at her aunt's house in Kensington some three months before the downfall. Her womanly gifts should have made an appeal to any man who became well acquainted with them, and I do not wonder that the young soldier surrendered to the spell.

Very simple in all her ideas, not a little afraid of the world, yet gifted with an imagination which years of solitary reading had stimulated, she seemed to be at once the woman and the child; wise above her years, yet afflicted by those ideals for which woman often pays so dearly. Fear of her father forbade that immediate acceptance of the soldier's advances which her heart dictated. She returned to Borrow Close, and was followed there shortly by the captain himself.

What was my astonishment to hear a few days later that Sir Borrow had refused all discussion of the matter, and in one of those violent paroxysms of temper, with which neither God nor man could reason, had ordered the captain from his house.

To give him his due, Southby played a man's part in this affair. He interceded warmly for his sister, returning from South Africa for that purpose. The scene between father and son is remembered at the Close as the culminating episode of an estrangement as discreditable to one as to the other. Passion dominated it, and set finality upon it. No word was spoken between these two men until the end.

Three months later Southby was a convict, and I remained the one man who visited the baronet in the days of his shame.

II

These are the events of sixteen months ago. I have already disclaimed any intention of dwelling upon the intimate days of sorrow which followed after. "The evil that men do lives after them," and while for the world the tragedy was but a nine days' wonder, it lay heavy upon the house of Borrow. No longer did the old baronet receive the visits of the few friends hitherto admitted to the Close. He shut the doors alike upon the old world and the new. His daughters saw no one but the servants and myself. In their turn, his neighbours shrank from him. Men had come to say that lust of gold drove Southby to the crime, and to believe that the boy was less guilty than the father.

The one man who stood by the stricken family was Captain

Kennington, who owed so little to the baronet. Now, in the darkest hour, he came forward to demand Evelyn's hand anew. It went without saying that she would not accept him. A rare type of womanhood, the very fact that she loved was the barrier between them. Nothing, she felt, could ever blot out the shame of this happening, or minimise its consequences. The harvest of sin was not gathered in Parkhurst Prison, but here in the ancient house, where women reaped with sickles of tears.

My own relations to Harriet were, God be praised, but superficially affected by Southby's downfall. We had learned to know each other so well before the trouble came that it but set a seal upon our mutual sense of help and sacrifice, and although I knew that she would not marry me immediately, I left the future to lead us as it might. Sir Donnington himself now seemed to find in my society the sole consolation of his declining years. He did not go to church, but I visited them for worship early every Sunday morning, and was always at the Close to supper when in residence at the rectory.

So the months rolled on, and time, the healer, came to our aid. The bitterness of fear and doubt had passed down and given place to a brave attempt to face the future. We made many plans for Southby upon his release, and were determined to start him in a farm in South Africa if we could. Kennington went so far as to visit the prison and see the convict. His own father was one of the visiting inspectors, as it chanced, and so an advantage was permitted him.

He told us that he found Southby quite resigned to his fate, and he spoke of him as a man who was convinced that he had not committed a crime, but had been the victim of those who had betrayed him when they discovered that nothing was to be extorted from the baronet.

Parkhurst, it seems, is the gentleman's prison, and Southby was in aristocratic company there. I confess that the intimation was not without its saving humour, and permitted some reflection upon the permanence of those social aspirations which could afflict men even in a prison. Better, it appeared, to pick oakum with a lord than to earn an honest living among plebeians.

Kennington spoke of cheerfulness and of content, but I remembered afterwards one phrase in his letter which should have struck me as significant. Prison makes strange bedfellows, and so far as man may have a confidant in captivity, Southby had found one in a man by the name of Mester.

"This fellow," said Kennington, "is the cheeriest soul possible. He has been well educated in France, where he fell upon evil times. Then he became chauffeur to an Austrian baron, entered a motor-car factory at Suresnes, turned his attention to flying at Issy, and finally was accused of a savage assault and an attempt to rob an old lady at Dover who was about to establish him in a motor-car business there."

Mester declared to the end that the crime was the work of others. He protested that he was the victim of circumstances, and that the clues upon which the police convicted him were false. Nevertheless, he was found guilty and sentenced to four years' penal servitude upon the day following Southby's conviction.

Between these men a strange friendship took root. Each believed himself wrongfully convicted; each could sympathise with the other. And just as Mester declared that he would bring the old baronet to his senses when he got out, so could Southby interest himself in Mester's story, and implore certain old colleagues on the Press to investigate it.

As we know, one great novelist has already busied himself with the affair, and is convinced of the man's innocence. Admittedly a person of no stable character and unquestionably the associate of thieves, there would yet seem to be a doubt whether the graver crime were committed, and quite a reasonable supposition that the police may have been in error.

Mester himself did not hesitate to affirm that if he were free for a month he would establish his innocence beyond all question. So convinced was he of this that he appears to have told Southby quite plainly that he would escape from Parkhurst if the opportunity presented itself.

I thought nothing of the matter at the time, and, indeed, the threat must be one often made by prisoners to whom crime has not become a habit and the cell a refuge. But I confess that astonishment was no word for it when, a few weeks later, upon opening my morning paper, I read that two men had escaped from Parkhurst, and, despite the efforts of the police, were still at large.

"Southby and Mester," I said to myself. I was not wrong, as you shall presently hear.

III

Here was an upset if you will, and one to send me running to the Close with the tidings. Sir Borrow himself I would not tell, dreading the effect of the news upon a mind so deranged; but Evelyn and Harriet heard me eagerly, and the former I began to suspect was already in possession of the story. This fact did not in the beginning impress me as it should have done. Some letter, I thought, must have come from Southby himself, and yet had I reflected upon it I would have perceived that such a thing was hardly possible under the circumstances.

The man had escaped but yesterday, and even had a letter been posted from the Isle of Wight or the mainland on the previous evening, it would not have reached Borrow Close at nine o'clock. Later on I discovered, quite accidentally, that Captain Kennington hinted at some such possibility in a letter received on the previous day, and whatever thoughts the discovery suggested, I kept them strictly to myself. The immediate thing was the excitement the news occasioned at the Close, and the momentous events which must follow upon it.

For my own part, I was early of the opinion that the fugitive would swiftly be overtaken, and that that would be the end of the matter. Their escape, briefly narrated in the newspapers, had been admirably contrived. It appears that they scaled a high wall at a moment when a heavy mist drifted across the island from the mainland, that they then crossed an enclosure in which other prisoners were at work, climbed a second wall by the aid of a silk ladder, which they left behind them, and so made their way to the sea.

Authority believed that their flight was there cut short, and that they had not succeeded in reaching the mainland; but another account spoke of a mysterious motor-boat which had been seen recently off St. Catherine's Point, and, remembering Mester's acquaintance with the motor fraternity and its less desirable characters, the writer of the report seemed to be of the opinion that this might have some connection with the matter. The latter, I must confess, occurred to me as a plausible deduction. These flying people are unusually clever. They possess a daring which is proved, and their resources are many. I detected now the meaning of Southby's friendship for this undesirable mechanic, and I saw that the men were pledged to make the attempt together. For the moment it looked as though they had succeeded.

It was a little before nine o'clock when I arrived at the Close, and not until after lunch that I left. As usual, Sir Borrow spent the morning about his gardens, and kept me some while with him speaking of this plant or that with which I was always familiar, but never naming the son who would succeed to this splendid inheritance. When he retired to his study at twelve o'clock, I took the girls aside and resumed a conversation so full of meaning for us all. Naturally, we asked each other many questions which we were unable to answer. Where would Southby go if he reached the mainland? Could he get money? Would he return to Borrow?

"If he comes here," said I, "he is lost! It will be the first place the police will watch!"

Harriet agreed with me in this. Yet where else could he go with any prospect of getting money, by which alone ultimate success could be assured?

We thought of many places, but of one with conviction. Sir Borrow's sister, the aged Lady Rosmar, then lived at Bath. She had been staunch to the boy as far as her means permitted, and might be still a friend to him in such an emergency as this. We decided that Harriet should go to Bath without loss of time, in case she could be of any assistance there. Evelyn and I, meanwhile, would watch and wait at Borrow. God knows what we hoped to do if the boy came there, yet I think we both prayed for his coming.

It seemed such an impossible thing that he could evade the hue and cry which must attend this flight. Yet if he did evade it, might not we take up his burden and start him in that new life wherein so much might be achieved if the lesson had been truly learned? Foolish the hope may have been, yet it came natural to those who had suffered so much, and over whom the prison gate was ever the emblem of a terrible sorrow. We believed that Southby would come, and in ten days' time our faith was justified. He was there at Borrow Close, the police upon his heels, his own father ignorant that the house harboured him. Of such dire things have I now to tell in the story that comes after.

IV

I have said that we supposed the house would be watched by the police, and in this we were not mistaken.

Frequently, in the few days immediately prior to Southby's return, I had seen strange men in the park, and more than once I had been stopped upon an idle pretence and questioned concerning Sir Borrow and his affairs. Such a subterfuge would have deceived no one, and, fortunately, I was able to deal with the men quite frankly.

"You are a police-officer," I said to one of them.

And he did not deny it.

"The lad's sure to come here, sir," was his answer, "and, if he does, we shall take him. There isn't a road within ten miles we are not watching."

We fell to other talk, and chiefly of the escape. Officially the police thought there had been some connivance on the part of the warders, but of this I naturally knew nothing.

"The young men had a lot of friends between them," the detective said, "and as for Lionel Mester, he knows half the crooks in Europe!"

I replied that in such a case the friends in question might be expected to shelter their comrades.

"And," said I, "it is idle to look for your men here. Surely you know of the relations between Sir Borrow and his son?"

He was much interested in this, and questioned me closely—a proceeding I did not resent under the circumstances. A few days later I was stopped in the park by an American lady and her daughter, who pretended to be much interested in the old place, and asked me if it were not possible to get permission to visit it. In these I recognised also the agents of the police, and I put them off with what excuses I could; not that it would have mattered at such a time, for Southby had not then returned. He was to come three days afterwards, at dead of night, and the two who were to know of his coming would have stood at nothing for his sake. They were his sister Evelyn and Wellman, the butler, who had loved Southby as his own son.

It was from Wellman himself that I had the news at nine o'clock on the following morning. He came carrying a pretended letter from Sir Borrow, and not until we were alone in my study, and the door shut behind us, did he dare to speak freely.

"Mr. Southby's home, sir," he said in a whisper. "He's in the priest's room."

I feared to speak for a moment. Instantly I had visions of the hunted lad, fleeing from thicket to thicket of the forest he knew so well, and finally gaining that deep glen wherein is the subterranean entrance to the Close. That he had thought of it when none of us remembered! Of course, the police would know nothing of that. The very servants, save Wellman alone, are in ignorance of the existence of the passage, and locally it is believed that it perished long ago. Sir Borrow let them think so.

It was one of his humours to have the place opened up by the engineers who came from London to sink his artesian well. He liked to go to and fro as he pleased, to catch his servants when they least expected him. And so he used the priest's room for the purpose, or did use it until the tragedy happened. Nothing afterwards interested him. The secret chamber remained unopened after Southby was convicted. The rest of us, I think, had almost forgotten its existence.

The chamber lies at the western end of the long gallery. There is an octagon tower there, with an ancient stone staircase cunningly built within its walls. To this you gain access from the gallery by opening a panel upon the right-hand side of the smaller chimney. The room lies at the foot of one flight of stairs, and is lighted from two narrow windows giving upon the battlements. These are filled by stained glass of the fourteenth century, and show former abbots of Borrow in alb and chasuble. The room itself is large and commodious, and has a fireplace and an alcove for the bed. Those who desire to go from it to the forest descend the staircase until they find themselves in the old crypt which dates from Saxon times. The subterranean passage leads from that to Adam's Thicket, where it enters an ancient well, long dried up, and now but a pit of grass and bramble. I did not doubt that Southby had gained the forest by a devious route and had made his way by one of those paths which no stranger would discover. And so he had gone straight to the priest's chamber, and thence to Evelyn's bedroom.

"He waked her about one this morning," said Wellman, who still appeared to be trembling with the excitement of the news. "They wouldn't let you know sooner, sir, for fear of the police. Miss Evelyn is dreadfully afraid that the squire will find out, and so I came to you at once. Lucky for us, it was only yesterday afternoon that Superintendent Matthews searched the Close from garret to cellar. He must have had wind that Mr. Southby was on the road."

I was astonished to hear this.

"Superintendent Matthews—yesterday!" I exclaimed. "Is it real-

ly possible, and Miss Evelyn told me nothing of it? But, of course, it
may have been difficult to send. Does he know anything of the
priest's hole, Wellman? Surely you don't fear that?"

He shook his head, being a man of uncommon caution.

"They know a great deal too much nowadays, sir—more's the
pity. The question is, what are we to do with the young master,
since Miss Evelyn is at her wits' end? She would be pleased to see
you at the Close, indeed and she would. It's a hard task for a young
lady, as you can well imagine, sir."

I agreed, and, putting on my hat, went over with him immediately. Our way lay through Adam's Thicket, and I confess that I
suffered some alarm when a stranger appeared upon our path not a
hundred paces from the ancient basin by which the passage is
reached. He was a short, thick-set man, wearing a serge suit with
black leather leggings and a peaked cap, and when he saw us he
stopped abruptly for a moment, then turned his back upon us and
pretended to light a cigarette while we passed.

"He is no policeman," I said to Wellman, when the stranger was
out of hearing. The old servant agreed with me.

"But he might be an inquiry agent, sir. I've heard tell in London
of the tricks they play with their clothes. Don't trust him too far."

"I am not going to trust him at all," said I. "The fellow looked to
me as though he were a chauffeur."

"A bad lot, believe me, sir. There's been few honest men upon
wheels since they robbed us of our horses. A man wants the nose of
a setter to keep track of such as him. I wouldn't trust one of them
with a silver-plated soup-ladle, upon my word I wouldn't.'

I told him he was a laudator temporis acti, but as that conveyed
nothing to him we pushed on, and found Evelyn in the boudoir.

She was dreadfully agitated, but Sir Borrow being there, no word
of the affair might pass between us. The baronet plainly thought
that his daughter had become hysterical, and when I was alone with
him he hinted that she must have had some news from that d——d
scoundrel.

"Whatever it is," he added, "I don't want to hear of it or of him.
It would be a great day for me if the fellow were six feet
underground, and I hope to God he soon will be. That's the truth,
Cope, and none of your philosophy can change it. I have no longer
a son; I am trying to forget that I ever had one."

I shrank from his anger, knowing well how little such a man

would suffer a rebuke. Happily, he set out to drive into the town almost immediately, and Evelyn and I went at once to the priest's hole and interviewed Southby. He was in a sorry plight, I must say, his face and hands torn by the brambles of the thickets, his clothes splashed with mud, his beard unshaved, and his eyes bloodshot. I thought also a little delirious from want of food and exposure, and he talked incoherently of ships and the sea, of men who had betrayed him, and of others who were his friends. By-and-by, when he became calmer, he told me that the ignominy of prison affected him to such an extent that he would have gone mad if he had remained at Parkhurst.

"I couldn't have done it, Cope, by God I couldn't," he said. "You don't know what it means to a man who has lived as I have. I had to go or it would have been all up with me. If they take me I will shoot myself. That's an oath and I'll keep it."

"But," cried I, "whatever will you do, Southby? You must know that we cannot long protect you here."

He laughed defiantly, pushing the black hair from his forehead quite in the old way.

"Lionel will do it," he said. "I trust Lionel. He got me out; he'll see I don't get in again. You must know Lionel. He's a white man all through, and the prison that can hold him has got to be made. Why, it was his idea about the motor-boat—who else would have thought of it?—his and his friend at Hendon. They picked us up in the cover at high tide, and we were landed at Hayling Island before morning. I knew we should get through when Lionel undertook it."

"Then," exclaimed I, quite at hazard, "Captain Kennington knew nothing of it?"

His brow darkened at this. He looked at Evelyn curiously, and appeared afraid to speak out.

"No, I don't trust Kennington—not much. Mind what you're doing in that quarter, Evelyn. Kennington isn't thirty cents—you remember it."

She flashed out at this, a girl of spirit and a good heart.

"Do not say a word against Captain Kennington!" she cried. "He is the only friend you ever had who remained staunch to you. You should be grateful to him."

He still persisted, though with a weakening resolution.

"That may or may not be. It's my opinion he tried to give us away, and I shall stick to it. Now, get me a drink for heaven's sake. I am as dry as a camel."

She fetched him a brandy-and-soda, and he drank it eagerly. It was already a danger to pass to and from the long gallery, and I began to perceive the peril of the situation. Let the servants know and sooner or later the news would go to the village, and thence to the police. When we discussed it frankly between ourselves there seemed but one solution. Evelyn must be ill, and Harriet must be recalled from Bath to wait upon her. Meanwhile, Wellman must have a confidant, and none seemed better suited to the purpose than Turner, the head housemaid. Sooner or later this woman would discover us. We determined that it should be sooner, and, calling her to the conference, we put our fortunes into her hands. Good woman, she had a brother of her own, and Evelyn was beloved by them all.

We made our plans, and for the moment they were successful.

Harriet, unfortunately, could not return from Bath, her aunt being taken seriously ill and really requiring her assistance. Evelyn, however, feigned an indisposition very cleverly, and although it put me to some conscientious difficulty, I suffered myself to think of the greater good of that unhappy family and to acquiesce. Nevertheless, I understood that it was but a brief respite. The perils of the situation were manifest. Any day, any hour might discover us, and we began to go as those who feared their own shadows.

Perhaps my fears may have been responsible for a delusion, but there were moments when I thought that Sir Borrow suspected us. His manner became suddenly aggressive, and he questioned me more closely than he had done for a long time. Had I heard from that "d——d" son of his? Was Evelyn worrying about "the worthless scoundrel"? To all of which I responded with what wit I could, though God knows my position was difficult. Later on I discovered him in Evelyn's bedroom, and that very night, after dinner, he spoke of Kennington. Oddly enough, his opinion of that gallant soldier was exactly that of his son. He did not trust him, doubted his record, and stigmatised him most unjustly as a penniless adventurer. As to my knowledge the captain is in possession of an income of eight hundred pounds a year, I resented the slander, and did not fear to speak my mind. The result was a sharp quarrel, and the expression upon his part of a shabby apology, with which in any other circumstances I would have been far from satisfied. As it was, I had to bear with him, and to listen while he told me that, whatever happened, he would not have Kennington in the house again. Then he went off to his study, I to the priest's room to tell them of my suspicions.

Southby had always been afraid of his father. My news alarmed him, and he did not hesitate to affirm that the old man would deliver him up to the police should he be discovered at the Close. Evelyn herself appeared to be of the same opinion, and when we were alone she confessed the terror of her situation.

"Captain Kennington is coming here at the week-end," she said.

I told her what Sir Borrow had said, and it did but alarm her the more.

"Sometimes I wish I were dead," she declared.

And I, who knew how much that gentle soul had suffered, prayed to God that strength might be granted her.

The following night I was to meet Lionel Mester in the thicket, and to experience an apprehension more acute than any I had yet suffered in this woeful affair.

It was the Sabbath eve, and I was returning from the Close to the choir practice in our beautiful old parish church. A hundred yards from the well's head, where the secret entrance lies, I met again the short, thick-set man whom Wellman had declared to be a detective. This time he stopped, and begging me to step aside into the thicket, he introduced himself immediately.

"You'll have heard of me, sir—Lionel Mester, Mr. Southby's pal."

"Yes," I said, "I have heard of you. Why do you come to this dangerous place?"

"Because there's something Southby must know, and it can't come any other way. You see him every day, and can take this letter to him. I've been hanging about nearly a week trying to get it delivered. Usually I don't trust devil dodgers—not much. But you've got a decent mug on you, and I'm going to trust you. Take him this letter, and tell him, if he acts on it, it's all right and the wheels go round. Otherwise I do a double watch, and be d——d to it! Lord, I've been sleeping on stinging nettles for a week, and that's about enough of it! Tell Southby so, and you'll see no more of me."

He thrust a bulky letter into my hand, and was about to say more when we heard a sound of footsteps, and instantly he plunged into the undergrowth with the agility of a wild-cat. He was shod, I saw, in rubber-soled shoes, and carried a formidable stick; but the quickness of his movements was the surprising thing, and uttering but one word "police," he disappeared from my view. For my part, I thrust the letter into the inner pocket of my coat and at once regained the path. Fifty paces further on I passed Superintendent Matthews, and exchanged a good-night with him. He appeared to be in a hurry, and was going towards the Hall. But he did not stop to gossip with me, as he usually does, and for that I was grateful.

It will be understood that this unexpected turn perplexed me very much. I had expected that Lionel Mester would come to Borrow sooner or later, but now that he had come I perceived how considerable a danger he must be to us all. It was not to be hidden from me that I myself might be the victim of this unhappy family, and must answer to the law for the part that I had played. So much I was willing to do for a woman's sake, but now that discovery trod upon our heels, and all the shame and suffering of exposure hovered in the shadows about that ancient house, I confess that my courage almost failed me. The letter seemed a damning document which would convict me in any court. Yet I determined to deliver it, and that very night, about ten o'clock, I went up to the Hall and put it into Evelyn's hands. Upon my return an unknown man followed me through the thicket, and watched me enter the rectory. I believe that he was a police officer, though whether he were so or not mattered little since the letter was delivered.

That night I slept but ill, fearing so many things, dreading the peril of a situation which had become almost intolerable. The next day was the Sabbath, given almost entirely to the schools and the church, and it was not until we sat down to supper at the Close that I got the news of Evelyn. She had given out that she was a little better, and would sit down with us. The few words we exchanged in the porch when I said "Good-night" to her were of some moment, though not unexpected.

"Southby is going to-night," she said.

I answered, "Thank God," for I knew that none of us could stand the strain of it much longer.

And so we parted, and I was never to see her alive again. So brave, so gentle she was, blessed among women truly, an offering to man's sin, a martyr for whom men's tears should fall. They heard a loud cry in the house a little before midnight. Sir Borrow was awake, and first upon the scene. They found her lying at the foot of the circular staircase which leads down from the long gallery to the secret room.

Evidently there had been a struggle. A jagged bar of iron lay upon the stairs at her feet. The lamp she had carried was shattered; the very window in the angle of the octagon was broken, and the glass littered about. What was not a little remarkable was the discovery of nine pounds in gold wrapped in a yellow kid glove, the very shape and colour of the gloves always worn by Captain Kennington.

She was dressed in a long bedgown, I should tell you, and wore a dressing-gown over it. The door of the secret chamber stood open, but no one was to be discerned within. Southby had fled the house. Sir Borrow and Wellman alone stooped to the assistance of the stricken woman.

She was quite dead, a terrible wound in the throat having deprived her of life almost instantaneously. Naturally the police were called upon the instant, and not a moment was lost by them. Beaters began to search every thicket of the forest round about; there were motors abroad upon every road. Yet nothing was discovered, not a shadow of a clue to be found. Even Captain Kennington could offer no suggestion. I discovered to my surprise that he had come to Borrow on Saturday evening as he promised, but hearing Evelyn's story had gone to the town to sleep. The hue and cry waked him—to such a morn as few men are called upon to live.

And so here is this terrible crime committed, and no man to be brought to justice for it. God send us enlightenment that the guilty may be punished!

Proofs of the above mystery story have been sent to

Mr. G. K. CHESTERTON,

the creator of that famous detective of fiction,

"FATHER BROWN."

This is quite a new idea of story-telling, and Mr. Chesterton has entered into the spirit of the scheme with characteristic enthusiasm. His, or, rather, "Father Brown's," solution of The Donnington Affair will be embodied in a complete story which will appear in next month's PREMIER.

I am now in negotiation with other famous fiction detectives, and for the present I will merely mention that the next pair of stories in this series are in the capable hands of

SIR ARTHUR QUILLER-COUCH

and

BARONESS ORCZY

FATHER BROWN
SOLVES

The Donnington Affair

The Donnington Affair

It was natural, of course, that we should think of calling in expert opinion on the tragedy; or, at least, something subtler than the passing policeman. But I could think of few people or none whom it would be useful to consult thus privately. I remembered an investigator who had taken some interest in Southby's original trouble; merely because I remembered the curious surname of Shrike; but report told me that he had since grown rich and retired, and was now yachting inaccessibly among the Pacific Islands.

My old friend Brown, the Roman priest at Cobhole, who had often given me good advice in small problems, had wired that he feared he could not come down, even for an hour. He merely added—what, I confess, I thought inconsequent—that the key might be found in the sentence, that "Mester was the cheeriest soul possible."

Superintendent Matthews still carries weight with any considering person who has actually talked to him; but he is naturally in most cases officially reticent, and in some cases officially slow.

Sir Borrow seemed stricken rigid by this final tragedy; a thing pardonable enough in a very old man who, whatever his faults, had never had anything but tragedy upon tragedy out of his own blood and name.

Wellman can be trusted with anything up to the Crown jewels; but not with an idea. Harriet is far too good a woman to be a good detective. So I was left with my unsatisfied appetite for expert advice. I think the others shared it to some extent; I think we wished a man different from all of us would walk into the room, a man of the world outside us, a man of wider experience, a man of experience so wide—if it were possible—that he should know even one case that was like our own. Certainly none of us had the wildest suspicion of who the man would be.

I have explained that when poor Evelyn's body was found it was clad in a dressing-gown, as if she had been suddenly summoned from her room, and the door of the Priest's Room stood open. Acting on I know not what impulse, I had closed it to; and, so far as I know, it was not opened again till it was opened from within. I confess that for me that opening was terrible.

Sir Borrow, Wellman, and I were alone in the chamber of slaughter. At least we were alone till a total stranger strolled into the room, without even pulling the peaked cap off his head. He was a sturdy man, stained with travel, especially as regards his leggings, which were loaded with clay and slime of innumerable ditches. But he was entirely unconcerned, which is more than I was. For, despite his extra dirt and his extra impudence, I recognised him as the fugitive convict, Mester, whose letter I had so foolishly passed on to his fellow convict. He entered the room with his hands in his pockets, and whistling. Then the whistling ceased, and he said:

"You seem to have shut the door again. I suppose you know it's not easy to open again on this side."

Through the broken window which gave upon the garden I could see Superintendent Matthews standing passively among the shrubs, with his broad back to the house. I walked to the window, and also whistled, but in a far more practical spirit. And yet, I know not why I should call it practical, for the superintendent, who must have heard me, did not turn his head, nor so much as shift a shoulder.

"I shouldn't worry poor old Matthews," said the man in the peaked cap in a friendly tone, "he is one of the best men in the service, and he must be awfully tired. I expect I can answer nearly all the questions that he could." And he relighted a cigarette.

"Mr. Mester," I replied with some heat, "I was sending for the superintendent to arrest you!"

"Quite so," he answered, throwing his wax match out of the window. "Well, he won't!"

He was gazing at me with a grave stolidity. And yet I fancy that the gravity of his full face had less effect on me than the large, indifferent back of the policeman.

The man called Mester resumed.

"I mean that my position here may not be quite what you suppose. It's true enough I assisted the young fellow to escape; but I don't imagine you know why I did it. It is an old rule in our profession——"

Before he could finish I had uttered a cry.

"Stop!" I cried out. "Who is that behind the door?"

I could see, by the very movement of Mester's mouth, that he was just about to answer, "What door?" But before the lips could move he also was answered. And from behind the sealed door of the secret chamber came the noise of something that was alive, if it were not human, or was moving, if it were not alive.

"What is in the Priest's Room?" I cried, and looked round for something with which to break down the door. I had half lifted the piece of jagged iron bar for the purpose. And then the horrid part it had played in that night overwhelmed me, and I fell against the door and beat on it with feeble hands, only repeating, "What is in the Priest's Room?" It was the awful fact that a voice, obscure but human, answered from behind the closed door, "The Priest!"

The heavy door was opened very slowly, apparently pushed by a hand no stronger than my own. The same voice which had said "The Priest," said in rather simpler tones, "Whom else did you expect?" The door swung out slowly to the full compass of its hinges, and revealed the black silhouette of a stumpy, apologetic person, with a big hat and a bad umbrella. He was in every way a very unromantic and inappropriate person to be in the Priest's Room, save in the accidental detail of being a priest.

He walked straight up to me before I could cry: "You have come, after all!"

He shook my hand, and, before he dropped it, looked at me with a steady and singular expression, sad, and yet rather serious than sad. I can only say it was the face we wear at the funeral of one dear as a friend, not that we wear by the deathbed of any directly dear to us.

"I can at least congratulate *you*," said Father Brown.

I think I put my hand wildly through my hair. I am sure I answered:

"And what is there in this nightmare on which I can be congratulated?"

He answered me with the same solid face:

"On the innocence of the woman who will be your wife."

"No one," I cried indignantly, "has attempted to connect her with the matter."

He nodded gravely, as if in assent.

"That was the danger, doubtless," he said with a slight sigh, "but she's all right now, thank God. Isn't she?" And as if to give the last touch to the topsyturvydom, he turned to ask his question of the man in the peaked cap.

"Oh, she's safe enough!" said the man called Mester.

I cannot deny that there was suddenly lifted off my heart a load of doubt, which I had never known was there. But I was bound to pursue the problem.

"Do you mean, Father Brown," I asked, "that you know who was the guilty person?"

"In a sense, yes," he answered. "But you must remember that in a murder case the guiltiest person is not always the murderer."

"Well, the guiltiest person, then," I cried impatiently. "How are we to bring the guiltiest person to punishment?"

"The guiltiest person is punished," said Father Brown.

There was a long silence in the twilight turret, and my mind laboured with doubts that were too large for it. At last Mester said gruffly, but not without a kind of good-nature:

"I think you two reverend gentlemen had better go and have a talk somewhere. About Hades, say, or hassocks, or whatever you do talk about. I shall have to look into this by myself. My name is Stephen Shrike; you may have heard of me."

Even before such fancies had been swallowed up in my sudden fear at the movements in the secret room, I had faced the startling possibility that this escaped convict was really a detective. But I had not dreamed of his being so famous a one. The man who had been concerned for Southby, and since gained colossal prestige, had some claim in the case; and I followed Brown, who had already strolled down towards the entrance of the garden.

"The distinction between Hades and hassocks——" began Father Brown.

"Don't play the fool!" I said, roughly enough.

"Was not without some philosophical value," continued the little priest, with unruffled good temper. "Human troubles are mostly of two kinds. There is an accidental kind, that you can't see because they are so close you fall over as you do over a hassock. And there is the other kind of evil, the real kind. And that a man will go to seek however far off it is—down, down, into the lost abyss." And he unconsciously pointed his stumpy finger downward towards the grass, which was sprinkled with daisies.

"It was good of you to come, after all," I said; "but I wish I could make more sense of the things you say."

"Well," he replied patiently, "have you made sense of the one thing I did say before I came down?"

"Why, you made some wild statement," I replied, "that the key of the story was in Mester's being cheerful, but—why, bless my soul, and so it is the key, in a way!"

"Only the key, so far," said my companion, "but my first guess seems to have been right. It is not very common to find such sparkling gaiety in people undergoing penal servitude, especially when ruined on a false charge. And it seemed to me that Mester's optimism was a little overdone. I also suspected that his aviation, and all the rest of it, true or false, were simply meant to make Southby think the escape feasible. But if Mester was such a demon for escaping, why didn't he escape by himself? Why was he so anxious to lug along a young gentleman who does not seem to have been much use to him? As I was wondering, my eye fell on another sentence in your manuscript."

"What was that?" I asked.

He took out a scrap of paper on which there were some scribbles in pencil, and read out:

"'They then crossed an enclosure in which other prisoners were at work.'"

After another pause, he resumed:

"That, of course, was plain enough. What kind of convict prison is it where prisoners work without any warders overseeing or walking about? What sort of warders are they to allow two convicts to climb two walls and go off as if for a picnic? All that is plain. And the conclusion is plainer from many other sentences. 'It seemed such an impossible thing that he could evade the hue and cry that must attend this flight.' It would have been impossible if there *had* been any hue and cry. 'Evelyn and Harriet heard me eagerly, and the former, I began to suspect, was already in possession of the story.' How could she be in possession of it so early as that, unless the police cars and telephones helped to send word from Southby? Could the convicts catch a camel or an ostrich? And look at the motor-boat. Do motor-boats grow on trees? No, that's all simple. Not only was the companion in the escape a police detective, but the whole scheme of the escape was a police scheme, engineered by the highest authorities of the prison."

"But why?" I asked, staring. "And what has Southby to do with it?"

"Southby had nothing to do with it," he answered. "I believe he is now hiding in some ditch or wood in the sincere belief that he is a hunted fugitive. But they won't trouble him any more. He has done their work for them. He is innocent. It was essential that he should be innocent."

"Oh, I don't understand all this!" I cried impatiently.

"I don't understand half of this," said Father Brown. "There are all sorts of difficulties I will ask you about later. You knew the family. I only say that the sentence about cheerfulness *did* turn out to be a key-sentence, after all. Now, I want you to concentrate your attention on another key-sentence. 'We decided that Harriet should go to Bath without loss of time, in case she should be of any assistance there.' Note that this comes soon after your expression of surprise that someone should have communicated with Evelyn so early. Well, I suppose we none of us think the governor of the prison wired to her: 'Have connived at escape of your brother, Convict 99.' The message must have come in Southby's name, at any rate."

I ruminated, looking at the roll of the downs as it rose and repeated itself through every gap in the garden trees; then I said, "Kennington?"

My old friend looked at me for a moment with a look which, this time, I could not analyse.

"Captain Kennington's part in the business is unique in my experience," he said, "and I think we had better return to him later. It is enough that, by your own account, Southby did not give him his confidence."

I looked again at the glimpses of the downs, and they looked grander but greyer, as my companion went on, like one who can only put things in their proper order.

"I mean the argument here is close, but clear. If she had any secret message from her brother about his escaping, why shouldn't she have a message about where he was escaping to? Why should she send off her sister to Bath, when she might just as well have been told that her brother wasn't going there? Surely a young gentleman might more safely say, in a private letter, that he was going to Bath than that he was escaping from prison? Somebody or something must have influenced Southby to leave his destination uncertain.

And who could influence Southby except the companion of his flight?"

"Who was acting for the police, on your theory."

"No. On his confession." After a sort of snorting silence, Brown said, with an emphasis I have never seen in him, throwing himself on a garden-seat: "I tell you this whole business of the two cities of refuge—this whole business of Harriet Donnington going to Bath—was a suggestion that came through Southby, but from Mester, or Shrike, or whatever his name is, and is the key of the police plot."

He had settled himself on a seat facing me, clasping his hands over the huge head of his umbrella in a more truculent manner than was typical of him. But an evening moon was brightening above the little plantation under which he sat, and when I saw his plain face again, I saw it was as mild as the moon.

"But why," I asked, "should they want such a plot?"

"To separate the sisters," he said. "That is the key."

I answered quickly: "The sisters could not really be separated."

"Yes, they could," said Father Brown, "quite simply, and that is why——" Here his simplicity failed, and he hesitated.

"That is why?" I insisted.

"That is why I can congratulate you," he said at last.

Silence sank again for a little, and I could not define the irritation with which I answered:

"Oh, I suppose you know all about it?"

"No, no really!" he said, leaning forward as if to deny an accusation of injustice. "I am puzzled about the whole business. Why didn't the warders find it sooner? Why did they find it at all? Was it slipped in the lining? Or is the handwriting so bad as that? I know about the thing being gentlemanly; but surely they took his clothes! How could the message come? It *must* be the lining."

His face was turned up as honestly as a flat and floating fish, and I could say with corresponding mildness:

"I really do not know what you are talking about, you and your linings. But if you mean how could Southby get his message safely to his sister without the risks of interception, I should say there were no people more likely to do it successfully. The boy and girl were always great friends from childhood, and had, to my knowledge, one of those secret languages that children often have, which may easily have been turned afterwards into some sort of cypher. And now I come to think of it——"

The heavy-knobbed umbrella slipped from the seat and slammed on the gravel, and the priest stood upright.

"What an idiot I am!" he said. "Why, anybody might have thought of a cypher! That was a score for you, my friend. I suppose you know all about it now?"

I am certain he did not realise that he was repeating in sincerity what I had said in irony.

"No," I answered, with real seriousness; "I do not know all about it, but I think it quite possible that you do. Tell me the story."

"It is not a good story," he said, in a rather stony way—"at least, the good thing about it is that it is over. But first let me say what I least like saying—that you knew well. I have thought a good deal about a certain kind of intellectual English lady, especially when she is at once aristocratic and provincial. I think she is judged much too easily. Or, perhaps, I should say, judged much too hardly; since she is supposed to be incapable of mortal passions and temptations. Let her decline champagne at dinner, let her be beautiful and know what is meant by dignity in dress, let her read a great many books and talk about high ideals, and you all assume that she alone of her kind cannot covet or lie; that her ideas are always simple, and her ideals always fulfilled. But, really and truly, my friend, by your account of it, the character was more mixed than that. Evelyn feigned an indisposition very cleverly. Assuming her to be blameless, I cannot see why she needed to feign anything. But, anyhow, it is scarcely one of the powers given to the saints. You 'began to suspect' that Evelyn already knew about the escape. Why didn't she *tell* you she already knew about it? You were astonished that Superintendent Matthews had called, and she had been silent about it; but you supposed it was difficult to send. Why should it be difficult to send? You seem to have been sent for whenever you were really wanted. No; I will try to speak of this woman as of one for whose soul I will pray, and whose true defence I shall never hear. But while there are living people whose honour is in cruel danger undeservedly, I simply refuse to start with the assumption that Evelyn Donnington could do no wrong."

The noble hills of Sussex looked as dreary as Yorkshire moors as he went on heavily, prodding the earth with his umbrella.

"The first facts in her defence, if she needed one, are that her father is a miser, that he has a violent temper combined with a rather Puritanic sort of family pride; and, above all, that she was afraid of him. Now, suppose she really wanted money, perhaps for a good purpose; or, again, perhaps not. She and her brother, you told me, had always had secret languages and plots; they are common among cowed and terrorised children. I firmly believe myself that she went a step further in some desperate strait, and that she was really and criminally responsible for the false document with which her brother seemed to be seeking financial help. We know there is often a family resemblance in handwritings almost amounting to facsimile. I cannot see, therefore, why there should not be a similar family resemblance in the flaws by which experts detect a forgery. Anyhow, the brother had a bad record, which goes for a great deal more than it ought with the police; and he was sent to gaol. I think you will agree that he has a very good record now."

"You mean," I said, curiously thrilled by the very restraint of his expression, "that Southby suffered all that time rather than speak?"

"Rejoice not against me, Satan, mine enemy," said Father Brown, "for when I fall I shall arise. This part of the story really is good."

After a silence he continued:

"When he was arrested, I am now almost certain, he had on him some letter or message from his sister. I hope and believe that it was some sort of penitent message. But whatever it was, it must have contained two things—some admission or allusion that made her own guilt clear, and some urgent request that her brother should come straight to her as soon as he was free to do so. Most important of all, it was not signed with a Christian name, but only 'Your unhappy sister.'"

"But, my good man," I cried, "you talk as if you had seen the letter!"

"I see it in its consequences," he answered. "The friendship with Mester, the quarrel with Kennington, the sister in Bath and the brother in the Priest's Room, came from that letter, and no other letter."

"The letter, however, was in cypher; and one very hard to follow, having been invented by children. Does that strike you as paradoxical? Don't you know that the hardest signs to read are arbitrary ones? And if two children agree that 'grunk' means bedtime and 'splosh' means Uncle William, it would take an expert much longer to learn this than to expose any system of substituted letters or numbers. Consequently, though the police found the paper, of course, it took them half-way through Southby's term to make head or tail of it. Then they knew that one of Southby's sisters were guilty, that he was innocent; and by this time they had the sense to see that he would never betray the truth. The rest, as I said, was simple and logical. The only other thing they could do was to take advantage of Southby being asked to go straight to his guilty correspondent. He was given every facility for escaping and communicating as quickly as possible, so long as the police could secure the separation of the sisters, by Mester getting the other one to Bath. Given that, the sister Southby went for must be the guilty one. And when, through those awful nights, the police gathered round you thick as wolves and still as ghosts—it was not for Southby they were waiting."

"But why did they wait for anyone?" I asked suddenly, after a silence. "If they were sure, why didn't they arrest?"

He nodded and sighed:

"Perhaps you're right. Perhaps it's best to take the Kennington case here. Well, of course, he knew all about it from the inside. You yourself noticed that he had privileges in that prison. It will grieve you, as a law-abiding person, to learn that he used his power to intercept what had been decided. A good deal can be done by missing appointments. A good deal more can be done by not missing people—vulgarly known as hitting them. He used every chance, right or wrong, to delay the arrest. One of the thousand small, desperate delays was 'feigning illness.'"

"Why did Southby call him a traitor?" I said suspiciously.

"On exceedingly good grounds," said my friend. "Suppose you had broken prison in all innocence, and your friend sent his car for you and it took you back there? Suppose your friend offered to get you away in his yacht, and it took the wrong course, till overtaken by a motor-boat? Suppose Southby was trying to get to Sussex, and Kennington always headed him off towards Cornwall or Ireland or Normandy, what would you expect Southby to call him?"

"Well," I said, "what would you call him?"

"Oh," said Father Brown, "I call him a hero."

I peered at his rather featureless face through the moony twilight; and then he suddenly rose and paced the path with the impatience of a schoolboy.

"If I could put pen to paper, I would write the best adventure story ever written about this. Was there ever such a situation? Southby was kicked backwards and forwards, as unconscious as a football, between two very able and vigorous men, one of whom wanted to make the footprints point towards the guilty sister, while the other wanted to twist the feet away at every turn. And Southby thought the friend of his house was his enemy, and the destroyer of his house his friend. The two that knew must fight in silence, for Mester could not speak without warning Southby, and Kennington could not speak without denouncing Evelyn. It is clear from Southby's words, about false friends and the sea, that Kennington eventually kidnapped Southby in a yacht, but lord knows in how many tangled woods, or river islands, or lanes leading nowhere, the same fight was fought; the fugitive and detective trying to keep the trail, the traitor and true lover trying to confuse it. When Mester won, and his men gathered round this house, the captain could do no more than come here and offer his help, but Evelyn would not open the door to him."

"But why not?"

"Because she had the fine side of fear as well as the bad side," said Father Brown. "'Not a little afraid of life,' you said, with great penetration. She was afraid to go to prison; but, to her honour, she was afraid to get married, too. It is a type produced by all this refinement. My friend, I want to tell you and all your modern world a secret. You will never get to the good in people till you have been through the bad in them."

After a moment he added that we ought to be returning to the house, and walked yet more briskly in that direction.

"Of course," he remarked, as he did so, "the packet of banknotes you took through to Southby was only to help him away and spare him Evelyn's arrest. Mester's not a bad fellow for a 'tec. But she realised her danger, and was trying to get into the Priest's Room."

I was still brooding on the queer case of Kennington.

"Was not the glove found?" I asked.

"Was not the window broken?" he asked in return. "A man's glove twisted properly and loaded with nine pounds in gold, and probably a letter as well, will break most windows if it is slung by a man who has been a bowler. Of course, there was a note. And, of course, the note was imprudent. It left money for escape, and left the proofs of what she was escaping from."

"And then what happened to her?" I asked dully.

"Something of what happened to you," he said. "You also found the secret door difficult to open from outside. You also caught up that crooked curtain-rod or window-bar to beat on it. You also saw the door opening slowly from within. But you did not see what she saw."

"And what did she see?" I said at last.

"She saw the man she had wronged most," said Father Brown.

"Do you mean Southby?"

"No," he said, "Southby has shown heroic virtue, and he is happy. The man she wronged most was a man who had never had, or tried to have, more than one virtue—a kind of acrid justice. And she had made him unjust all his life—made him pamper the wicked woman and ruin the righteous man. You told me in your notes that he often hid in the Priest's Room, to discover who was faithful or unfaithful. This time he came out holding a sword left in that room in the days when men hunted my religion. He found the letter, but, of course, he destroyed it after he had done—what he did. Yes, old friend, I can feel the horror on your face without seeing it. But, indeed, you modern people do not know how many kinds of men there are in the world. I am not talking of approval, but of sympathy—the sort of sympathy I give to Evelyn Donnington. Have you *no* sympathy with cold, barbaric justice, or with the awful appeasements of such an intellectual appetite? Have you *no* sympathy with the Brutus who killed his friend? Have you *no* sympathy with the monarch who killed his son? Have you *no* sympathy with Virginius, who killed——. But I think we must go in now."

We mounted the stairs in silence, but my surging soul expected some scene surpassing all the scenes of that tower. And in a sense I had it. The room was empty, save for Wellman, who stood behind an empty chair as impassively as if there had been a thousand guests.

"They have sent for Dr. Browning, sir," he said in colourless tones.

"What do you mean?" I cried. "There was no question about the death?"

"No, sir," he said, with a slight cough; "Dr. Browning required another doctor to be sent from Chichester, and they took Sir Borrow away."

NOTES AND SOURCES

'The White Pillars Murder' was first published in *English Life*, January 1925. It was reprinted in Ellery Queen's *To The Queen's Taste* (1949), but never included in any of Chesterton's own books.

'The Tremendous Adventure of Major Brown' was published, to establish copyright, in a single 24-page stapled booklet by Shurmer Sibthorp in December 1903. It appeared in the June 1904 issue of *The Idler*, and was collected in *The Club of Queer Trades* (London and New York: Harper, 1905).

'The Singular Speculation of the House Agent' appeared in the September 1904 issue of *The Idler*, and was also collected in *The Club of Queer Trades*.

'The Garden of Smoke' appeared in the October 1919 issue of *The Storyteller*, and was collected in the UK edition of *The Man Who Knew Too Much* (Cassell, 1929). It was omitted from the US edition, and from later reprints.

'The Hole in the Wall' appeared in *Cassell's Magazine* (September 1921), and 'The Bottomless Well' in *The Storyteller* (July 1921); both were collected in *The Man Who Knew Too Much*.

'The Three Horsemen of the Apocalypse' and 'When Doctors Agree' appeared in the issues of *The Storyteller* for July and November 1935, respectively. Both were collected in *The Paradoxes of Mr. Pond* (London: Cassell, 1937).

'The Shadow of the Shark' and 'The Finger of Stone' appeared in the issues of *Nash's Magazine* for December and February 1921, respectively. Both were collected in *The Poet and the Lunatics* (London: Cassell, 1929; New York: Dodd Mead, 1929).

'The Donnington Affair' appeared in the October and November 1914 issues of *The Premier*. Hitherto uncollected.